Hearts Out of Hiding

MELISSA HUMPHRIES PIERCE

Address all personal correspondence to:
Melissa Humphries Pierce
Email: melissahumphriespierce@gmail.com

Individuals and church groups may order books from the author directly, or from the publisher. Retailers and wholesalers should order from our distributors. Refer Deeper Revelation Books website for distribution information, as well as an online catalog of all our books.

Published by:
Pure Heart Publications
(Division of Deeper Revelation Books)
Stories That Change Lives Forever
P.O. Box 4260
Cleveland, TN 37320
423-478-2843
Website: www.deeperrevelationbooks.org
Email: info@deeperrevelationbooks.org

Pure Heart Publications assists Christian authors in publishing and distributing their books. It is an honor and a blessing to help produce and promote literature that is written for the glory of God and the advance of His kingdom. Please note that final responsibility for design, content, permissions, editorial accuracy, and doctrinal views, either expressed or implied, belongs to the author.

In Loving Memory of

JOSHUA JAMES HUMPHRIES
7/18/1977 – 5/7/2020

Part One

"So all of us who have had that veil removed can see and reflect the glory of the Lord. And the Lord-who is the Spirit-makes us more and more like him as we are changed into his glorious light." 2 Corinthians 3:18 (NLT)

CHAPTER 1

W hile picking up the prescription bottle of anxiety medication and swallowing a double dose, Ciara prepared to perform well for another Caldwell Thanksgiving. She held the pills in her right hand while steering the car with her left. Shaking the half-empty bottle, she swore loudly and bit her bottom lip. A precious cache. Not enough. A lump formed in her throat as she wiped a tear from her cheek. For the first time in five years, her fiancé, Cameron Shivers, was not beside her. The passenger seat was empty.

She spotted lukewarm smoothie pooling on the woodgrain console of her car and smear marks trailing to the carpet. Her pulse raced as she touched the empty seat and looked away from the smoothie mess. She inhaled and exhaled, letting her breath escape in one long sigh. Slow and steady.

Adjusting the shoulder strap and leaning forward, she looked out to the winding road ahead. Ciara turned on Ridge Road to the private mountain chalet rented for the Caldwell family. Her family. The dash clock displayed 5:30. She stared at the navigation and tapped the time 6:02. How could he? Why did she have to make this trip alone?

Ciara could always persuade Cameron until now. For years, he pursued her. This time was different. Her influence was gone, and he chose to stay in the small town of Bayport, Alabama. Gone were all the wedding plans poured over for months. "Stupid town, stupid people,"

7

mumbled Ciara.

"Nothing's changed." The last words of Cameron surged through her mind. She thought about his somber face turning from her gaze. She bit her lower lip, trying to stop the quiver when remembering his strong hands pushing her away. Cameron had held her slim waist before stepping back and dodging her hand as she reached for him.

Looking out at the road ahead, Ciara's eyes widened as blinding car lights headed toward her. Her wheels drifted to straddle the center line, and she fought to pull back to her lane. A blaring horn sounded, and she gripped the steering wheel until her knuckles turned white. The oncoming car swerved, sending a dust cloud above the road. She found her lane and the yellow and white lines came into full view. She spoke four words, "God, please help me."

Ciara's tires rumbled under loose gravel beside the pavement. "Focus, I need to focus," she said while scooting to the steering wheel. Hot tears fell from her chin, and she blew her nose into a napkin. Her freshly manicured nails reflected the glow from the streetlight as she tilted the rearview mirror.

She craned to see from the passenger window. The only thing in sight was a thick forest of trees with occasional short, unlined roads between. Lifting her chin to the mirror, she looked at her dilated pupils. Large, black orbs rested on her sunken face. She blinked and focused on light coming from oncoming traffic.

She waited for the medication to take effect. Doubling the dose of valium curbed the churning in her stomach, but her thoughts still raced. She would call the doctor. She needed relief and would soon run out of pills. Images of a handsome face flashed before her. Shaking her head back and forth, she squinted and looked through the slits of her eyes at the curve ahead.

Ciara reached for her stomach with one hand and felt a rumble moving to her chest. Alone. Vulnerable. Cameron was truly turning into a pastor. She had planned a trip to Atlanta to look for wedding dresses after Thanksgiving. No dress needed since her last meeting with Cameron. Her mind replayed him walking away as the harvest moon reflected on her new red sports car. It was final. He chose the people of Bayport Community Church. Not her.

The drive was in sight beyond the cedar trees lining the hills. Ciara turned at the small break in the trees. She slowed and ascended the drive to the mountain chalet. Navigating the steep paved area, she swore under her breath. At the top, sat a monstrosity of a van. Ciara's sister, Jan, Jan's husband, Luke, and their four small children, must have gotten the same invitation. All six could fit in the large vehicle comfortably.

Turning the wheel and congratulating herself on landing off center and on the grass, Ciara fell back into the driver's seat. None of the nephews would scratch her new car this far off the drive. She smiled when she thought of the enormous bow that once sat on top of her sports car for her twenty-fifth birthday. She got the new BMW from her parents and Cameron gave her the ring. Her eyes darted to her left ring finger naked and exposed. Nothing there.

Ciara counted breaths while reaching for the visor. A little lipstick and a smile and no one would know she was upset. Performance ready. She frowned while applying mascara. The jet-black liquid coated her lashes but didn't disguise her constricting pupils or red eyes. The side effects of doubling the dose were hard to cover.

What would this Thanksgiving weekend be like without Cameron? By now he should've grown tired of the small town and needy people. If he had come with her, he could've helped her dad at his church. There were opportunities to keep the large church functioning. Her dad, Jack Caldwell, senior pastor of Vero Beach Community Church, trusted Cameron and would've given him back his position as college and career pastor. He could also have helped in the family real estate business. The Caldwell family were well-known for pastoring and gaining wealth in real estate.

Ciara rehearsed, leaving early and meeting with her friends. She wouldn't stay in the chalet long, since her close friends, Matt and Stephanie, were announcing their engagement soon. This wasn't good for Ciara since she was currently without Cameron; however, it would provide an excuse to stay away from most of the family activities.

Ciara picked up her phone and looked at the display. No messages from Cameron. She saw five unread text messages: one from her dad; three from Stephanie, and one from her brother, Jack Junior. That was odd. She hadn't had a conversation with Jack Junior in over three years. She read his message twice. "We need to meet after dinner tonight." Ciara reached for her purse and absently pushed the bottle of valium to the bottom. As the medication took effect, Ciara settled. A calm came to her mind, and she began to relax.

While Ciara sat in the driver's seat of her new car, she caught sight of her father through the second-floor window. He moved the curtain slightly. She was sitting alone. Her father's heart would ache for her. "Daddy, I am going to get Cameron from Bayport. He and I need this time together." Ciara's text from yesterday was at the head of her father's message feed. The last conversation her dad had with Cameron Shivers was related to her and it left him concerned.

She continued watching from her car as her dad descended the stairs. The A-frame window provided a view of a large staircase and her mother, Carol, entertained the small children with a movie and board games. The TV flickered with animated characters and a large chandelier cast light inside and out. Ciara cringed when she thought of the overstuffed couches and chairs draped with various toys, toddler shoes, and a new infant seat.

Her youngest niece, Grace, was beautiful and looked like Ciara. Ciara had platinum blond hair around her face and her warm hazel-brown eyes changed colors with her moods and dress. She looked at her eyes again. The mascara and eyeliner masked some of the puffiness, and she began waving at her eyes, drying any excess moisture.

Her phone alerted, and she looked at the display. Another text message from Stephanie. She sighed and read the text asking her to join the special celebration later that evening. She would give an answer to her friend after talking with her father. Her dad left several text messages earlier coaxing her to be a part of the family get-together this weekend. This mountain chalet was rented to make sure she wouldn't resist coming.

Ciara saw her dad's graying head before his body emerged from the front door. Her mood improved when she saw him. She would convince him to let her skip the whole ordeal for Thanksgiving. She smiled and moved to hug him. It was much colder in the Smoky Mountains of Tennessee than she expected.

"I'm glad I packed my warm jacket and boots," she said as he kissed the top of her head.

"Ciara, we need to talk," Jack said. Lines formed around his mouth as he grimaced before letting out a sigh.

Still being dressed for the Florida climate, Ciara stifled a shiver. Jack stepped back, looking into her eyes. He was best at seeing through the cold, aloof exterior she liked to maintain. She laughed nervously and looked down to her bear arms. "Wow, it's colder than I expected, Daddy."

Jack's eyes met Ciara's again for a fleeting moment before she turned and looked away. "I'll get your luggage. Do I need to send for the troops to help? I know how you pack." His breezy tone put her more at ease.

"I only packed three suitcases, Daddy. If you hadn't insisted on us coming to the mountains instead of Hawaii like last year, I wouldn't need the third one." She moved toward the car. His brows raised when she came with him. She met his stride and hit the trunk button on the keyring. Two of her expensive Italian leather suitcases were stacked neatly in the trunk and one in the backseat.

She turned toward the backseat while Jack slid the other two out of the trunk. Once he put the matching luggage on the sidewalk, he lifted the handles to navigate the walkway to the front steps. She followed him and took the moment before the steps at the massive double-door entrance to mention Matt and Stephanie.

"They're planning an important dinner tonight at Buckhorn Inn. I'm invited to witness a great moment. He's going to propose to her after the main course. It's all perfect," said Ciara.

"I'm glad to see you enjoying your friends so much." Jack smiled while placing his arm around her shoulders.

"Even if my stuck-up friends probably just want the

optics of the best social media post?" Ciara questioned. The post would make its way to every envious person in her father's congregation.

"Sweetheart, tonight everyone in the family will be eating a special dinner for Thanksgiving. We need to meet tonight, so your brother can get back to Orlando. I really want all of us together. Can't you meet with Stephanie tomorrow. I'm sure the event will be posted for all to see," said Jack.

Ciara and her brother, Jack Junior, both embraced an expensive lifestyle and chose friendships over the gospel message. Ciara's eyes narrowed, and she fought the urge to say something back to her father. He was not impressed with Matt and Stephanie. It always angered her. Her father's infatuation with modest living and simple people baffled her. It made no sense and left her uncomfortable.

"Please, honey, don't make it difficult. I want all of us to be together this time. You can do whatever you like tomorrow and the rest of the weekend for that matter," said Jack.

Her shoulders relaxed. Ciara paused before speaking and turned toward her dad. She felt her eyes droop from the valium and needed to lie down soon. She could handle this compromise. She only had a brief time in captivity to play the family role before she could shop and hang out with her friends for the remainder of the weekend. Besides, she already knew the proposal events play by play. It was either spend the evening with her family or Stephanie's.

"Okay, Daddy. I need to go to my room and rest. I left my hotel early this morning. I would like to lie down before dinner," said Ciara.

It was decided then. She followed him inside and

gave the customary embraces before excusing herself upstairs. All her family were there and accounted for, except for her brother, who was expected to arrive just before dinner. Her mother, Carol, moved toward her and stopped when Jack waved her away.

As Ciara ascended the stairs, her pulse raced at the sight of her mother's face. It was twisted with concern, and deep lines creased her brow. Jack gave Carol a half-smile and winked. Her mother's face softened, and she continued to rock baby Grace on her shoulder, cooing at the young infant.

One hour later, after sleeping soundly, Ciara rose from the large king bed and looked around the room. The rustic timber walls adorned with lace-white curtains were illuminated by a large floor lamp. She sat with her toes laced in an oversized chenille rug beside the bed. Everything in the room was oversized, leaving her feeling small. It was great not sharing a room, but she felt silly being alone in such a large space.

The adjoining bathroom was empty, and she took the opportunity to take a quick shower and put on make-up before she joined the dinner preparations downstairs.

Jack Junior would be in the other room and Jan and family would be on the ground floor. The chalet boasted room for twenty people and the downstairs accommodated most of them.

She stood at the hardwood-lined bathroom mirror and braided her long, blond hair to one side. The braid fell below her shoulders and her big, brown eyes were exaggerated by the frame the braid made of her face. She hummed softly and smiled.

"Now, I'm ready," she said while reentering her room and closing the bathroom door behind.

She faintly heard movement in the other room and

called out a quick, "Hello, Junior?"

"Hi Ciara, I guess we're suitemates again," he said while locking the bathroom door. Jack Junior turned on the faucet and she figured he was getting a quick shave before joining the family.

As Ciara descended the stairs, she saw Jan, who smiled and pointed to the water pitcher and ice. Ciara took the cue and began filling the crystal drinking glasses at each place setting. She smiled softly at her mother. Carol arranged the enormous wood table with the Thanksgiving bowls and plates. Carol and Jan spent half an hour arranging the centerpiece and chairs. Ciara busied herself, placing silverware beside each plate.

The food was catered, but Carol brought family dishes to add a cozy feel. The whole table could be photographed for the cover of a magazine, but still had family charm. She wiped her cheek and grasped her husband Jack's hand. Carol and Jack glanced occasionally at each other. They sat close and laced their fingers together.

Jack Junior reached for his phone and scrolled through a text. His frown caused Ciara to move closer and ask, "What's up?"

"I've got a new guy driving from Atlanta to get me to sign something...he's almost here. This dinner needs to begin already." He shuffled in his seat and reached for his water glass.

"Goodness, Junior, you got a poor guy driving here on Thanksgiving? At least invite him in to eat." Ciara frowned and drank deep from her water.

"Good idea sis, scoot over and grab a chair." Jack Junior smiled broadly while texting.

Ciara felt warm despite the chilly weather. For the first time in two days, she did not ache for Cameron. Her mind whirled about the trips she would take in the spring. She was free. She would go to Europe now that Cameron wouldn't distract her. She hummed and tapped her nails on the white tablecloth. The nap earlier and being with her dad and mom at the beautiful mountain chalet was good medicine.

Ciara watched her niece, Grace. The quiet baby slept soundly and barely moved when Jan passed her to Luke. Ciara's experience with the other children included a lot of screaming and crying. Jan's husband, Luke, took the older children to the aquarium earlier, leaving only baby Grace. Now, they were back at the children's table. Ciara didn't even mind the constant chatter, since the children were at the small table, away from the adults.

Jack Junior looked up from his cell phone mid-text. He didn't change from his suit. He shed his coat and stayed in his dress pants and shirt. He barely made it to the chalet in time for dinner. At that moment the doorbell rang. Jack Junior excused himself and returned with a young man dressed for the office and carrying a large Manila folder.

"Dad, mom, family, this is my newest hire, Bryant Ward. He's driving back to Orlando tonight, but I had him stop by to sign a few things." Jack stood beside Bryant and took the manila folder while motioning for him to sit beside Ciara. Her brows raised as her eyes met the young man's dark-brown ones. He smiled broadly.

"Ciara suggested we invite Bryant for dinner. No objections, right?"

"Of course not." Carol stood and grabbed another plate and drinking glass. She smiled warmly at Bryant and returned to her seat. "I'm glad you are here, Bryant. I'd hate for you to miss Thanksgiving."

"Thank you, ma'am. You saved me from a Thanksgiving dinner at a diner on the way back to Orlando."

Bryant winked and looked around the table. His stark-white shirt contrasted with his smooth, brown skin. Ciara wondered if he might be Native American or Hispanic. His impeccable English and his charm at the Caldwell table added to his mystique.

"Driving here from Atlanta was a blur. I spent the time on the phone negotiating a deal. My plan to buy another high-rise is in the works," Jack Junior whispered to Ciara while sipping tea. Bryant moved back in his seat allowing Jack Junior to look fully at Ciara.

Jack Junior's jaw tensed. "It is risky and would tie up a sizable amount of capital, but I want the business to grow faster than it's been for the last forty years." He locked eyes with Ciara. She shifted in her seat and nodded in understanding. A twinge of concern at his declaration to tie up capital caused her to swallow hard.

She knew better than to argue with him at the family table and looked at her dad sitting on the other side of Jack Junior. Jack sat facing Jan and Ciara could only see the side of his face. Her dad would not let Jack Junior do anything too risky.

Ciara turned back as Bryant's eyes darted to the folder resting on the table beside Jack Junior, and her pulse raced. What would be so pressing that an employee would drive here on Thanksgiving?

"Ciara, you seem happy and I'm curious about the absence of your fiancé. Wasn't Cameron invited tonight?" Jack Junior looked directly at Ciara again.

"Cam is not with me tonight. He's at his new church." Ciara cleared her throat and looked away from Jack Junior.

Bryant leaned forward and blocked her view of Jack Junior. Relief flooded Ciara as she sat back in her seat. At least this new guy was running some interference.

She welcomed the diversion and remained quiet.

She thought about her credit card. She knew how to go through money. That was fine for Jack Junior, because he understood her. Now she figured he would attempt to negotiate her expenses right after dinner, stay the night, and leave early in the morning. This would allow him to get back before dinner tomorrow.

Ciara looked at Jan. She did not have superficial wants. She would not be easily bought and might pose a threat to Jack Junior's ambition. She was the wild card, because she had a big heart capable of giving away large portions of her wealth.

"Heavenly Father, thank You for the time we have together tonight. We are enjoying family and want to thank You for our many blessings. We are humbled by the goodness You've shown us and grateful for the feast before us. Bless the food and continue to be with us throughout the rest of this year. In Christ's name we pray. Amen," Jack prayed.

As he finished his prayer, each family member began lively chatter and passing dishes around the large table. Ciara found her appetite for the first time in weeks and piled turkey, dressing, and a cranberry concoction on her plate. She laughed at the sight of the turkey hanging off both sides of the platter.

Bryant Ward politely passed bowls and ate quietly beside Ciara. His left hand brushed her right hand several times as he reached for his tea glass. The touch was electrifying and left Ciara feeling awkward. Why was she responding to this stranger? She attempted to scoot to the left, but bumped into Luke, her brother-in-law, who sat at the end of the table. This caused her to move again toward Bryant.

Bryant leaned toward her and whispered, "Sorry, I'm

a lefty. I should've asked to sit at the kid's table. I'm always taking someone's dining space."

Ciara's eyes locked with his and she stammered, "No,
you're fine. I just thought I'd give you some room." She
looked away and was thankful when Luke stood to help
Jan with the children at the other table. Bryant unsettled
her with his intense eyes. They were dark and reflected the candlelight. She wanted to continue to study his
handsome face but turned and focused on the kid's table
instead. For once, she welcomed their animated movements and constant chatter.

Jan and Luke took turns leaving the table to arrange
child-sized plates while balancing little Grace on one hip.
It was amazing to watch the exchange of the baby and
various platters. Jack Junior sat next to Jack and talked
incessantly about business and future deals. Carol ate
slowly and smiled broadly. As the large bowls of Thanksgiving sides were being emptied, stories from childhood
and the new ones being lived out were free flowing.

"My new housekeeper, Nora, walked into my bedroom
while I was in the shower and yelled at me for leaving
my pajama pants on the floor." Jack Junior laughed until
tears formed in his eyes. "I would have placed a formal
complaint if she didn't look eighty-years-old and wear ac-
tual rubber-soled nurses shoes. She's about four-feet-tall
and wears her gray hair in a bun. She makes a mean la-
sagna and scrubs my baseboards until they sparkle, so I
guess I'll keep her around," said Jack Junior.

Everyone shook their head in agreement with his decision. Carol's eyes darted to Jack Junior's, and she said,
"Pastoring is demanding and rewarding, but also very
sacrificial. We are glad someone is taking care of you
when we're not around."

Carol's eyes widened and locked with Jack's. His

expression was hard to read, but Ciara saw a slight nervous twitch in his lips. She waited for her father to speak, and her stomach turned when Carol's hand went to her short-cropped hair and twirled the graying strands at the nap of her neck.

"Now that our bellies are full, and our hearts are light, I'd like to speak to everyone," said Jack.

Carol smiled, and her gaze moved carefully to each of her children's faces. Ciara moved in closer while Jan grabbed Luke's hand. Ciara watched as Jack Junior leaned back and crossed his legs in front while clasping his hands together. He looked just like their grandfather with his confidence, swagger, and the premature lines around his eyes. Ciara turned back to look at her father.

"After much prayer and many discussions with your mom," Jack looked at Carol and winked, "we have decided to stop pastoring and managing the business. We plan to move to the mission house in Honduras." The collective gasp and incredulous stares from Jan, Luke, and Ciara gave him a chance to continue, "It's been time for me to move on for a while. I didn't have the chance while you kids were in college, and we had other obligations."

"Daddy, you're not old enough to retire. What about the church? What about Caldwell Real Estate? Who will manage it now that Uncle Jim is sick? You can't leave him with his heart like it is," said Ciara. All eyes went to Jack Junior as Ciara's questions ended. She looked directly at her brother's smug face. He knew, and he was up to something.

Ciara sat frozen while her sister Jan moved to their mother and hugged her tightly. Tears began streaming down Jan's cheeks. "I knew it. I knew God was talking to you last fall," said Jan as she embraced her father. "Daddy,

Luke and I will help in any way. Just let us know." Jack's eyes filled with tears as Jan hugged him.

Ciara pushed back from the table, spilling the remainder of Bryant's tea glass in his lap. He reached for his cloth napkin and began sopping up the tea from his black dress slacks. "I'm sorry," Ciara said weakly. She fumbled for her napkin and moved to help Bryant clean up the spill. She felt heat rise to her cheeks as he stood beside her and dabbed at his clothes. Iced tea dripped from his shirt and onto the floor. She handed him the cloth napkin and sat back in her seat.

Her usual calm demeanor fled as she dropped her head and studied her designer shoes. What could she say now? She was being cut off from her parents' income. She couldn't survive on the allowance Jack Junior would give her each month from the company. A ringing was starting in her ears. Her parents were leaving to go to a third world country. What about her? She raised her head and caught her mother's eyes. Ciara did not try to mask the hurt.

"What about me?" Ciara mouthed to her mother. She stood up in a grand gesture and walked toward the front entrance. She pushed and pulled, trying to get the deadbolt to disengage. Finally, it clicked open, and she burst through to the large porch lined with six, full-size rocking chairs.

"Ouch!" Ciara yelped as she hit her shin on the back of one of the chairs. She immediately regretted her exit. The cold, night air made her skin goose pimple, and her breath came out in a fog. Her silk blouse provided no warmth, and she immediately crossed her arms in front of her chest. Her eyes darted around in panic as her mind replayed the events of the evening.

How did she miss this? She was usually aware of

everything her mom and dad were planning. She was the one who planned their vow renewal last year. She was the one who booked the chalet for this trip. The betrayal of the moment was threatening to overtake her. Now there was a new feeling she rarely felt. She was afraid.

As she turned, she found herself face-to-face with Bryant. He studied her eyes before offering her his jacket. She stood looking at the jacket and then took it. She draped the large men's trench coat around her small frame while counting her breaths. The two stood facing one another for a few awkward moments before Bryant spoke.

"I should be going." His eyes caught Ciara's and he smiled. Her heart fluttered and she quickly lowered her gaze from his.

"Here's your jacket." Ciara began to take the jacket from her shoulders as Bryant motioned for her to stop. His fingertips grazed her trembling hand, and she fought the urge to grab for him. She wanted comfort from more than a jacket. She imagined him holding her and shook her head to rid the thought. It made no sense that she desired this from a man she didn't know.

"Keep it. Maybe I'll see you in Orlando and you could give it back to me? Who knows? I certainly don't need it as much there," he spoke softly while pointing toward a silver sedan parked at the top of the drive.

"Thanks," Ciara said as Bryant walked to his car and waved goodbye. Her shoulders slumped when his taillights disappeared. An ache started in her chest at the sight.

The coat was warm and smelled lightly of men's cologne. The scent was clean and woodsy. She snuggled it to her body thankful for its warmth. Then she thought of

Cameron. He should have been there for her. The hurt and frustration grew until the pounding of her heart reached her ears. "I am really alone," she yelled to the night sky. Then she closed her eyes and breathed deeply, dropping into one of the wooden rocking chairs.

She could forget the horrible night and join her friends at Buckhorn Inn, but she knew it was too late. The events of the evening couldn't be undone, and she would have to live with the consequences. She wiped a tear from her cheek and pulled the coat closer, refusing to return to the warmth of the chalet.

"I'll just stay out here and freeze. I hope that makes all of you happy," Ciara spoke through clenched teeth. Her breath came out in puffs and her teeth began to chatter. Her only hope was in the chalet, but she could not bring herself to go back in. Not yet. Not until she had control. Not until she had a plan.

CHAPTER 2

The night passed in a blur. Ciara remained on the porch until she could no longer endure the cold and her fingers were numb. Both her parents embraced her as she reentered the chalet great room. As they led her to the fireplace to warm up, Ciara sat and focused on her parents soft voices.

"You can come visit any time and we will be back quarterly," Carol said. Ciara grinned with her lips tightly closed. She could not say what she really thought. She didn't want them to leave, but more than that, she didn't want them to give up their income. It was a large part of her income.

She also listened to the other side conversations as she warmed herself by the large fireplace. After she felt warm enough, she hugged them all and said goodnight.

Ciara tiptoed into Jack Junior's room. She would find his plane ticket information and intercept him tomorrow. His bed sat untouched with one lone hard-shell suitcase perched beside it. She grabbed the handle and looked for the zipper compartments. There were none on the outside. She would have to open his luggage and look inside. She unpacked the socks from the netting, looking for any sign of paper or documents. She would take the same flight to Orlando in the morning if she could find the ticket. It was not with the socks.

"Where would you put your travel plans, Junior?" She whispered in the dark room. The only light was cast by the bathroom between their rooms, and Ciara squinted to see the contents before her. She lifted his khaki slacks and felt a small zipper on the right-hand side of the case. She unzipped the pocket and found the printed papers shoved inside. As she took a photo with her phone, she heard deep male voices at the bottom of the staircase.

Ciara's hands trembled as she methodically arranged Jack Junior's clothing and placed the suitcase back against the side of the bed. She crept back to the bathroom and closed the door at the same time he entered his room. She locked the bathroom door and sat on the closed toilet seat. Her heart pounded. His footsteps stopped at the bed, and she moved to unlock the door.

"Goodnight, Junior," Ciara said softly.

"Goodnight, Ciara," Jack Junior said.

She spent the next two hours scheduling a flight to Florida. She was stunned and hurt, but her instincts told her to stay engaged with the situation. Her only chance to maintain the life she desired was to talk to Jack Junior. Unfortunately, Luke had cornered her brother, and it was growing too late for her to get his attention tonight. Besides, she needed time to get her emotions in check and take more valium to calm her nerves.

Early the next morning, Ciara woke in the mountains of Tennessee. A deep fog enveloped the tree line just above the road at the mountain chalet. The Caldwell family rose early. The frantic movement was much different than the previous day of family leisure and feasting. Jack Junior quickly grabbed an apple and hugged all present in the great room before making his way outside. Carol and Jack followed their son to his rental car while Ciara pushed the curtain aside and peeked from the large bay window.

Jack Junior pumped his dad's hand and embraced his

mother before tossing his bag in the passenger seat. Ciara adjusted the lacy curtain while locking her eyes on Jack Junior.

Thirty minutes later, she handed her car keys to her dad, trading for his rental car. Her dad's shocked expression at her announcement to fly back made her pause before she smiled and reassured him, "I just need to be back home."

"Ciara, it can wait. You need to be with us," said Carol.

"I'm fine, you two. I want to talk with Jack Junior and get my head wrapped around all the changes," said Ciara as she embraced her parents and held out the rental keys. Her dad and mom would be a little more crowded in her sports car, but she couldn't worry about that.

Ciara arrived in Knoxville a half hour after Jack Junior. She parked the car under the rental sign and rushed to catch her flight to Orlando International Airport. She would be back home in four hours, making this the quickest family trip yet. She was the only one who hadn't settled with Jack Junior and hoped she could find some leverage when talking with him.

Jack Junior had the sole responsibility to work out the details now that Jack Sr. was stepping away. Jack Junior was close to having complete control and his final negotiation would be with her. The company was split four ways. Uncle Jim, Jack Junior, Jan, and Ciara. Jack Junior had gained the confidence of everyone and would be acting on everyone's behalf. Everyone but Ciara.

Ciara could imagine him crunching the figures in his mind and considering whether a complete buyout or a percentage each quarter would be better to offer her. She would probably swoon at the one-time, sizable amount, but she might also want a wage to support her lifestyle. It wouldn't be cheap dealing with her, and Jack Junior would have to give her plenty.

She fumbled with her small carry-on. She was relieved one of her luggage pieces fit the criteria for the plane's overhead compartment. Shoved in the small suitcase were her essential toiletries; her expensive high heels she never got to wear this trip, and one men's trench coat. Ciara smiled when she thought of the coat. Her skin warmed at the thought of pulling it close to her. The mysterious Bryant Ward had left a lasting impression on her and try as she may, she could not shake the thought of him.

"I wonder what you are doing the day after Thanksgiving, Mr. Bryant Ward," she whispered under her breath while riding the escalator to her gate.

Ciara walked toward Jack Junior. He raked his hands through his short, black hair and let out a sigh. He had not seen her, and Ciara studied him before approaching the sitting area. Earlier that morning, Jack Junior took a quick shower and didn't bother with his usual hair gel and blow-dryer routine. He dressed in slacks and a long-sleeved buttoned shirt which encapsulated his casual wardrobe.

His brow creased and tiny, fine lines formed around his eyes. Most business partners and many of his close companions did not realize Jack Junior was only thirty-four. He carried himself much older and had been an integral part of the real estate company since Ciara was a teen. He skipped the college fraternity life and never showed interest in friends his age.

Jack Junior stood with his shoulders squared and his carry-on perched at his feet. He smiled broadly until he saw Ciara. She walked to the terminal sign. The surprise of seeing her needed to work to her advantage.

Jack Junior squinted his eyes.

Ciara stopped at a row of seats and sat in the front row facing Jack Junior, who stood by the terminal counter. She felt her phone vibrate and opened her newest text. She skimmed Stephanie's biting words. Ciara felt a tinge of guilt for leaving her best friend on her special engagement weekend. She would have to make it up to Stephanie.

She looked from her phone and met Jack Junior's eyes. She raised her hand in a quick wave. She felt silly as Jack Junior's frown deepened and he walked toward her. He stood over her and peered down.

"What are you doing here, little sis? You're missing the family weekend." Jack Junior stepped back allowing her to grab her carry-on and put her cell phone in her designer purse. Ciara pointed to the terminal number and raised her ticket to her brother's nose.

"Flying back home to Vero Beach." Ciara lowered the boarding pass and met his eyes waiting for him to challenge her. She was ready to fight. In fact, she welcomed the opportunity to let someone know how she truly felt. Her temper was flaring, and she hoped her brother would say something inflammatory.

Jack Junior recoiled from her anger and stepped back from the challenge. He slowed his breathing while backing away. He pulled the handle of his carry-on to his waist and pivoted on his heels to face the counter.

"Good afternoon passengers. This is the pre-boarding announcement for flight 197. Please have your boarding pass and identification ready. Regular boarding will begin in approximately ten minutes time. Thank you." At the announcement, Jack Junior moved from the counter and made his way to the line. Ciara followed him closely and stood beside him.

"You plan on boarding first class, huh?" He pulled out his ticket and handed it to the waiting attendant while smirking at Ciara. She followed his lead and did likewise. She boarded behind him and followed to sit next to him in the middle aisle.

"How did you get on this flight on the day after Thanksgiving, little sis?" asked Jack Junior.

Ciara smiled sweetly and remained silent for the first hour of flight. She sat quietly partly because she didn't know what to say to her brother and partly because exhaustion settled on her as soon as she sat down. The usual, restless anxiety she was accustomed to was replaced the last two days with a lack of energy to do anything.

Her head rested on the pillowed seat, while she sipped the seltzer water. Jack Junior sat with his laptop open, and his phone perched beside it. He took Ciara's cue to stay quiet, however, he was not resting. Instead, he began calculating numbers and looking through architectural drawings.

"What kind of building would need that many sprinklers? That's kind of excessive...don't you think?" Ciara broke the silence and questioned the plumbing blueprint page on Jack Junior's laptop screen. She knew about design from her college days.

The interior design class she attended used a software that mimicked the engineering floor plan in front of Jack Junior. Ciara paid close attention in the designing class a year ago and made an excellent grade. Her anxiety escalated during college. She graduated with an associate degree in business and hoped her parents would accept that as her college accomplishment.

The first panic attack she suffered in college left her dependent on valium to handle stressful situations. No one knew she was on medication, and she planned to keep it a secret. A muscle twitched in her face while her breathing raced slightly. It made no sense she would feel this exhausted and at the same time feel the tension.

Her hand slipped into her purse and found the pill bottle at the bottom. She would take one more. It had been three hours and she could get more after the week-end. Ciara reasoned with herself. It was worth it to be as calm as possible while sitting here with Jack Junior. She slipped the pill into her mouth and swallowed hard.

Thirty minutes later, Jack Junior turned to Ciara and shut his laptop. She wondered if he might reveal the details of his plan with her. What were the implications of exposing the deal to the family before all the company was in his firm control? It probably was risky to involve the whole family. Jack Junior would need the freedom to reinvest in more property after this flip and they may stop him from investing Caldwell money in the first place.

The family would want to maintain the cash flow and would also want to distribute any profit. He would not be able to act on his plan until the lawyer had everyone's signature. Knowing Jack Junior, he would be patient and wait for two more weeks. Soon he should be able to go ahead with the purchase.

"Ciara, things are going to change once we all meet with the lawyer. Are you prepared? You need to understand I am not Dad. I have a company to run, and I can't be distracted from doing what I need to do," Jack Junior said as a flight attendant walked the aisle offering beverages.

Jack Junior's eyes locked on Ciara's. Did he think she was emotional or unaware of the full implications of the family meeting? Ciara's instincts led her to remain calm.

She was scared, but not weak. He would not feel sorry for her now. He frequently described her as a spoiled young girl full of drama.

Ciara sniffed and looked at Jack Junior's forehead. She changed her expression to a blank stare and said the only words that came to mind, "What kind of deal do you want to make with me?"

She had no idea what influence she had. The second valium was starting to take effect while her heart rate slowed and breathing leveled. Ciara always expected her dad to handle everything of consequence. For a fleeting moment, Jack Junior looked surprised and recoiled. This brief show of emotion on his face gave Ciara some added confidence.

"You only need to sign as silent partner and leave the details to me. You'll get your share as it comes in or you can get a very sizable amount," said Jack. He was familiar with her lifestyle, and she figured he said the last part as a bonus. She wouldn't have to do anything but wait on the profits or manage her own one-time sum.

Ciara's shoulders relaxed against the smooth leather seat. He would be like her dad. She could live her life and let Jack Junior run the company. She started to agree to his proposal until a nagging thought overtook her. Could she live the life she wanted without her parents' help? Junior wasn't going to give her more money and he would probably give her even less after the deal.

Why was he quick to pay her off and out of the picture? What did he have planned in the future that needed her signature? Jan and Uncle Jim had not signed as silent partners. They left Jack Junior in control of the company but could join board meetings as needed. She wondered why he was proposing she be a silent partner.

Ciara's mind raced to the blueprint page again. There

were enough sprinklers in the floorplan for a hundred rooms. Her pulse raced. He had big plans he wasn't sharing with any of the family. Why leave everyone out? She needed to prove to Jan and possibly Uncle Jim to trust her more than Jack Junior if any of them were going to benefit from his deal. At that moment the only card Ciara had to play was her one vote to Jack Junior's majority. She was very outnumbered, but still had her one vote. What was her vote worth to him?

Ciara smiled at her brother sweetly and turned toward the seat in front of her. "I think I'd like to talk to a lawyer before I sign. Let's agree to let this go for now. Can we?" She never experienced this feeling of power before and smiled broadly at the seat in front of her.

Jack Junior squinted his eyes slightly and pumped his fist. She was exasperating him. She knew he had to think quickly before everything spun out of control for his plan. What could he do with her? She only wanted more money, and his instinct would tell him that no amount would ever be enough. Involving another lawyer would cost precious time.

"I've been thinking you should put that fresh college degree of yours to good use. Instead of staying on the sidelines, why don't you come to work in the office. We could use another Caldwell to wheel and deal," said Jack Junior. Fear returned to her eyes. He found the right currency. She didn't want to work or be responsible for the company.

"I...I didn't quite finish my bachelor's degree and the office is in Orlando. I live an hour from there...It's not easy relocating." She saw the smile playing at the corner of his mouth. She was trapped. She had only two choices. Either go to work with Jack Junior and watch him closely or become a small shareholder giving Jack

Junior control over the company. Her uncle and sister had agreed to do it. Obviously, her dad conceded too. She couldn't bring herself to allow her brother to take her share or influence. Something told her he planned to cut everyone else out of his big scheme and she wasn't going to allow him to do so. Her wealth depended on it.

"I'll do it."

CHAPTER 3

Two years later in a small Alabama town called Bayport, Cameron Shivers sat opposite his good friend Mary Jolly and looked across to his future mother-in-law Deborah Westin. He was Mrs. Westin's pastor and was growing into the role more each day. Since he relocated to Bayport, he was getting used to being known simply as Pastor Cam. He smiled at the thought as Mary sat down across from him.

"You want to sell your beautiful bay front home? Hasn't it been in your family for a long time?" questioned Mary.

Deborah Westin's daughter, Annie, lived in Bayport and worked as a chef of a local restaurant to help her mother afford to keep their family estate. It was expensive and took everything they earned just to make ends meet. Cam and Annie were recently engaged, and he was surprised when Mrs. Westin called him for a meeting about her house. Now he understood.

Mrs. Westin looked at Cam and said, "You belong with a rare breed of men who still understand chivalry and work very hard to care for people. You and Annie need this break."

Cam smiled and looked at Mary who nodded in agreement. It was a sacrifice for him to pastor the small congregation. His and Annie's wedding was postponed while they considered their next steps. Something had to change. It took a lot of prayer and sacrifice, and now Mrs. Westin was determined to go through with a plan to set Annie free.

"It's time, Annie needs the chance...she's worked far too long just to keep us in that house. Besides, it's time for someone to restore it to its grandeur. We've just been ignoring the big issues," said Mrs. Westin as she squared her shoulders. Her wrinkled hand clasped her pocketbook and turned white as she squeezed the pink leather.

Mary sat for a moment. Mary didn't say she disagreed that Annie needed a break, but this was a big decision. "Annie may not even want you to give up the property. Maybe she would want it passed down to her," Mary said.

"You know Annie doesn't want that house. She wants to move on and live life. It's only been an albatross since she was old enough to contribute to the family income." Mrs. Westin's words echoed Cam's thoughts.

Mary moved around her huge mahogany desk and sat beside Mrs. Westin. She reached for her hand and held it with both of her larger ones. The older woman's hand disappeared between Mary's strong grip.

"Why did you come to me? I'm not in the real estate business any longer and my son has relocated the Jolly company to Atlanta. He probably wouldn't be best at finding a buyer," said Mary as her eyes met the older woman's. Mrs. Westin's expression was firm.

"I want to surprise Annie with the money to buy a storefront and start her restaurant. I've been talking to Charles at The Teardrop Restaurant, and he's agreed to let me purchase one of the smaller ovens, a refrigerator, and a few odds and ends to get her started. Of course, he doesn't know why I want the items." Mrs. Westin's eyes twinkled, and a grin replaced her former nerve-racked demeanor. She was enjoying herself.

"You've thought a lot about this," said Mary.

"I came to you, Mary, because I know you. You still run this amazing ministry here at Bayport Rehabilitation Clinic. I trust you and I believe you can help. Can't your son recommend someone? Surely, he has some idea," said Mrs. Westin.

Mary sat quiet for a moment and picked up the new family photo displayed on her shelf. Her handsome son with his wife Tia and toddler granddaughter, Marianna, were all smiling at the camera while sitting in a grassy area flanked with high rise buildings. Mary smiled at the candid photo. "I'll make a call to him if you're serious. Maybe he can put us on the right track," Mary said.

"Let me know as soon as you can. There's only one place I can find in our little town that would be a good start up place for Annie's restaurant. I've seen her looking up a place beside Glenn's bakery. I found it in Annie's search history on our computer. At first, I couldn't understand why she would be looking at storefronts in downtown Bayport. Then it hit me...she's thinking about a restaurant. It's small and old but is in a prime location." Mrs. Westin smiled at Cam.

"That is a great location right beside Glenn's Bakery," said Cam.

"Especially after all the publicity from the street revival," Mrs. Westin said as she rose to her feet and in a grand gesture straightened her back. Her peach suit gave her a rosy look and made her silver hair shine in contrast. She was a classic and the step she took today revealed even more about her. She was willing to sacrifice her family property for Annie and his happiness.

"Well Lord, You never cease to amaze me. Annie will finally get her chance," Mary said with her gaze resting on the ceiling of her office.

The next morning Cam pulled out of the angled parking space on the corner of the Twice Blessed Consignment Shop. His small studio apartment was situated above the store, and he was growing anxious to move from the small quarters.

It wouldn't be long until he and Annie had their own place together. The sky was overcast in Bayport, but Cam's mood was light. The drive to the Bayport Community Church took less than ten minutes, but he planned a detour by Glenn's Bakery this morning.

It was close to two years since he met Annie Westin and the whole community experienced a beautiful awakening to God. His pulse raced, and he wiped at his sweaty palms. Annie was going to be happy. He smiled broadly. He massaged his shoulders and spoke, "Wedding plans, restaurant plans, and finding our own home is next."

As he turned onto the historic street, Bayport Way, the glass front window covered with white butcher paper came into view. He couldn't see in, as he slowed his truck to a crawl in front, but he imagined what it looked like inside. One corner of the paper was rolled down from the top revealing a mostly intact drop-down ceiling. His mind whirled with ideas, and he said a quick prayer while moving through the street.

Cam called Annie as she made her way through the back streets of Bayport to The Teardrop Restaurant. She giggled as she spoke, "I'm actually going to marry a reverend." He imagined her playful smile, and her mood sounded light as she talked about their future together. Even heading to The Teardrop restaurant for long hours of work didn't affect her good mood.

Last night Cam prayed with her after researching more about the storefront beside the bakery, "Lord, You know what's best...I trust You." Cam fought the urge to tell her all the recent plans with Mrs. Westin, but he didn't dare ruin the surprise.

Cam heard her engine shut off as she parked at the southern cuisine restaurant. "Today will be long and laborious, but tonight we will meet up to look through apartment listings and plan our future," said Annie.

Cam smiled and whispered, "I love you, Annie Westin."

"I love you too, Cameron Shivers." Annie's voice sounded strong and determined.

That same morning rain splashed the window outside Ciara Caldwell's office suite in Orlando, Florida. The usually beautiful skies were overcast as an autumn storm close to tropical storm proportions landed. She arrived early morning around 8:20 and forced herself to look over the quarterly report again before a 9:00 meeting. She phoned her doctor and listened to his nurse explain, "Dr. Lowell will do more evaluations before giving you more medication. Can you come in two weeks?"

He didn't believe she was under more stress at her job, but at least he gave her another prescription for nerves. Ciara opened the bottom drawer and counted the remaining pills for the third time. Frowning, she realized she wouldn't have enough medicine to last until the middle of the month when her new prescription would be valid. Her nails drummed a restless beat in time with the pattering rain while she drank deeply of the expresso she picked up on the way to work.

She looked down at her pasty white arm and out the window. The unusual amount of rainfall and the lack of daylight hours available after office hours, left her desperately in need of a tan. Her designer business suit in tasteful cream blended in with her blond hair, leaving her washed out and looking as gloomy as she felt. She wasn't sure the valium was what she needed now. She needed something that would give her energy too.

Ciara focused on each mundane report given every Tuesday. Where was the exciting reveal Jack Junior had been planning for almost two years now since the family meeting at the lawyer's office? Back then she had been surprised when her dad agreed with her decision to work at the company. "Sweetheart, I think that's a great idea and just what your Pop would want. Jack Junior and you have always reminded me of him." Jack had smiled and wiped a tear from his cheek.

She knew enough about the business now to know her presence in the company slowed the progress and possibly cost Jack Junior the deal he was trying to finalize two years ago. He postponed the purchase to fight her for control. If she quit now, she would lose her influence. She could let Jack Junior buy her out of the share and get this over with. It would be a sizable amount, but not near what would come if she would just be patient. She had to outlast her brother.

It was wearing on her to sit and be patient. She whispered as she typed, "New BMW for sale close to Orlando." If she couldn't get out of the office at least she could look for a new car. Her car was two years old and was losing its new car appeal. Jack Junior wasn't going to give her a new car like her parents had done. She would have to buy it herself, since her parents didn't have the means any longer.

She looked at the price prominently sprawled under the description and grimaced. That wouldn't do. Her share of the company was holding steady at the precise amount she had been receiving two years ago. The only difference was now she paid her own way with rent and expenses. She moved from the screen and let it turn to the screen saver. She didn't want Jack Junior to walk by and see her search. He would rub in that she no longer had the means to buy a new car.

Ciara thumbed through recent texts on her cell phone. The alerts to recent properties came in each day and gave her an adrenaline rush. A newly built condominium with full beach views and club access was now available. It wasn't in her price range, but in time, she could be the one to make the upgrade. Instead, she penciled in beside the date an old client and printed the MLS listing. The thrill of pushing the information to the seekers kept her engaged and on task despite her anxiety.

Sometimes she would branch out of the receptionist role and suggest properties for clients. Most of the time it would prove to be the right fit. She was good at matching people and property. It made sense to her. The Drayer family would snatch this latest listing up for their daughter. It fit the young twenty something.

Ciara was smart and Jack Junior reluctantly admitted it to her last week in front of Bryant Ward. The affirmation felt good especially with Bryant hearing. In the last two years she learned very little about him. He was driven to succeed, and nothing was going to get in his way, so she steered clear of him. She saw him once or twice a week at board meetings and that was it.

Ciara thought about the men's coat in the back of her closet. Bryant's coat. She never mentioned it and he never brought it up. His mysterious dark eyes were difficult to read and left her feeling confused. Her pulse raced when he was near. She avoided him most days. She knew less about him than she knew of the custodians in the building. In the last meeting with Jack Junior, he surprisingly partnered her with Bryant. Her heart raced and she fidgeted in her seat at the thought. Why did Jack

Junior want them working together? She didn't trust her brother's motives.

Wind and torrential rainfall whirled around the two-story building lined with palm trees front and back. Ciara's eyes went to the desk calendar filled with meetings and phone numbers. She spent most of her day answering clients and scheduling visits to properties. It was something she did well.

At that moment, Ciara's eyes darted to the hall outside her office. Bryant filled the entrance to her office. He leaned against the door frame and cleared his throat, motioning to the seat across from her desk. Ciara nodded in agreement while he sat down across from her. Bryant had an uncanny knack for surprising her when she was off her game. This moment was no exception.

"Are you ready for the meeting? We need show what we've been working on," said Bryant.

"We need to actually work together then." Ciara frowned. Since being partnered last Tuesday, they had not met even once. He smiled and extended his long legs in front of her desk.

"You feeling alright, Ciara? You look a little pained." Bryant leaned back in the small office chair and crossed his arms over his head. His black hair was gelled and fell on his forehead in one swoop. He was handsome and terribly ambitious.

"I am in pain...my doctor won't listen when I tell him I need a refill." Ciara couldn't believe she let it slip she was on medication. She felt like a schoolgirl who couldn't talk plainly around the hunky jock. She had to think fast. He would tell Jack Junior she needed anxiety medication. She couldn't let him know.

"Oh?" He leaned forward and locked eyes with Ciara's. The lamp light from her desk danced in his chestnut brown eyes. His mouth parted slightly, and his eyebrows raised. His hair fell forward, and she fought the urge to push it back.

"I have an old ankle injury and it acts up when it rains," said Ciara.

Jack Junior would remember the summer she spent in an ankle boot in twelfth grade if Bryant said anything. Jack Junior grudgingly took her to physical therapy for two months, while she couldn't drive herself. She pulled her gaze from his and looked down at her ankle. She was thankful the rain kept her from wearing her usual stilettos. Instead, she wore chunky pumps.

"You should get your doctor to prescribe you some medication for that. There's no need for you to suffer," said Bryant as he looked at his phone and moved to stand.

"My doctor did prescribe me medicine, but I lost my prescription and can't get another for a month," said Ciara. Her lie kept growing and she was beginning to feel vulnerable and exposed.

"What do you need? Just something for pain? I could get you something to get you by. My dad's a doctor." Bryant smiled widely revealing his white teeth and dimples.

"Well...I don't want to bother you or your dad." Ciara's heart pounded. The bottle in the drawer wouldn't last long. Not for two more weeks.

"No bother, I'll talk to him this afternoon and bring you something tomorrow. The weather isn't getting better for the next few days, and I don't want to see you suffering like this," Bryant said.

He turned his phone display toward Ciara showing a picture of a pale middle-aged man with light brown hair wearing a gray suit. The title, Richard Ward M.D, was sprawled under the picture. Ciara's eyebrows raised and she looked from the phone display to Bryant.

"You don't look much like your dad," she said.

"I look like my mother. She's French Creole from Louisiana. We have dark hair and skin. My dad is mostly Irish and German. I'm a real mixture of many cultures. I like to think I'm mostly like my Louisiana relatives, though, handsome, and full of southern charm." He winked at Ciara.

Ciara reached for her coffee and took a big gulp of the lukewarm liquid. Bryant was certainly handsome. She felt heat rise to her cheeks as she smiled and pointed out of the window. She said, "It's raining."

Just then, Bryant's phone chirped another text message while he backed out of Ciara's office. She heard him answer a call and waited until his footsteps were out of her hearing.

"I can't believe I just told him it's raining," she whispered and turned to her computer screen.

Ciara traced the date with her finger for several seconds before remembering today marked two years since she last saw Cameron. Her stomach turned, and her pulse raced again, but this time for her ex-fiancé. Her life was different now. Her aspirations had been to travel and get away and here she was stuck in an office. What was Cameron doing now? Ciara wiggled her computer mouse and watched the screen turn on again. She typed 'Bayport, Alabama' into the search engine and clicked on a news story close to the top.

It was an article in Southern Shores Magazine. Ciara saw the magazine a few times a few years ago when she was interested in finding shops and houses in Bayport. She researched thoroughly when she thought she might be living there with Cameron. The article mentioned a religious experience. Ciara squinted at the picture and enlarged it full screen. It was a picture from a bakery on a city street.

People were bowing their heads and a man was standing at a podium. She caught her breath when Cameron's form came into view beside the man at the podium. In the photo Cameron stood straight with his hand clasping a young auburn-haired woman beside him. She was tall, slender, and very pretty. Ciara's stomach churned at the sight. A sadness enveloped her like a smothering blanket too warm for the season.

Was she jealous? Ciara scrunched up her face and rolled back in her chair. At that moment Jack Junior walked into her office and gave a quick nod. He raised his eyebrows in question.

She moved to minimize the computer screen, but the other search engine screen was on the car dealer site. Ciara paused mid-stride. Frozen. Her eyes raised to Jack Junior, and she blurted, "What do you need?"

"Can't a brother check on his little sis?" Jack Junior said while circling her desk. He pushed at the computer screen turning it. Rain continued to pelt the window and the wind gave a loud howl.

"I was researching." Ciara hoped Jack Junior wouldn't see Cameron in the web image, and she minimized the photo in the frame.

The picture shrank into the article and the city name, "Bayport- Bay of the Holy Spirit" came into view as Jack Junior questioned, "You thinking about religion? Ready to get back to church?"

"No...I was researching property. I've heard there's a thriving market in Bayport, Alabama." Ciara raised her chin proud of her quick comeback. Talk business and get him off the trail of her personal life. She couldn't let him see her vulnerable.

"You want to invest in property in Alabama?" Jack Junior began tapping his chin while he considered her statement. "We don't have a presence there in that market. Someone would have to relocate there to get it up and started."

"You should move there, Junior. It would give you a chance to get out of this saturated market and expand," Ciara spoke quickly and longed for distance from him. She smiled and crossed her arms in front. Jack Junior moved from the screen and sank into the office chair across from Ciara's small desk.

He picked up a photo of his parents. They looked different with the Honduras jungle and white, cinderblock building in the background. Jack's suit was replaced with jeans and a polo shirt and Carol wore casual jeans and a flowered, button-down blouse. The photo on Jack Junior's shelf was of his parents at their vow renewal. The ceremony photo was regal. The expensive attire ranked them at the top of the class of his associates and friends.

"Oh no, I couldn't leave the CEO role here in Orlando. But maybe a partner could...maybe one who has researched it so well." Jack Junior added emphasis to the last part. His eyebrows raised, and he lowered his chin. The challenge was made. Ciara knew he was growing accustomed to constantly bantering with her. His eyes searched her face.

Ciara shrank in her chair. An awkward silence fell. He wasn't going to back down. Her mind raced and then settled on the idea of getting away from Jack Junior. She liked the idea of distance. She could come back to Orlando for important meetings. Maybe this would be her chance.

"Alright then, I'll do it. I'll go and show you the untapped market of such a beautiful place not inundated with high-rises and prefabricated buildings." Ciara couldn't believe what she just agreed to do, but she couldn't back down.

"Oh God, what am I doing?" Ciara whispered under her breath when Jack Junior looked at his cell phone screen. She held the armrest of her computer chair attempting to stop the shaking in her hands as she watched Jack Junior text. He then reached across her desk grabbing her desk phone. He punched his assistant's line and began giving orders.

"We need to add a special impromptu item to our agenda...yes...I'll explain in the meeting." Jack Junior dropped the phone back into its base and smiled broadly at her. She could tell he was pleased with himself. Jack Junior's movements and facial expressions were mechanized. He was a machine; every emotion and thought controlled. For once in two years, she felt sorry for him. He would never enjoy anything but power.

Back in Bayport, Cam walked about in the wood paneled sanctuary of Bayport Community Church lit only by stage lights. The overcast skies outside did not provide enough sunlight for the stained glass to illuminate the room. The stage lights were floor mounted and reflected soft colors on the backdrop, leaving Cam mostly free of any possible distractions. He loved the sanctuary either in a very quiet, reverent state or packed full of music and people praising in full abandon. He chuckled at the thought of this contradiction in himself.

Cam spent the morning studying Old Testament passages while listening to The Matrix instrumental soundtrack. Now here he was in total silence kneeling before the altar, "Lord, there's more. I know there's more. We're growing, but it's not the same as when You came before...on the streets of Bayport. Send us out.

Give me a purpose and lead me to the lost and hurting."

As his prayer continued, the afternoon sun shone briefly through the blue and purple stained-glass casting light midway through the chairs and carpeted aisle. Cam sat up and walked to the light calm and still. As he stood in the light, he watched as it disappeared before him leaving only shadows.

"Only those in the dark need the light," he said softly. Cam's prayers asked for uncomfortable circumstances, and he didn't want shadows to enter his peaceful town, "Lord, help us be ready."

CHAPTER 4

⁓

The month of November went by in a blur for Cam and Annie, and they reeled from Mrs. Westin's decision to sell the family property. A new real estate company relocating to Bayport gave the Westins top dollar and asked them to move quickly so renovations could begin.

Cam was a little concerned the company was affiliated with Caldwell Realty, but quickly dismissed the thought when he realized it was a new company started up recently. The Caldwell's weren't the type to be intimately involved with a small town like Bayport. It probably had little to do with the Caldwell's themselves. He couldn't live his life avoiding everything about Ciara Caldwell and her family.

Documents were signed with the Caldwell representative, Bryant Ward, who sat across from Deborah Westin at closing. "That young man was so slick he slid when he walked. It took Mary a good forty-five minutes just to knock him off his high horse and get down to business," said Mrs. Westin. She met Cam and Annie for lunch after the meeting.

Annie was amused at her mother's retelling of Mary Jolly negotiating beside her son, Bernard Jackson. "I wish I could've been a fly on the wall. I hate dealing with business, but that would've been worth all the mind-numbing details of real estate," said Annie.

At the Westin House, Cam and Annie stood outside the beautiful bay front home and stacked boxes. After pushing the last box piled high with antiques, a tear collected and threatened to roll down Annie's cheek. Cam held her close and kissed the top of her head as she pressed her finger into her lid and absorbed the moisture. The weather was playing tricks on Bayport and decided to give its inhabitants a mock summer day. Temperatures were threatening to climb into the low eighties by afternoon. Cam could see the bay water lapping on the shoreline, while the sun warmed the rocky sand. Christmas was in seven weeks, and nostalgia was hitting the Westins hard. This would be the first holiday out of their home. Cam figured it was only a matter of time now and there would be a solid date set for their wedding.

"I feel a strong urge to toss off my tennis shoes and walk the shoreline to the water's edge," said Annie. Instead, she took deep breaths, closed her eyes, and waited. A calm fell over her in soft waves tickling her skin as Cam watched goose pimples form on her arms. The corners of her mouth turned up into a contented smile as she said goodbye to the only home, she and her mother's family had known for nearly seventy years.

The trunk barely closed on the overstuffed box. Cam and Annie abandoned the idea of adding Mrs. Westin's hanging basket planters. They would have to balance in the floorboard of Annie's car. She drove away from the white two-story colonial house and did not look back in the rear-view mirror.

"We should have brought my truck. I thought you said the movers only left a few things." Cam winked and shifted in the seat and peered around a floor lamp propped between them.

"It is a few things. My car's just small," Annie laughed. Her smile faded and she sighed deeply.

"I pray you serve your new owners well," said Annie

as the house came into full view of her side mirror. With that final prayer, Cam clasped Annie's hand as she turned uphill toward the main road and started the twenty-mile journey to her new apartment.

In Orlando, Bryant and Ciara looked across the conference table at Jack Junior. Bryant's face tensed as he waited to hear news. Jack Junior set up the important meeting. The last time there was a meeting like this, Bryant was given the negotiating deal for property in Bayport, Alabama. Bryant's eyes darted around the room and Ciara wondered if he might sit on his hands to keep his nerves at bay. The breathing technique learned from Jack Junior at the negotiating table would help. She watched Bryant take deep breaths and exhale slowly.

Jack Junior's gaze rested on his protégé. Jack Junior was less than ten years older but acted more like a father with his son. Ciara saw the same hunger in Bryant's eyes and the undaunting focus of a man ready to achieve.

"How's the Madison deal going?" asked Jack Junior.

Bryant sighed and fell back in his seat. Jack Junior was stalling. He knew Bryant was anxious to talk about future deals not past ones. Ciara would soon be well on her way to Bayport. Jack Junior mentioned the investment in the property was a fair deal and would keep Ciara busy with renovation details. Ciara knew more than she let on. Jack Junior was most likely giving her enough room to fail but not enough to hurt the company.

"It's almost a wrap. We're just negotiating warranties and closing costs." Bryant reached for his laptop to pull up the latest email while Jack Junior reclined with his hands clasped behind his head. Outside the Orlando sun shone brightly illuminating the side brick and almost blinding Bryant through the window. The shades needed to be drawn tighter but neither man moved to alleviate the problem. Instead, they both locked positions across from one another.

Bryant didn't shrink back and moved forward into Jack Junior's space. He read the email and closed the computer locking eyes with Jack Junior. Bryant didn't show weakness. The best Jack Junior could do was hold his own with him.

"I've got a proposition for you. As you know we are expanding our market. You did so well with the Bayport deal that I can't think of anyone better to oversee the project in Bayport." Jack Junior leaned on the conference table resting on his elbows waiting for Bryant's reply. At that moment the sun poured through the window at Bryant's eye level. He closed his eyes and drew back shielding his face from the onslaught of light.

As Bryant leaned back, he backed away in his resolve. Ciara almost felt sorry for him. Why would he need to be in Bayport, Alabama to babysit her? She was obviously expected to fail. What would possibly be the motivation behind sending Bryant? The silence between the two was growing long and awkward. Bryant had no advantage and wasn't coming up with a rational retort.

Bryant's annoyance and pride were threatening to surface, and Ciara knew Jack Junior was excellent at dealing with emotional people. He'd taught Bryant and Ciara well to use surprise and emotion as an advantage. Ciara waited and prayed Bryant would come up with a good idea to change Jack Junior's mind. Bryant distracted her. She worried the attraction she felt would expose her vulnerability more and steal her focus.

"I don't think that's a good idea," said Bryant. Ciara wilted in her chair. Bryant's reply was weak, and Jack Junior's attempt at surprise was working. He must have thought Jack Junior was going to have him negotiate the high-rise deal he researched for the last three months. Ciara caught glimpses of the floor plan when Bryant left his laptop open. With Ciara gone, it was time to act. Jack Junior was cutting Bryant out. He was sticking him with her while he used Bryant's research to make the deal.

"It's only temporary. There are deals here that will be postponed for a while. It's just a matter of time," said Jack Junior while moving to close the blinds. It was a humane gesture to put Bryant more at ease, however the sun moved lower and only a soft glow remained. Too little, too late to offer any relief, but it worked to Jack Junior's advantage. The smugness was masked well, and he plastered his winning smile.

"When do you plan for my departure? There are some deals I need to finalize here in Orlando. Can it wait until after Christmas?" Ciara knew the answer to the questions, but Bryant had resorted to small talk in his present defeated state. He half-listened, half-sulked while Jack Junior plotted the next few months of his life. He would leave soon and finalize any deals before Christmas remotely from a little bay front town he had visited only once and never wanted to see again. Now he'd be living there in no man's land with her.

Two weeks later Ciara's journey was well underway. She took two pills on the drive to Bayport. Bryant's dad supplied her with three times the amount of her current prescription. He told his dad an old college friend, a two-hundred-and-eighty-pound former football player, was dealing with a chronic back injury and needed some relief.

Now Ciara was alternating the valium with pain pills. This helped bring clarity to her reeling mind. In four short weeks, she planned to move to Alabama, gave up her lease on her posh Orlando apartment, and agreed to live in a massive colonial house by the bay. She would oversee the remodel, look for buyers, and establish a presence for Caldwell Realty.

Ciara sipped her diet soft drink and ate almonds while following her electronic navigation. The screen showed the map of her travel thus far and she was relieved she only had two hours remaining until pulling into her new drive. She masked her hollow eyes and thin frame brought on by her lack of appetite and nervous energy, with baggy clothes and full-coverage foundation make-up. Making a good impression as she entered town was at the top of her list.

Ciara stopped off-road and bought protein shakes. She was losing weight. Each video chat with her parents brought concerned looks and comments. She consumed mostly liquids and snacks and try as she may, she could not muster an appetite. Switching doctors helped keep the valium coming, but the new doctor wouldn't give her anything stronger for nerves than what she was already taking. The added pain medicine from Bryant kept the anxiety at bay, but she worried about her nerves when that was gone.

Back in Bayport, Deborah Westin, red-faced, put the home phone on its charger base. "I could kill somebody right about now."

Cam watched as her temper mounted at the news she just received. He drove as quickly as he could to be with her. He listened as she called Mary Jolly to get the details. All her efforts to get Annie's storefront were failing because of "one rich girl from Orlando's whim." The Caldwell company snatched up the storefront for their business over two weeks ago. The new company was going to be run by Ciara Caldwell.

"Oh God, why would she come here? Annie's dream is dying. Please help us, Lord," Cam whispered.

Negotiations were quick and final. Bernard Jackson had inside knowledge of the shenanigans and illuminated what he suspected from the Caldwell family. "It is the youngest daughter's pet project to move to Bayport and start a side business for the company," he explained over the conference call with Mary. Mrs. Westin's family property was sacrificed to Ciara's whim.

Cam called Mary Jolly quickly, dismissing himself from Mrs. Westin, and dropped his head in prayer. "God, You know all things and You saw this day coming. Help Mrs. Westin and Annie right now. They are going to need You to deal with this situation," he prayed.

Cam knew more than he told Mrs. Westin. The time would come to explain how the youngest Caldwell was connected to him. He just didn't want to add any fuel to the fire. It was not the time to expose Cam's past to his future mother-in-law. It was only a matter of time before the whole ugly truth would surface.

Cam followed Mary as she rose, grabbed her jacket making her way out the back office, past Director Jeremy Clay's office and into the front lobby of the Bayport Rehabilitation Center. It was just a couple of years ago that she made a sacrifice herself to keep the rehabilitation property instead of selling. The deal was tempting and large, but in the end the needs of the clients won her heart and kept the clinic safe and sound. Cam had counseled her through it.

Tonight, she was eating at The Teardrop Restaurant with him. It was their ritual to meet to share Annie's culinary excellence and wonderful company. This night was especially charged with drama. "Why is that girl moving here? She doesn't know who she's messing with." Mary breathed deeply trying to settle her temper.

Cam saw Mary willing herself to relax and he thought about the relationship God put together two years ago after Ciara Caldwell's failed attempt to derail him from the ministry in Bayport. That Thanksgiving service at the church had been a real turning point for him and shortly after he began dating Annie Westin.

"God, You got this. Nothing this girl does can stop Your plan," Mary prayed with Cam at their usual table at The Teardrop restaurant.

Cam refolded his napkin several times before crushing it into a ball. His earlier conversation with Mrs. Westin kept rolling over in his mind. He needed Mary more than he could ever remember. She was a surrogate parent to him when he first arrived as pastor of Bayport Community Church. Cam attempted to call his dad and get advice, but only got his voicemail. His parents lived in North Carolina and were an hour ahead. He looked at his watch's digital display, 6:03.

He was supposed to be at the church by 7:30 to lock up and critique the choir's latest song, but he doubted he could handle seeing anyone right now. He texted Harold Hartline, the Glenn's Bakery owner and close friend to lock up and give his apologies.

"My first inclination is to give Ciara Caldwell a good tongue-lashing, but I'm resisting," Mary said as she took his hand in her own. Her long-manicured nails painted silver locked over Cam's hands and her ebony hands warmed his. He relaxed a bit and looked directly into Mary's soft, brown eyes. Faint lines were showing around her eyes and for the first time he thought she must be quite a bit older than him. She looked a little more tired than usual.

"Lord, I pray You give Cam wisdom and strength.

Nothing happens to us that You don't allow. Let us know what to do and speak. And Lord, please help me not to kill that little vixen. Amen." Mary looked up from Cam's hand and smiled sweetly.

"You're gonna be OK. God's plan is still active. You just got to pass a few more tests. Don't let this get you down," said Mary.

Mary waved the server over to the table and ordered two meat pies for them. As the server filled two glasses with water and placed silverware on the table, Cam looked up and breathed a sigh, "You are right. I will pass this test. It's a test. Annie and I will get through this." His shoulders relaxed as he thought about Annie in the back of the restaurant.

Right now, she would be dipping plates of food and steadily reading orders. She was a talented chef full of life and beauty. Her circumstances were changing despite not getting the storefront for her restaurant and despite his ex-fiancé's intrusion into their lives and beloved town. "I'm getting her out of The Teardrop, storefront or no," said Cam.

"That's the spirit. Think outside the box, Cam. You have an opportunity to move on with the wedding and God will show you an alternative to the storefront," said Mary.

Cam's mind began racing. Try as he may, there was no good alternative to the storefront. It really was the best location. It was prime real estate that needed some repairs but would have given Annie the chance to stretch her talents beyond a couple of menu items at The Teardrop. It was next door to Glenn's Bakery and Harold Hartline, the co-owner, had hoped they would be neighbors.

"Have you thought about how you are going to break the news to Annie. She needs to know who purchased her family home and the storefront." Mary didn't want him to neglect telling Annie and Mrs. Westin the full truth. It mattered the news be broken by Cam in the best possible way instead of them stumbling onto the heart-breaking reality.

"I am going to talk to Annie tonight. We planned to go to the coffee shop after her shift since she doesn't work tomorrow." Cam's face looked pained. The dread was settling on him, "Why would Ciara move here? Why the Westin house?" questioned Cam.

"The good Lord only knows...that girl is lost. My gut tells me she's desperate. Stay strong and stay clear of her as much as possible. I'll run interference if need be." Mary winked at Cam and tried to draw out a smile. Her searching eyes looked on for a full five seconds before he cracked a weak smile.

"Now that's the best thing I've heard all night. Ciara doesn't know what she's in for." Cam chuckled at the thought of Ciara running into Mary and he almost felt sorry for his ex-fiancé.

Cam peeked in on Annie as she wiped her brow and lifted her eyes to the ceiling of the restaurant kitchen. Tonight, it felt especially hot and cramped to him. Cam wondered if a familiar feeling of entrapment was threatening to surface. It had been two years since she spoke of the feeling. "Lord, help me to reach her. I don't want her to ever get back to that place," Cam mumbled.

Her blue eyes darted to the back door and Cam remembered her recollection of her frequent trips out back for fresh air before the new security system was installed. She had taken up smoking for a short while before she rededicated her life to the Lord at the Thanksgiving service two years ago. She pushed her auburn hair back into her bun and refocused on her task. Cam decided not to disturb her and wait for a better chance to talk with her.

She didn't have time to peek her head out to Mary and Cam and he felt an unsettling in his stomach from earlier. Annie said her mother was acting strange and complaining more than usual about the apartment space. When Annie suggested they put up the foyer Christmas tree since they had to abandon the thought of hauling out the ten-foot great room heirloom spruce, Mrs. Westin frowned and waved off the suggestion.

"I don't understand my mother. Why did she give up her house? Nothing is making sense. I want to get married and leave The Teardrop. Now that it is a possibility, I'm not feeling any more settled." Annie texted on her break.

Cam texted back one word, "Praying."

The digital clock on the wall showed 7:04 and Cam knew Annie would leave tonight at ten and not delay for anything or anyone. He would be waiting to get coffee and she wouldn't be back home until midnight or later. She wouldn't be able to talk to her mother until tomorrow.

"We're getting to the bottom of all this soon. I can't stand being left in the dark." Cam remembered her words from earlier.

At 10:00 sharp, Cam stood at the kitchen entrance while Annie tossed her apron and said her quick goodbyes. They moved to his truck parked beside her little sedan and climbed in quickly. After a curt greeting and a sweet kiss, they made their way to the coffee shop. The streets of Bayport were lined with Bradford Pear trees donned with white twinkle lights set to come on at dusk and to fade off at midnight.

Cam navigated the small lane with his pickup truck.

His right-hand clasped Annie's tightly while his left hand rested on the steering wheel. She sat quiet in the passenger seat. Cam was afraid small talk would send him over the edge and he'd finally break down from the day of nerves.

The apartment guidebook sat between them like an exclamation mark to the fact that they were responsible for Mrs. Westin's misfortune. Annie turned her face toward the window and Cam looked down briefly feeling the weight of the moment settle on his shoulders. Annie didn't know the half of it. Mrs. Westin hadn't told her daughter about the storefront.

The beautiful, sleepy street displayed traditional Christmas decorations lining windows and displaying an occasional wooden reindeer or sleigh. Even with all shops closed tight, the streetlights and decorations left a festive, lively atmosphere. Across and four doors down from Glenn's Bakery, the coffee shop was the only place open for business. Its digital sign shone brightly indicating its open status.

Three compact cars were parked curbside, and the outside tables were full of teenagers out for the weekend. Cam chose to skip over two streets and come in back avoiding the storefront next to Glenn's Bakery.

Down the street, Ciara drove into the parking space in front of the storefront beside Glenn's Bakery. It was 10:22 and she couldn't believe her eyes. The street looked exactly like the website photo. On this trip to Bayport, she was driving these streets trying to avoid Cameron Shivers, not find him. She remembered the church was nearby and hoped he was there or home in his consignment shop apartment.

Ciara shivered despite throwing on a jacket and tennis shoes. She stood in front of the storefront sorting through keys to open the double glass doors. What a humble start. She sighed and turned toward the pear tree illuminated by Christmas lights. As she found the key, bright headlights blinded her. She shrank back and waited for the driver to park completely. Her heart leaped as she waited to address the occupant of the luxury sedan. She sighed deeply when Bryant's face came into clear view.

"Bryant, what on earth are you doing here so soon." She stood at the shop door as he rose from the leather seats and stretched his legs in a grand gesture. He then twisted his back and rolled his shoulders. His wrinkled shirt was untucked from his designer black trousers.

"Hi, partner. Looks like we got a lot of work to do here." Bryant moved past Ciara retrieving the key she held out in front of her body. He nimbly opened the glass door and felt along the right wall for lights. She rubbed her hand where his warm skin had touched hers. It had been a while since she felt a touch like his. She shook her head, back and forth and dropped her hands to her side.

Bryant said, "I called ahead and made sure there is electricity and to get the contractor in early morning to begin converting the space into a respectable office. I may be stuck in a little town with two traffic lights, but I don't have to suffer along with them."

Ciara walked the length of the room and shook her head. She balled her hands into fists and shook one to the ceiling, "I hate my brother. I've never taken it this far and I know that God is very displeased with me saying it, but I hate my brother," Ciara spoke through clenched teeth as she looked at her surroundings.

After finding the bathrooms and the back-office, she wilted into one, lone chair left from the previous owners.

It was covered in dust and had a wobbly leg. The place was old and a mess. The once white tiled floor was now mostly gray colored, and the ceiling tiles contained multiple water stains. Bryant knelt in front of her.

She lowered her head and fought the urge to vomit the protein shake she'd made earlier for lunch. She had no groceries and hadn't managed to unpack her kitchen supplies since she arrived. "God, it's over. He's finally trapped me and sent his lynch man to complete the job." Ciara lifted her head and cleared her throat while looking into Bryant's warm, brown eyes.

"It's not as bad as you think. A little paint and the help of some skilled carpenters and we could have this office looking very respectable," said Bryant.

Bryant counted floor and ceiling tiles and wrote down the numbers for the contractor. He stopped in front of Ciara again and studied her for the first time in a long while. He'd sat across from her for months and never really looked closely. Ciara knew men found her attractive and figured she looked vulnerable in the dusty chair. Her blond hair was falling around her face and she wore tennis shoes instead of office heels. He'd never seen her like this.

"Jack Junior will see to it that I fail. Why even try to make this work?" Ciara was too tired and defeated to play her typical role of aloofness and control. She sank back into the fabric of the chair. It was dusty and smelled like a greasy french fry. She recoiled and shot forward, placing her elbows on her knees.

"I'm not going to let him take us down. I'll fight him to the end. He messed up when he sent me to you," Bryant seemed to say this more to himself than to Ciara. He kneeled in front of her again, taking her small shoulders in his hands. "Look at me. We can do this. He messed with the wrong two people when he put us together."

Ciara looked into Bryant's eyes. It was there. She believed him. She still didn't quite trust him, but he was telling the truth. Bryant needed this plan to work and now they both had a lot at stake. She slowly stood before him and motioned for him to follow her as she made her way out the front glass doors to her car. She popped the trunk latch and walked around as Bryant followed. His hands were tucked in his pockets and his gelled hair fell onto his forehead.

There in the back of the car was a lock box with her costly jewelry. It contained a menagerie of gifts and family treasures, but Ciara was drawn to the other contents. The pain pill bottle was in there too. Bryant watched closely and moved toward her when she leaned deep into the truck.

She was not dumb enough to drive across two states with a bottle of medicine prescribed to another person in clear view. She trembled and removed the box. The key to the lock box hung around her neck on a small gold chain. She pulled it over her head and walked back into the storefront with Bryant. His questioning eyes were met by her determined ones.

"Bryant, I need you to keep this key and box for me. I'd like for it to be kept here. There are things that matter very much to me in there. I just don't need regular access." She handed the box to him and put the gold chain around his neck, "Keep it safe."

Ciara's trembling hands were giving away her current state, but her voice was strong and clear. She was making a stand and needed him to help her find the willpower. He opened the box and found more than family heirlooms. The pills. Bryant lowered his eyes and nodded in agreement. Their eyes locked and a small tear escaped from one of Ciara's eyes.

"Let's find a greasy spoon that's open late. I need to eat. I don't want to eat, but I've got to eat," Ciara said this to Bryant while brushing aside the tear. She turned and walked to her car. He moved back to the front and turned out the store light and locked the door.

"You need my help. It's the only way we're going to make this work," Bryant said while following her to the car.

Ciara sat in the passenger seat of her little sports car, and Bryant took the cue to get in the driver's seat. He checked to see if his car was locked tight and pushed the lock button on the keyring twice while listening for a beep. He would retrieve it later tonight. Neither talked while he found the highway leading away from the bay. She thought about the pancake house she passed on her way into Bayport and gave directions to Bryant.

"I never thought I'd be taking you to a place like this, but just maybe this could be a step in the right direction for you," said Bryant.

Ciara watched him closely. Bryant rubbed his temples and tapped the dash. He frowned, and his jaw tightened as he looked over at Ciara. She massaged one of her shoulders and fought the urge to vomit. It was a good thing she hadn't eaten. The pills she took earlier with the soda and nuts left her feeling nauseous and empty.

"I'm sorry I am a little off my game tonight. I really shouldn't have taken the medication on an empty stomach." She clasped her trembling hands together in her lap.

Bryant sighed deeply and said, "My dad spent his whole life taking care of people and worked long hours at the hospital never really living for himself. My mother finally had enough and divorced him. Her bitterness spews out each time she recalls the events and schedules of their lives focused on hospital rotations and skipped vacations."

Ciara was surprised Bryant felt the liberty to tell her about his parents. They never talked about anything personal before. The long drive and recent events were exposing more than just Ciara. She looked forward and did not comment.

"My first real girlfriend from high school was a real damsel in distress. I wasted many important moments of my senior year with a young woman who was bound for trouble," Bryant continued, "She skipped school and began drinking every weekend. Our senior prom was ruined by her getting drunk and yelling at me because I insisted on taking her home. My mom said I was just like my dad. Always taking care of other people."

Bryant looked to Ciara and whispered under his breath, "How did I get here again? God help me." Ciara counted the light poles as they passed overhead. She couldn't find the words to reply. He knew about the pills and couldn't say anything about it since he had given them to her. She gave them back and left them in his hands. She knew he suspected her of using the pain pills to cope with stress. Her present state after driving in earlier was obvious to anyone including herself.

She wanted to eat and go to sleep. Bryant could say what he wanted. She wasn't his girlfriend and had no desire to use Bryant for more than a business partner to get the Bayport extension to the company off the ground and profitable.

"My private life will get better once I get settled here," she whispered into the passenger window.

That same night Cam willed his eyes to look at Annie and not out the coffee shop window. He spotted a red sports car and almost jumped at the site. Either his mind was playing tricks or Ciara just rode by in the passenger seat of a red BMW. The same car she sped away in two years ago. Annie seemed in no mood to hear any deep revelations tonight. He wasn't sure if she had any idea what he was about to tell her. He only knew her face mirrored his own discomfort.

"I can't understand. Why would my mother sell her house and move into an apartment? She's unhappy and I feel like I'm to blame somehow," her words trailed off as she picked up the oversize mug and took a long drink. She peered over the cup and slowly lowered it. "Are you alright? You look like you just saw a ghost."

Cam took her hand in his, letting his fingers squeeze tightly while looking into her eyes. She wore minimal make-up, and her hair was in a loose bun on top of her head. Auburn tendrils escaped around her face. She looked adorable tonight and he hated to introduce the issue this late after her long day of work at the restaurant.

"I know why your mom is so discontented. She discovered something today that made her very upset. She's been planning a great surprise for you and found out the plan has failed," he said.

"What plan? What did she find out? Why keep it from me? This is all so strange. I feel like everyone around me has gone crazy and decided to protect me like a child. I am a grown woman, and I can take the news," said Annie.

"Do you remember me talking about my ex-fiancé, Ciara Caldwell? I told you about her family and their real estate business?" He searched her face to see if anything was ringing a bell. She moved her hand away and slumped into the oversized chair.

"I do remember you saying her father was your

former pastor and he owned a company. What does this have to do with my mother?" Annie rubbed her temples.

"Ciara's company bought your mother's property... your property. I didn't know it was the Caldwell family who made the deal. It never occurred to me they would have any direct dealings here in Bayport. They're all from Orlando." Cam spoke slowly and smiled weakly. His shoulders slumped.

"Why would they do it then? I don't understand." Annie leaned on the table. She rubbed her shoulders and Cam knew they were knotting. He felt sorry for her when she moved to rubbing her temples again; she often had migraine headaches form behind her eyes. It had been a long time since she had shown these symptoms.

Annie watched Cam's face, "Why are you so upset about the company buying property in town."

For a split second he could not mask his anger and she saw color rise in his face.

"Do you still have feelings for Ciara? I've always heard there is a thin line between love and hate," said Annie.

"Ciara is moving to Bayport and will be living in your family property. And the worst part is she bought the storefront next to Glenn's Bakery. Your mom has been looking into buying it for you. It was supposed to be a surprise for Christmas." Cam balled his fist and frowned with the declaration.

Annie closed her eyes and Cam watched her shoulders sink. "I'm frustrated I was not given any say in the matter," Annie mumbled, "What made everyone think I need to be rescued? The storefront dream has ended. Just like that. A manipulative girl from your past just traipsed into our life and took everything from us," said Annie.

Cam looked at Annie's long fingers laced together. Her knuckles were turning white as she squeezed them tight and said, "I never thought I could feel this way about you. I feel like your past is ruining my life."

Cam felt the blow and sat quiet not wanting to react. She only said what they were both thinking. He leaned closer to Annie. His hands moved to the table. He looked up and felt his face getting hot. Tears threatened to come next.

"I've got to get a hold of myself...it's not your fault," said Annie as she shook her head and stood abruptly.

"Annie, you need some time to sort through this. I don't know what to say. I'll take you to your car. You need to talk to your mom," Cam said while rising to stand in front of her.

Cam placed a tip on the table and reached for Annie. She reluctantly took his hand. His knees felt wobbly, he was exhausted, and the incessant sound of chatter in the coffee shop was likely adding to Annie's headache.

As they made their way out the door and to the curb, Cam slid into the driver's seat. An exhaustion he couldn't push away descended like a heavy shadow on his shoulders leaving him numb. "God, we really need You now," he prayed aloud while looking at the top interior of his truck.

CHAPTER 5

⌒⌒

Three weeks later, Ciara stood inside Glenn's Bakery as Harold Hartline turned on the sign. He was part owner and baker and explained to Ciara that everyone called him Hartline. She came next door to meet him and hoped to get the word out about Caldwell Realty. He and Mrs. Rosita Glenn, his business partner and close friend, worked long hours completing orders before the end of the week.

Hartline said, "I was welcomed into the family two years ago and Mrs. Glenn became like a mother to me. Bill, her late husband, was like a father to me and their daughter, Katrina, is very special to me," he said the last part and grinned.

Ciara listened quietly while standing at the shiny glass counter. The signature cake for the bakery was untouched and sparkled under the recessed lighting above the heavy, glass cake cover. She moved closer to inspect the icing. It was delicate and pale yellow. Her stomach growled, and she patted it and moved away from the display.

"Where is Katrina now? I haven't seen a young woman here," Ciara said.

"She's in Europe training as a baker," he pointed to the map behind the counter, "in Italy for six months and then to France for another six."

"I'd love to join her about right now," said Ciara as a saw sounded next door. She frowned deeply and sighed.

"Christmas day falls on the weekend, giving the

bakery several workdays to finish before closing midday on Christmas Eve," Hartline said changing the subject. He was a little older than Ciara and reminded her of herself. His wiry frame and brown eyes were like Ciara's own.

"Southern Shores Magazine decided to devote a full-colored page for the bakery, and it has been difficult to get my head out of the clouds and back to reality today." Hartline smiled and patted the signature cake display.

"I have plenty to be grateful for, but I can't really get the big head. I'm just two years sober. And to think I couldn't make it two hours just a few years back." Hartline stared at Ciara. She felt his perusal and looked away a little uncomfortable with his statement. Did he think that she drank? She took anxiety medication, but she was not a user. She tensed and thought about the pain pills she had taken from Bryant. It wasn't her medication, and she knew it wasn't legal, but she didn't think she abused them.

Bayport weather was warmer than usual, and Rosita Glenn poked her head in the front through the double revolving doors. "Turn the thermostat, Hartline. Will you?" She waved at Ciara and let the doors fall behind her as she moved past enjoying the cooler temperature in the bakery front. She was petite and spoke with a heavy Mexican accent.

"Yes ma'am, that'll be the second time this week we've had to run air-conditioning. Merry Christmas." Hartline smiled and put on the Santa hat decorating the feature cake display. He pointed to the cake and said, "This is the same cake from my late grandmother's recipe with some tweaks by Katrina. It put Glenn's Bakery on the map for many people in the region and landed

Katrina a scholarship to study abroad."

We added a sugared lemon with mint leaf to the top giving it a festive feel for the season. I wonder how many ways we can decorate this same cake for the rest of the year. "This is getting ridiculous," said Hartline. Ciara smiled and laughed with Hartline glad he was no longer talking about addiction.

"Have you gone to Caldwell Realty? Sounds very busy next door." Rosita pointed to the wall adjacent to the bakery. Saws whined, and nail guns popped unsettling the instrumental Christmas jazz song playing louder than usual from the bakery speakers. She raised her eyebrows and a small smile played at the corner of her mouth as she looked at Ciara across from Hartline. Her black hair had streaks of gray and her brown skin was flawless.

"Ciara Caldwell has come to visit us. I don't want to disturb them while they work next door." Hartline smiled tightly and nodded to Ciara.

Ciara waved to the older woman and smiled. Rosita said, "Come over anytime and get something to eat." She looked at Ciara's small frame and frowned.

Rosita picked up a plate of muffins and extended it to Ciara, "No thank you, Mrs. Glenn, I've already had my breakfast this morning," Ciara lied.

She could not bring herself to eat the sweetened chocolate muffin. She survived on health shakes and organic fruits and vegetables. It had been a while since she had eaten anything with that much sugar and flour. "I need to get back, but I appreciate your offer. I will see you around." Ciara walked to the door while Hartline moved to unlock it for her. The bakery would open in the next couple of hours, and they would work for many hours to fulfill the Christmas orders.

Later that morning, Cam talked with Hartline at a small table close to the back exit of the bakery. Hartline frowned as he talked about Annie not moving in next door to open her restaurant. Before the Caldwell family bought the storefront, it was working out perfectly for the bakery and restaurant to work together on the beautiful historic street.

"I haven't had time to go over there but she's visited here," said Hartline. "My plan was to help you guys get the business up and going."

Cam said, "But now, all is spoiled."

"I already feel a drawback. The real estate company seems out of place. It's the kind of business that should be on the new build sites closer to the interstate." Hartline waited for Cam's reply while Rosita Glenn listened.

"I agree with you, man. We've got to pray for the situation. It is breaking Annie's heart, and Mrs. Westin is furious. I'm sorry you are having to deal with Ciara and the Caldwell family; some of them are easier to reason with than the others, unfortunately, Ciara is one of the others," Cam said this quickly behind clenched teeth. His raw emotion threatened to emerge.

"We should make ourselves neighbors. It is the right thing to do." Rosita Glenn's kind expression prodded Hartline. She pronounced each word carefully while her strong accent added emphasis.

"What would the Lord have me to do?" asked Hartline.

Cam watched as Hartline dutifully opened the display and pulled out the featured cake. It had aged for twenty-four hours, and the smell of the bright yellow filling permeated the glass enclosure. The knife sliced through the creamy pale-yellow icing revealing the white cake with mango filling. "I guess I'll bring the bakery best and my claim to fame. It'll be my sacrifice unto the Lord." Hartline walked past Cam and shrugged his shoulders. Cam took that statement as his cue to exit behind Hartline.

He walked out the glass doors into the waiting sunlight as the midday holiday crowd was ramping up for Christmas. He carefully made his way to the rear parking lot. He did not want to run into Ciara. It would be better if he avoided her right now. He cranked his truck and drove south to the Bayport Community Church. "I have much to pray about today," Cam said to the bright blue sky.

Back at Caldwell Realty, the glass door opened while Hartline entered carrying a white box. Bryant didn't look up. His sleeves were rolled up and he had a notepad in hand. It was up to Ciara to play the receptionist here too. She walked to Hartline, and frowned at his serious expression, "Hi again...What can I do for you?"

"Hello, I thought I should come over and officially welcome you to Bayport." Hartline offered the box to Ciara and stepped back a full stride. His weak effort at friendly conversation was less than inviting and he looked as if he might leap for the door. Ciara figured the renovations were bothering him.

"Is this the signature cake? I know a thing or two about bakeries. I'm not easily impressed." Ciara was in her element now. Her travels and lifestyle gave her very refined tastes. She opened the box and held the cardboard support up to her nose and smelled deeply. "Yummy," she said as her stomach growled. She put her finger up indicating she wanted Hartline to wait.

She retrieved the plastic fork and napkin in the plastic bag in his other hand. The plastic fork provided her with a full bite of icing, filling, and cake. As she chewed, a smile played at her lips, and she looked fully in Hartline's waiting eyes.

"Wow, now that's good! Orlando has nothing on Bayport finest. Heck, Italy has nothing on this. You should really market this. I think you got something here," said Ciara.

"You do, huh. Well, I'll think about that sometime," said Hartline as his eyes darted to the door.

At that moment, Ciara's eyes rested on Hartline. His eyes moved from the door to her trembling hands. She couldn't hide them, and her eyes were droopy. She swayed slightly and giggled. She was intoxicated. She shouldn't have taken an extra pill at lunch. Hartline would know all the signs. Her puny frame and unsteady walk pointed to her lack of control and extra valium. His face twisted in concern, and he reached out to her. Ciara swayed slightly to the left and focused on standing still.

"If you need a reference, I'm just next door," Ciara said weakly in her breeziest voice. Something about Hartline was distressing her, he was a noticer. He saw her trembling and he made eye contact a little longer than she liked. The last person to do that was her doctor who refused to give her more medication.

"I'll keep that in mind. See you around." Hartline walked over to Bryant and shook hands. As Bryant motioned for the carpenter to shut off the saw, Hartline waved him off and just pointed next door. Bryant smiled and nodded and gave a thumbs up. Over the whine of the saw, he mouthed, "See you around."

"Lord, why do I have to be so anxious all the time?" Ciara whispered to herself as Hartline stepped to the door.

Hartline exited, and Ciara's gaze followed as he made his way out the front entrance and onto the sidewalk.

That same day at the bay front, Cam and Annie parked at the top of a hill overlooking the gray-brown water. Mary was meeting them for lunch. The smell from the hotdog stand wafted up making Cam's stomach growl. Annie stepped out of her car waiting on Mary in the steady line of people forming from the docks and street. Cam followed quietly and didn't make small talk or hold Annie's hand.

One lonely Christmas wreath decorated with chili pepper string lights hung on the truck side. The cook busily made orders while Tony Glenn, Rosita Glenn's grandson, greeted each customer. He shared Rosita's beautiful brown skin and rich black hair; however, his green eyes were different. They were like his grandfather's, Bill Glenn. Cam thought of Bill and smiled. He had been his first friend in Bayport, and it had been bittersweet conducting his funeral service. They all missed him greatly. Tony kept busy filling orders from the commercial fishing and shrimping crews either coming or going out to sea for a catch.

Cam and Annie watched Mary park at the top and join them in line. They stood by a banner swaying beside the truck. Sprawled across the banner were the words, 'Closing soon.'.

"Sorry I'm late. I didn't realize how crowded it would be." Mary looked around with big eyes as she stood behind the couple. The famous sauce still brought in the business.

"I don't know what we are going to do when he closes the stand. Where will we go to get dogs like this?" Mary's question was somber. She moved forward and gave her order. Both women's faces were serious.

"He's really shutting it down the first of the year." Annie joined Mary and Cam at the picnic area. It was warm enough to sit outside. Mary sat across from them extending the basket with the hotdog smothered in fresh relish and special sauce.

Mary said, "Maybe the hotdog will lighten the mood and fill our bellies. I feel so hollow right now." Cam lowered his head and said a quick prayer over their food.

"He's ready to call it quits. Rumor has it the special sauce recipe will go to the grave with him." Annie smiled at this statement.

"Hmm. Well, that's not good for me. I only have two places to eat as it is. The Teardrop when you are there and here. It's a crying shame, I tell you," said Mary.

Mary took an oversized bite of her hotdog and chewed quickly. The burst of flavor fully filled Cam's mouth as he took his first bite. The crowd moved, and Cam saw down to the brown water. A pelican cried out stalking the fishing vessel docked on the wharf hoping for some scraps of fish. "I know how you feel crazy bird. My meals are about to be scarce too," Cam whispered to himself.

"I wonder how much a food truck costs?" Annie made small talk while she nibbled on the last two bites of her meal. Everything was out of sorts these days. It was hard to find anything that hadn't changed except for the one thing Cam knew she desperately wanted to change-working at the Teardrop. That stubbornly remained.

"Why don't you go and ask him now the line is gone. Might be worth checking out," Mary said the last statement like a dare. The wink she gave pushed the idea and caused Cam's stomach to flop.

"It doesn't hurt to ask," Cam said quickly and nodded his head up and down. Annie smiled while raising her brows.

"You two think I should run a hotdog stand? That's

a crazy idea. What would I do with a hotdog stand? Burly fisherman and smelly docks. No thank you." Annie breathed out and shook her head, no. She looked down at the dock and on cue an annoying seagull grabbed at a fish head sending pieces of flesh flying onto the wooden planks of the boardwalk.

"Food trucks move around, Annie, and they don't all sell hotdogs," Mary said this calmly while grabbing for her friend's hand. Annie's hand was thin but strong. So capable of creating beautiful food. Only a few people knew of her talent, and they weren't enough to launch her into her own place. She needed a lot of money and investment.

"It doesn't hurt to ask." Mary smiled broadly for the first time in days. Her nodding head prompted Annie to action.

Cam looked at the truck scrutinizing the weathered exterior. The tires were old and planted in four inches of dirt and sand. The silver top and white panels were streaked black.

Tony sprayed the small jutting counter with a bleach concoction and wiped vigorously while Annie cautiously approached the window.

"Is Ned close?" Annie spoke softly, and her voice trembled slightly. Ned turned around from scrubbing the flat grill top. His hands were steady, but the lines around his face and the hunched back showed signs of a hard-working life. Most likely six days a week with ten-hour days.

"Hi, miss Annie, chef extraordinaire. Did you enjoy your lunch?" He gave a rare smile and moved to the recently sanitized counter. He absently stirred the oversized crock pot while flexing his left hand to work out the cramps.

"Hi Ned...congratulations on your upcoming retirement. Must be nice to think about sleeping in and having Saturdays off?" Annie leaned on the counter. The smell of the grill and sauce were still permeating the area despite the large exhaust fan running atop the truck.

"No ma'am...I'm going fishing. Instead of feeding the fishermen, I'm joining them," he chuckled, and the tension relaxed in his face.

"What about the truck? Are you selling it?" Annie's brows raised in question. She smiled and looked back at Mary who continued to grin and mouthed, "Good girl."

"Well, yes I am...can't think of anyone who would want to buy it. There just isn't a demand around these parts. I ended up with this old girl because my storefront was ready to be condemned and now five years later." Ned stopped mid-sentence and looked Annie in the eyes, "You interested?"

"I think I am...I-I-I could possibly buy it...for a decent price...and maybe move it someplace else...I don't know." Annie's eyes darted around the truck and down the bank to the murky bay water lapping at the dock.

"Breathe, you got to breathe, so you won't pass out," Cam said.

Mary smiled and moved beside Annie offering a hand to steady her. The ground slanted toward the bay and Annie looked as if she might tumble any minute.

Ned said, "I'll meet with you on Monday. I'm sure we could work out a deal."

After dropping Annie off at The Teardrop and driving back to Bayport Community church, Cam knelt in his office to pray. His thoughts were racing. Annie had asked about a food truck and a disturbing image of Ciara kept coming to his mind.

He'd caught a glimpse of her earlier while passing

the storefront. He did not expect her to be outside, and he almost didn't recognize her. She looked hollow and ten pounds lighter. Her signature blond locks and designer clothes were familiar, but that was all that gave any indication it was Ciara.

"Heavenly Father, I feel such a heavy burden for Ciara. Something's wrong," Cam prayed.

CHAPTER 6

Christmas day in Bayport brought with it a cold front and misty rain. Ciara video chatted with Bryant as he navigated the street to the office. She saw Glenn's Bakery locked tight with the closed sign prominently displayed in the window in the background. The gloom created by the rain caused Ciara to frown at the site. The street was abandoned except for Bryant, who parked in front of Caldwell Realty.

Ciara flew to Orlando two days earlier, but Bryant stayed in Bayport. She watched through the small screen of her laptop as Bryant sat behind his new office desk and scrolled through real estate properties on his laptop. The video conference had just begun.

"The new paint smell is giving me a doozy of a headache," said Bryant while massaging his temples. His gelled hair escaped to his forehead. His stark, white button-down shirt was unbuttoned, and his sleeves were rolled up to his elbows exposing his tanned arms.

Ciara sat in her old bedroom in Orlando. Bryant didn't plan on attending his own family celebrations. "Sorry, Mom, I'll come home as soon as I can," said Bryant into his office phone while Ciara waited.

Earlier that week she overheard his conversation with his dad. Bryant wanted a chance to get some things finalized to establish the company presence in Bayport. He hadn't realized how thin the walls were and Ciara overheard most of his conversation.

"She's complicated with her constant questions and

perfectionism. I can't get anything done," Bryant had said to his dad.

He showed Ciara the sizable check from his dad delivered on Christmas Eve. "The money will help me make a deposit for a bay front cottage. I've decided to rent for the next few months," said Bryant.

"Bryant, I hope you take a little time for yourself on Christmas. I had to hide in my room to chat with you. My family expects me to take Christmas day off," Ciara said.

"I'll have that luxury as soon as we turn a profit. Can you sign and fax the last bank statement?" Bryant asked as he flipped to his January calendar.

"Ok. I will as soon as I can. Well, Merry Christmas and I'll be back the first of next week." Ciara smiled weakly and moved to close her laptop.

"Bye, Ciara," Bryant mumbled.

Ten minutes after the video conference between Ciara and Bryant, Cameron Shivers parked in front of Caldwell Realty and walked to the double glass door. He rapped lightly on the door. Bryant Ward peered through the glass. Cam motioned for him to open the door while his other hand was shaking wildly to the sound of a sputtering diesel engine and the backing signal of a large truck. Bryant let Cam into the reception area.

"Who would be making a delivery on Christmas Day?" Bryant said while opening the glass door again propping it with one foot.

"Mr. Ward, I'm Cam Shivers and my fiancé and I are starting a food truck business next door at Glenn's Bakery. I saw your light and wanted to let you know what the commotion is about." Cam stood at the other glass door with one foot in Caldwell Realty the other on the sidewalk. He kept waving to the tow truck.

Bryant rushed to the door, and Cam let the door close.

Bryant pushed through to the sidewalk and stepped into the misty, cold rain. While running to the curb, he motioned for the driver to stop and stood three feet from the flank of the large tow truck. A multi-colored green and white food truck balanced with its front wheels on the tracks while the back tires met the pavement. Black streaks ran down the top of the truck and the front tires were stained grey from sand and soil.

"What are you doing? This is private property." Bryant moved to the driver's window of the tow truck and knocked furiously. The driver slowly lowered the window and tilted his head to one side while reaching for his cell phone. Cam squatted to check under the truck.

"Are you the one paying me triple to deliver this vehicle on Christmas Day? Can't imagine anyone wanting this for Christmas." The tow truck driver chuckled and looked through his text messages trying to retrieve the name of the person meeting him.

"No, I am not paying you and you've got the wrong location...this is not a food truck site or a...junkyard." Cam stood as Bryant's eyes narrowed for emphasis.

"I have the address programmed into my navigation and was told to park in front of Glenn's Bakery. Now this is the only Glenn's Bakery in these parts...I'm in the right spot." The driver opened his door, sending Bryant back two full steps. The cell phone alerted a new text and as the driver read the text, he moved to the back to unhook the large vehicle. Bryant looked on while rubbing his chin. Cam and Bryant watched as the truck lowered into four angled spaces in front of Glenn's Bakery. The back oversized tailgate fit within the last of the bakery's front parking with five inches to spare.

As the driver moved his tow truck forward and pulled around to the rear parking, a large gold Cadillac drove up and parked in front of Caldwell Realty. Mary, dressed in a bright green and red plaid jacket, climbed out of the driver seat while Annie and Mrs. Westin scrambled around the front of the gold car.

Bryant said, "How small is this town? I never thought I'd be dealing with you people again."

"Isn't it beautiful...I can't believe I really did it...I know it needs some paint and some new tires and some cleaning." Annie wiped tears from her cheeks and hugged all standing around her. She paused at Bryant with a questioning look and moved past him to place a money order into the hand of the waiting tow truck driver. Cam followed close behind her and watching Bryant.

"Woo...wee...I think we got our work cut out for us... but Merry Christmas anyway. This thing won't be driving anywhere, but it sure can sit well." A deep chuckle came from Mary as she walked slowly around the food truck. She met Cam's gaze and gave a wink.

"Well Pastor Cam, how are you with a pressure washer and paint brush?" Annie hugged his waist and kissed Cam quickly before following Mary in her appraisal of the truck. Her pen moved quickly as she wrote down a list of supplies needed. Cam smiled while Mary hurried Annie along.

"I'm anxious to get on the road to Atlanta for my Christmas festivities. Bernard, Tia, and Mariana are waiting on me to start Christmas dinner," Mary said.

Bryant cleared his throat and approached Mrs. Westin. She was holding a pink purse close to her chest and leaned against the glass window of Glenn's Bakery. If Cam ever conjured an image of an old southern belle, the silver-haired Mrs. Westin was the picture. Her strong eyes were moist with tears and her lips turned up in a contented smile.

84

"What is this truck doing here on this street? I manage Caldwell Realty Bayport now and ask that you all please move it as soon as possible." Bryant put his hands on his waist.

"I remember you...you made the deal on my house. I know about that spoiled young Caldwell. I hope she knows how to steer clear of us." Mrs. Westin squinted her eyes while biting her lower lip. Her small frame and bowed shoulders rose toward Bryant.

At that moment, Cam walked over to Mrs. Westin as she shooed Bryant away with her hands. They both left Bryant at the window and returned to their group.

"I don't understand what you people are doing. This is insane." Bryant looked past Mrs. Westin and Cam searching for someone to hear his plea. Mary Jolly furiously rattled off hardware items and the others followed her nodding at each declaration.

Cam stood where he had a clear view of Bryant. Bryant looked around the empty street with empty shops. He investigated Glenn's Bakery which only had a small light illuminating the front counter and register. It was closed and locked tight. He then reentered his own storefront as Cam smiled at Annie and took her hand.

Later that night, Cam smiled so broadly and so often that his face muscles were beginning to hurt. He didn't care, though. He pulled his large truck into the small parking place beside Annie's little car. His parent's rental car pulled beside him, and they walked to the apartment door with hands full of presents and treats.

Christmas was bringing many wonderful things for them. "On the first day of Spring, March 21st, I will be married," he mumbled to himself. The date would be set tonight, while they all huddled around the little tree in the small apartment now rented by Mrs. Westin.

Gifts were being exchanged and many Christmas treats were eaten, but the best part was coming soon. The uncomfortable conversation about Ciara Caldwell hadn't been brought up by anyone. Annie talked with Cam's mom while Cam's dad stretched his legs after the long drive from North Carolina. Cam was nervous when Mrs. Westin asked him to help her in the kitchen.

"Pastor Cam, I feel like there's something you need to get off your chest. Am I right?" Mrs. Westin's sharp eyes looked unblinking at Cam.

"Yes, ma'am. I haven't told you all I know about the Caldwell family." He cleared his throat and felt as if the small kitchen was closing in on him. He fought to find a way to explain himself. He met her gaze and took the older woman's hand.

"Ciara Caldwell was my fiancé. We were in a relationship for about five years before I came to Bayport. We broke off the engagement right after I became pastor." Cam's voice trembled while he waited for Mrs. Westin's reply.

Mrs. Westin's eyes widened as she moved back from Cam and rested on the quartz countertop. The kitchen and living room were connected by a bar with three barstools and Cam was relieved to see that the bar was completely covered by opened gifts and trays of food. They served to provide some privacy for the conversation. He could see the top of his dad's silver hair just beyond the barstools but couldn't tell if he overheard the conversation.

"Cam, that clears a lot of things up for me. I'm sorry that Caldwell girl is still causing problems for you." She moved toward him and patted his hand softly and winked, "Annie and you'll get past this."

"I...didn't expect you to be so understanding. Ciara

Caldwell bought your family property and the store-front and she likely did it to spite me. I feel responsible for the whole mess." Cam felt tears threaten and lowered his head.

"It's not your fault...God's still working things out for Annie and you." Mrs. Westin touched his shoulder and waited for his head to raise. "Look at that fiery redhead in there. She's not going to let that girl stop her. She's determined to make the food truck work and she's determined to marry you." She laughed at the last statement while pushing Cam toward the living room.

"That's true, Mrs. Westin." Cam smiled a crooked smile and sighed deeply.

"Let's join the others. Annie and you have something to tell everyone?" Mrs. Westin's eyes danced while she led Cam past the bar.

Cam's heart fluttered, and he felt light-headed. The roller-coaster of emotions was proving to be intense. He walked past his dad and patted his shoulder while moving to sit beside Annie. He waited for a few seconds before grasping her hand and pulling her to her feet.

All eyes looked to the two of them. Annie giggled while Cam cleared his throat.

"Mom, Dad, Mrs. Westin...Annie and I have some news." Cam looked down at Annie and nodded.

"Well, it's about time," Sam Shivers spoke under his breath with a chuckle and big grin.

"Annie and I have set a date. We've decided to get married on March 21st of this coming year." Cam grinned while Annie nodded her head.

"Oh, Annie and Cam I am so glad to hear it...Deborah, we've got so much to plan and just a little bit of time." Cam's mom, Teresa, moved to Mrs. Westin and gave her a big hug.

"We'll get it all done. I'm so proud of you two." Mrs. Westin squeezed Annie and grabbed Cam's hand.

"It'll be here before we know it. Come on Cam. Let's give these ladies some room and go check on the food." He laughed deeply while leading Cam to the bar. Cam nodded in agreement and joined his dad. His nerves were finally settling, and he just wanted to sit and enjoy the moment.

A little over a week later, the second day of January, Ciara sat in a small plane and fidgeted with the tiny silver tray on the back of the seat in front of her. Her small frame took up most of the seat and the man beside her used the arm rest between them leaving her plastered to the window. The accommodations on her economy flight from Orlando to Mobile was a far cry from her usual flying habits but were necessary on her current budget. The only contact with Bryant since the video chat was one text that simply instructed her to call him to pick her up from the airport.

"He is so controlling. I ought to just call a taxi," she mumbled under her breath. The man beside her raised his eyebrows and smiled. Ciara smiled back and looked out of the small window. She would call him, though, but only to save money.

Her face was drawn tight, and she couldn't shake her overall miserable mood. She kept replaying her dad's last words to her after driving her to the airport, "Ciara, we are very worried about you honey. Why are you so pale and thin lately? Is the job too much for you? I'll talk to Junior and get you back to Orlando as soon as possible."

Ciara smiled broadly and diffused her father's questions with a long string of excited renovation and real estate ideas for Bayport. This was enough to put her father more at ease. He relaxed and her mother who sat in the back seat, began giving suggestions and making plans to visit Bayport on their next visit home.

The landing in Mobile was rougher than Ciara expected, and her knees hit the tray table that was supposed to be put up for landing. After the landing, she made her way to the carousel to retrieve her luggage and was surprised to see Bryant already standing there. He didn't look up from his cell phone and she dove into the women's restroom to freshen up. She pulled out a clean, button-down shirt from her carry-on.

"Why is he already here? I was supposed to call him," she whispered to herself while rummaging through her bag.

She removed her t-shirt replacing it with the fresh shirt. Now she felt more presentable. She sighed into the mirror and practiced smiling. It had been so long since she smiled for real. "This will have to do. I look presentable and Mom's cooking has helped me flesh out a little," Ciara said this to the mirror and was slightly embarrassed when a toilet flushed. A young mom with a little girl in tow walked to the adjacent sink.

Ciara walked out of the restroom as Bryant reached for the expensive Italian leather suitcase and didn't think twice before snatching it from the carousel. She heard him mutter, "Only Ciara would have luggage this lavish on a budget flight."

He wheeled it around and almost hit Ciara who stood a little too close. She backed up two full strides and frowned. They walked together. His dress shoes clicked on the tile beside her. She hoped he would notice she had improved in her appearance and was smiling a little wider than she had been before her trip.

"Going home did you some good, I see," said Bryant.

"Yes, Bryant it has. Now that I'm back, I need you to take me by the office before home. I'd like to retrieve a few items and grab my laptop to work over the weekend." Ciara gave the directions while grabbing for her luggage handle. Bryant stepped back and let go of the handle in time for her to pull the large suitcase to her side. The brush with his warm skin made her hand tingle and she felt heat rise to her face. His eyes softened and locked with Ciara's.

"To the office it is...just one thing, though. Don't panic when you get there. I am in the process of speaking to the zoning board and city council about a little matter with the office." Bryant flashed his confident smile that didn't quite use the right number of facial muscles. Ciara's eyes widened, and her forehead wrinkled.

"Don't ask questions now. Just trust me...I'm on it. It will be better for you to see it rather than have me describe the situation." Bryant navigated Ciara to the parking deck and put her suitcase in the trunk of his sedan.

Back in Bayport, Cam pressure-washed the top and sides as Annie scrubbed the tires of the food truck. It was beginning to look presentable, and the kitchen was in great shape. It was obvious to Cam, Ned focused more on the interior than the exterior. Parking at the bay next to the commercial boat launch had its advantages for more rustic looks over the pristine historic streets of Bayport. Annie couldn't forgo the exterior update.

Glenn's Bakery, namely Mrs. Glenn and Hartline, had agreed to let them use the parking spaces in front, as well as hook up to their power. Running a generator would be too noisy and could possibly cost them the prime location if too many people complained.

Annie would have to pay for the electrical box upgrade to support the oven, stove top, and various electrical kitchen utensils, but she didn't mind. This was much preferred to purchasing a generator and buying fuel. Cam and Annie planned to pay rent and part of the power bill as soon as she got on her feet and started making a profit. Eventually, she would repair the engine and take the truck on the road, but she was taking baby steps.

Neither Cam nor Annie noticed as an expensive sedan pulled up three feet from the bumper of the truck. The occupants sat in the car leaving it to idle in the area in front of Caldwell Realty. Ciara sat frozen against the leather seat while Bryant talked on his Bluetooth to the City Clerk of Bayport.

"We don't see how it is possible to park that unsightly truck right in front of two respectable businesses. We have rights as well. Do expect to be hearing from our lawyers." Bryant pressed the end call button on his display and turned toward Ciara.

Ciara looked out of the car window in such a state of shock that Bryant grabbed for her hand and shook it trying to break her stare.

"My ex-fiancé is cleaning the ugliest truck I've ever seen outside of my new family business and now is embracing a woman who is covered in soap...I've really lost it," Ciara spoke softly.

She rubbed her eyes with her free hand and slowly looked to the driver's seat at Bryant, whose expression only made her more frightened and confused. He turned off the ignition.

"You were once engaged to a food truck guy?" Bryant questioned while he looked out of the window. He slowly raised his visor to get a better view. At that moment, the pair who were busily washing and scrubbing moved closer to the rear of the truck. The young auburn-haired woman threw a wet sponge at the man holding the pressure-washer wand. He ducked quickly letting the sponge fly past him and land smartly on the passenger window of Dryant's car.

"He's pastor of Bayport Community Church...not a food truck guy," Ciara whispered through clenched teeth while Cam approached the car to retrieve the sponge. His hand went to the sponge and his eyes locked with Ciara's.

Cam's silly grin slowly faded and was replaced with a slight frown. His handsome face contorted for a split second before he recovered his expression. He shivered and made his way around to Bryant who was rising from the driver's seat of the car. Cam stood before Bryant while Ciara still sat watching the entire interchange from the passenger seat.

"We are not in agreement with the placement of this truck in front of our business. When do you plan on moving it?" Bryant questioned.

"Annie owns this truck parked in front of Glenn's Bakery. They are personal friends and have given their consent for it to be here." Cam met Bryant's stare and refused to look away or back down. Ciara knew Cam had spent many years with the Caldwell family and was no stranger to the type of negotiators the family and business associates were. He probably saw the same smugness and superiority in Bryant that was present in Jack Junior.

Ciara walked slowly around the car and stood beside Bryant. "Cameron, I did not expect to see you here and especially under these circumstances." Her lips turned into a smirk and her eyes narrowed to slits.

"He's in the very circumstances he wants to be in." A strong female voice was heard a good three seconds before Mary made her way around the street side of the truck. The auburn-haired Annie was close behind and tucked her loose strands behind her ears.

"Mary Jolly, Annie Westin, meet Ciara Caldwell and Brian Ward," Cam said.

"Bryant Ward." Bryant extended his hand to Annie.

"I guess we will all be neighbors for the next while, so I always say let's be good neighbors." Mary chucked and patted Ciara on the back. The thrust from the pat sent Ciara lunging forward slightly. Ciara adjusted her stance and moved back two full steps. Her brows furrowed, and she practiced her slow breathing techniques. She squared her shoulders and looked from Annie's eyes to Cam's and then to Mary's. Each of them met her gaze.

"You guys stand out here and be neighborly...I got work to do," with this declaration she lowered her eyes and walked the few steps to the glass door and moved inside before anything else could be said.

As Ciara left the sidewalk, Cam watched as Bryant moved back toward the street and scrolled through his phone. Mary and Annie continued making the list for supplies.

Cam entered the bakery as Hartline talked with Mrs. Glenn. "I can't help but feel as if I'm sitting between fire and gasoline with Caldwell Realty and Annie's food truck," Hartline said while rubbing his chin. His eyes darted to the bakery entrance, and he smiled at Cam.

Cam walked to Hartline and sat looking at Mrs. Glenn. She smiled and said, "This reminds me of the time a doughnut chain tried to move onto our street and put us out of business. We prayed and worked hard until one day they moved to a parking lot." She chuckled and winked, "Competition isn't all bad. It really pushed at us."

"I don't know if this competition is going to be healthy

for all parties involved." Hartline looked closely at Cam. Cam caught the troubled expression on Hartline's face and gave a weak smile in return.

Cam walked to the front door and heard Mary's voice. He caught a few of her words and was drawn to join her at the front of the building. "If your many customers get hungry, Annie will be more than happy to feed them. She's a genius with food." Mary smiled broadly at Bryant while turning away toward the truck where Annie was busy rinsing suds down the storm drain.

Cam moved to the sidewalk and pulled on his wet coveralls as he approached Bryant. The dripping coveralls bunched up around Cam's middle section. The contrast between Bryant in his smart-fitting designer dress shirt and pants with Cam covered in suds was startling.

Bryant turned toward Cam and began to speak when Hartline appeared beside Cam. "How's it going out here? I thought I'd come out and check on things." Hartline looked to Bryant and patted Cam on the back. The gesture relaxed Cam and he turned toward Hartline smiling. "We're great, but I better get back to Annie. We won't last much longer in these chilly temperatures soaking wet." He smiled at Hartline and nodded to Bryant while following Mary to the front of the truck.

Cam overheard Hartline say, "How's Ciara?"

"She's fine except for this little issue." Bryant squinted his eyes and pointed to the rear of the food truck. "I got to get back to work...sure hope for everyone involved that it gets resolved quickly."

"Annie Westin has a permit and permission to park here. I think it'd be best if you just accept it." Hartline smiled and moved toward the bakery entrance. Cam saw him pause before opening the door waiting on Bryant's reply.

"Don't count on it," Bryant said smugly. Cam caught the innuendo and prayed Bryant was bluffing, but his gut was telling him they were in for the fight of their lives.

CHAPTER 7

C am chatted with Annie as she opened the truck window to blinding morning light. "The reflection from the store glass almost blinded me when I placed my magnetic menu on the side. I'm glad you can make it for lunch, Cam...I can't wait for you to see the truck and try my food." Cam listened while Annie pushed the speaker button on her cell phone and continued to chat.

Cam knew nerves and excitement would drive her hands to flitter about. She admitted she hadn't slept much the night before. Last weekend she spent long hours making meat pie concoctions before landing on a near perfect recipe.

Adding sides had taxed her creativity, and after three weeks of sleepless nights and solid prayer, Annie settled on adding special ingredients to the meat pies themselves. She then simply added a few spears of asparagus. She explained to Cam it was easier to stick with what she knew well. She had to figure out how to use supplies, time, and limited space now that she wasn't managing a restaurant kitchen.

"Oh, Lord, help her learn fast," Cam prayed a quick prayer while listening to her sweet voice. He imagined her moving about the tiny cook space.

Cam ended his call with Annie in time to answer Hartline's. Hartline said a quick prayer over the phone with Cam before opening the bakery entrance to customers. Cam was grateful Hartline was giving him an update.

"The morning flew by, and it was 10:00 am before I looked up. Two customers were already waiting at the bakery door." Hartline explained to Cam, "Two elderly ladies just came into the bakery and went directly to the cake decorating book on the counter. The street is quiet and only a few people seem to be braving the chilly temperatures to come outdoors."

"I'm glad there are a few people out in the cold, but I wonder how the slow season is going to affect Annie. The bakery is well-established, and you have a steady stream of party planners and special events to keep you busy year-round." Cam couldn't mask the concern in his voice.

The two men ended the call and Cam bowed his head over his office desk strewn about with sermon notes. His eyes rested on the title of his latest sermon series, "Anxious for Nothing." "Practice what you preach, Pastor Cam." He smiled and looked to the ceiling. "You got this."

Later that morning, 11:21 flashed on Cam's dash clock. He had hoped to be at the food truck by 11:00 when Annie opened, but bathroom and cleaning supplies were being delivered to the church, and he had to sign for them.

"Who ever heard of having to sign for toilet bowl cleaner?" Cam questioned.

He drove a little faster than usual to make it by 11:30. His stomach knotted, and he couldn't imagine eating anything in his current excited state. He would buy lunch at the truck, but he wasn't sure he would be able to eat it.

As Cam parked behind the bakery, he spotted Mary's Cadillac, several sedans, director Jeremy Clay's blue Honda, and three church member's SUV's. His heart quickened and warmed with the show of support. He parked in one of the last spots and sighed deeply before exiting his vehicle. As he emerged from the rear of the bakery, he caught a glimpse of Annie as she smiled sweetly and laughed at the church's head deacon. She passed a paper boat with a steaming white dough mound surrounded by asparagus spears.

She continued to take orders and spoke gently to four-year-old, Maddie, and Bayport Rehabilitation Director, Jeremy Clay. Jeremy held Maddie in one arm and balanced the other on a stroller where little John was bundled tightly in a coat and wrapped in a warm blanket. Mary kneeled beside him and made googly-eyes while Jeremy placed an order. Cam overheard that Jeremy's wife, Caroline Clay, was in the field writing a story for the magazine.

Cam got in line and waited his turn. He studied the menu and was surprised at the variety and clever uses of ingredients. While reading the menu, his appetite returned, and the coffee consumed earlier now left him empty. His stomach growled leaving him grinning from ear to ear. Gone was the anxiety plaguing him all morning.

Cam's pulse quickened when his eyes locked with Annie's. She wanted to make a good impression on him, and almost tripped over an extension cord leading to her mixer after spotting him at the end of the line. Cam overheard her telling Mary food temperatures were holding steady and the pies she made earlier were leaving the warming tray quickly.

He was proud of her for preparing the crowd-pleasing meat pie filled with au jus and tender meat. The smell alone had enticed several customers standing in line. He knew they were her friends, and he knew they were coming on this cold January day to support her, but he also knew Annie's food was excellent. The word would spread.

Cam reached the counter and celebrated inwardly to see several people from the neighboring businesses in line behind him. They trembled in their coats, but at the rate Annie was passing food out of the truck, they wouldn't have to wait too long. His smile was wide, and he winked at her, "Give me my regular."

"Oh no, Pastor Cam, not today...I've been saving a special pie just for you. No one else has ordered it and I want you to do the honors of being my first customer to try it." Annie fingered her engagement ring and reached for the waiting pie with her other hand.

The paper tray filled with dough and two dressed asparagus spears was passed to Cam's waiting hands. He forked the top flaky dough releasing the steam and aromatic filling. It smelled strangely familiar and as he bit into the pastry, he checked the menu looking for the description. At the bottom he found it.

"I'm eating a smoked sausage meat pie with special sauce," he mentioned to a man standing close to the front truck window.

He took a large bite and was surprised with the explosion of flavor. "You used Ned's special sauce?"

"He would only give it to me." Annie leaned out of the window and winked. She moved back into the truck while stirring the crock pot and checking ovens. Ned installed a small double oven he found at an RV sale in hopes of making his own hot dog buns and adding apple turnovers to his menu. His dream never materialized, but Annie was now fulfilling hers. Cam was grateful for that.

Later that afternoon, next door at Caldwell Realty, Ciara caught sight of her reflection in an abstract mirrored piece placed by decorators. It had enough glass pieced together to show her troubled eyes and taunt mouth. The distortion reflected her current mood accurately.

"I need relief... I can't do this. Seeing Cam and the red-headed Annie is too much," she said to herself.

The large office clock showed 12:00 pm. She reached for the half-empty bottle and shook it. It wasn't enough. She took her night dose and wondered how she would make it home and how she might be able to rest later. Sleep had alluded her most nights since returning to Bayport.

Her office phone blinked three missed calls and her desk calendar showed neat, small cursive on each day reminding her of the exasperating schedule Bryant wrote in for the last week of January and all of February. He somehow managed a strategic meeting with Bayport's mayor, four of Bayport's council members, and a reporter from a regional magazine for Saturday night. He was moving at a fast pace, and Ciara was not able to muster the energy and drive to compete with him.

He avoided her and made small talk any time he was around her. She was losing her influence and was at a loss to recover.

"I'm unfocused and I can't seem to rest...I need more pills," she whispered to her office walls.

She straightened, smoothed her blouse, and walked to her office door. While peeking out and straining her neck she caught sight of Bryant's smart, blue button-down shirt through the opened blinds to his office space. His head was lowered while he typed.

She raised her hand and began biting on her thumbnail while considering the best approach to get the pills. The nail biting was a recent development and embarrassed her enough to stay away from the nail salon this month. Her polish was growing off and chipped on both her thumb nails where she nervously nibbled them.

She looked down at her feet realizing she wore some very impractical four inch, high-heeled shoes today and had walked around in them all morning. It would be hard to fake the ankle injury. He wouldn't give her the key without a good reason. She walked to Bryant's office door and waited at the threshold.

As Ciara stood in the doorway, she watched Bryant finish his advertising proposal with Southern Shores Magazine and place the printout on his desktop. He then began to type out an additional op-ed on her. Ciara listened as he read aloud her credentials, "She's a smart woman with an eye for up-and-coming trends-next generation meet the youngest Caldwell," Bryant said. He mostly relied on what he knew about the Caldwell family and added heavy emphasis on the family name and less emphasis on Ciara as an individual.

Ciara cleared her throat and Bryant rubbed his eyes and raised his head following the noise. Ciara stood before him now and he jumped at the sight of her.

"Speak of the devil," he said.

She watched his eyes dart between her skeleton frame, swollen eyes, and trembling hands. "When did you get this bad?" asked Bryant.

She saw a momentary tenderness in his expression and his eyes bugged before he regained his composure enough to say, "Ciara, you scared me...how long have you been standing there? Are you sick?" He moved to position a chair across from his desk. He fumbled with an armchair while she stood on the threshold looking intently at the small shelf on the adjacent wall.

The armchair swallowed Ciara's small frame. "Do you think you are up for the meeting tomorrow night?

You seem so tired and distracted. I can tell you're feeling sick," said Bryant. Ciara started to speak, but Bryant held his finger up and looked back intently to his computer screen.

"Wait just a minute, Ciara...I got to get this last part finalized." He learned this stall tactic from Jack Junior, and it worked on her. She got quiet and her eyes darted again to the shelf. As he typed data onto a document, Ciara took a mental inventory of the contents of his shelf. Bryant followed her gaze and his eyes rested on the shelf. They both locked eyes on the lock box.

He rose quickly and searched her face. "You been struggling lately with that old ankle injury? Still in pain?" Bryant moved to the shelf and retrieved the lock box dropping it on the desk and grabbed his briefcase from the floor. He fished for the key in the side pocket.

Ciara's eyes raised to his and her brows knitted together. She slowly lowered her eyes while clenching her hands together in her lap. She stammered, "I have been having some trouble with it in this cold weather. I thought Bayport was still south enough to keep the frost away." Her voice was thin and trembled slightly.

She spoke quickly and breathlessly. They both looked at her small ankle twisted around the underside of the office chair. The high-heeled designer shoes strapped to her thin ankle conspicuously emphasized her deceit. Was he feeling guilty as her tempter? His brows creased and he rubbed his chin. He had bigger things to consider than babysitting her. Ciara knew he would give it to her.

Bryant found the key and in a grand gesture offered it to Ciara over the desk as he rolled his office chair forward to give her better access. As she reached for the key, he quickly clamped his hand shut and tilted his head slightly.

"You probably need to stay off your ankle for a while...I can manage tomorrow night while you rest," said Bryant. His smug expression and raised brows added emphasis to the wager.

Ciara smiled slightly and narrowed her eyes. She knew what he was proposing. He wanted to meet with the mayor and city council without her. She paused, nodding her head in agreement. She reached again for the key. Her eyes fixed on his hand waiting for its contents to be released. Bryant opened his hand dropping the key on the polished wooden surface with a thud. He left his office before she retrieved the bottle. A slight sinking feeling hit her hard, but she shook her head rapidly and sighed in relief when she thought about what she would feel.

"It'll be worth it," she spoke softly while grasping the key.

Ciara opened the box quickly retrieving its contents. She placed it back on the shelf and dropped the key in one of Bryant's desk drawers.

"I don't need this box anymore. I'll just take this prescription and get back to my Orlando doctor for more next month," she said.

As she left Bryant's office and slipped into her own, the bottle felt unusual in her hand. She turned it over revealing a man's name and the Oxycontin prescription directions. She felt a nudge in her mind and spoke quietly to herself, "Don't take this. It's not yours. You're better than this."

Ciara felt the flop in her stomach as she ignored the warning. Instead, another thought sounded loud and drowned all other voices as she spoke softly, "I can't make it alone. My anxiety is too much. I need to get through this tough place. I'll be back on top in Orlando soon. Bryant can stay in this one-horse town, and I'll give Jack Junior a run for his money. None of the family will question whether I belong at the negotiating table."

She took two of the pills from the bottle and chased them down with her lukewarm diet cola. She grimaced as the bitter pills lodged and she took another drink. Placing the bottle in her purse she researched the mayor of Bayport for thirty minutes while waiting on the pill's effects. Finally, Ciara rose from her desk and grabbed her purse, carefully making sure she had her car keys, wallet, her prescription valium, and the Oxycontin.

She bumped her shoulder into the alley door and winced loudly while exiting to her car. It was dark out and she could see a shadow of a person standing at the adjoining dumpster. She giggled lightly and waved over to her neighbor. Hartline waved back. She moved to her car struggling to keep her eyes focused.

At that moment, she tripped, spilling the contents of her purse on the hood and side of the car. Hartline moved quickly to help her. He knelt beside Ciara at the front bumper of her car while she looked through her phone trying to locate the flashlight. As her phone lit the paved lot, Hartline's eyes went to a prescription pill bottle. He reached for it at the same time Ciara noticed it within his reach. She bounded toward Hartline throwing him off balance. He crashed back on his bottom as Ciara grabbed for the bottle.

The light from Ciara's phone illuminated the bottle enough for Hartline to read aloud, "Oxycontin...James Drayer...Why do you have this bottle?" Hartline's face softened, and he scooted away from the scattered contents while Ciara continued to fill her purse shaking off dirt and gravel from her wallet and her various cosmetics scattered about.

"Thanks for your help but I can handle this myself." Ciara looked at Hartline sitting on the pavement beside her car and quickly pushed the prescription pain medicine into the deep part of her handbag. He rose and looked into her eyes while offering her a hand up from the pavement. She took it reluctantly and rose to her feet. She steadied herself and met his gaze. He looked for several seconds before dropping his gaze to the ground.

"I saw you fall and thought you might need a hand. I see that you are Ok." Hartline stood by Ciara's car while she opened the driver's side and slipped in, throwing her handbag in the passenger seat.

"I am Ok. I was just leaving for home. Thanks again for helping me," Ciara said. She shut her door quickly and turned the key. Hartline moved back as if a little afraid she might exit the parking space over his foot. He moved to the small curb between the back lots, and she saw him standing there as she backed up and waved bye. As he waved in return, Ciara realized he might have tried to stop her from driving.

"I've got to be more careful and only take extra medication when I'm not driving," she whispered while turning onto Main Street.

Later that night, Ciara pulled into her circle driveway feeling the effects of the combination of the valium and pain medicine. She stopped at the late-night smoothie and coffee bar and ordered the protein & bulk shake in its largest cup. She sipped the shake until her head ached from the freezing liquid. She couldn't handle the medication on an empty stomach. Her eyes were drooping and at the same time she felt her mind racing. She thought about her wardrobe and racked her brain trying to remember where the spas were in Bayport.

Ciara continued to hatch a plan and decided to join

the meeting with Bryant and their clients. She spent two hours locating a trendy spa that touted clients like local celebrities and a few regional ones. The next item on her agenda was to research the mayor, council members, and the Southern Shores Magazine.

She winced when she found the same article that prompted her to move to Bayport, but quickly looked past it and continued her research. By the time she felt satisfied enough to go to bed, her head was reeling, and she felt nauseated. The medication was doing a number on her stomach. She decided to eat a sandwich and drink some hot tea. Feeling better, she slipped in the bed and slept deeply for the first time since Christmas.

Chapter 8

Early Saturday morning, Annie and Cam pulled behind Glenn's Bakery. As Cam put the truck in park he reached for Annie and embraced her. "Happy Saturday, Baby." He kissed her hard and breathed deeply. Annie leaned into him and laughed lightly. Her blue jeans, white button down, and black apron already tied at her waste drove home the image of a casual chef. This endeared her to Cam even more. She could make the most casual of wardrobes look elegant and timeless.

Annie's hair was braided and fell on her right shoulder. Some wavy tendrils had already escaped and made a halo effect framing her face and forehead. Her crystal blue eyes which sometimes looked intense were warmer in the morning light. They were reflecting the sunlight bouncing from the red brick façade that wrapped the storefronts.

"Happy Saturday, Pastor Cam." Her eyebrows raised, and she lightly pushed him away creating some distance between them, "We only have two more months and..." He moved back slightly and raised her left hand leaving a kiss on her knuckles.

Cam was in love with Annie. His heart swelled more when he realized how nice it was to be marrying a woman with principles. She cared about her faith and didn't want to be too intimate before their marriage. He was accustomed to showing the voice of reason and making sure the physical part of the relationship didn't go too far in past relationships.

He shook himself and smiled sheepishly at the beautiful redhead in the seat beside him. He stilled his heartbeat and focused on the truck dash in front of him. The clock displayed 5:06. Getting ready for the lunch crowd at 11:00 started early. Annie wasn't going to cut corners or lower her freshness standards to trim off some preparation time.

"You ready to get started? I'm the sous-chef, right? I just chop things and grab utensils for you?" He looked concerned.

"Of course, you will be fine. It'll be fun. Don't worry." She tousled his hair and grabbed for her car door.

He held her hand and shook his head, no, while scrambling from the driver's seat and sprinting around the front of the truck. He opened the passenger door and helped her down. He grabbed both plastic tubs she brought from her apartment. They were heavy and off balance. She was strong to carry the tubs down two flights of stairs. He felt bad for not helping her to the truck earlier when he felt their weight.

As they unlocked the food truck and turned on the oven and grill top the truck hummed to life. Sweet, spicy, and savory smells began to fill the space and they promptly turned on the exhaust fan. Annie and Cam began the new daily ritual of the food truck business. It became warm and toasty in the truck quicker than Cam expected and he shed his pullover.

Before Cam could sit and take a breath from the constant chopping and storing of food items, it was time to open the serving window. The day was proving to be bright and beautiful despite the chilly temperatures of late January. Using tight quarters to cook, heating and storing food items for the lunch crowd, and navigating the small appliances became a constant drive. Cam and

Annie had little time for more than an occasional glance at one another.

A line formed on the sidewalk and Mary was second in line behind Hartline, who explained to Cam he had thirty minutes to spare before he would need to be back behind the counter himself. Tony was able to relieve him on Saturdays since being home from school.

"I would like to try Ned's Special. Heard it was good," Hartline announced to Annie and shook his head decidedly. "Can I have a cream soda too? We don't carry that fountain drink flavor in the shop."

Annie smiled and retrieved the paper boat filled with the smoked sausage meat pie covered in special sauce.

"Let me see if I can find that cream soda for you. It's probably in the bottom cooler." She knelt while Cam stumbled forward to Hartline.

Hartline met his gaze and said, "Can you come by the bakery when you get a chance? Jeremy Clay from the clinic is coming...maybe you could join us?" His intense expression and knitted eyebrows concerned Cam.

"What's the matter?"

Hartline shook his head, no, and replaced his serious expression with a wide smile as Annie rose from the cooler and passed the can of soda out the window. Cam moved back and nodded, yes, over Annie's head. "I'll come by around three, if that's Ok."

"I'll let Jeremy know to come then too. Bye." Hartline attempted his most casual shrug and turned toward Mary who stepped forward and winked at Hartline.

"Boy, you got to move on, so I can get my weekly fix from my favorite chef." She playfully pushed him aside and plopped her hand on the counter. "Now I need my special, honey. I skipped breakfast this morning and I have two recreational groups today at the clinic. I need my nourishment." Mary flashed her biggest smile making Cam ad Annie laugh in response.

"Mrs. Mary, you know you've been to this truck every day this week. I think you are well nourished. You've worn a path between the clinic and here with your massive car," Cam said this loudly while Annie filled the order.

"Never-your-mind about my nourishment. There's a lot of hungry mouths to feed today. The sunny weather has brought us all out of hibernation. I passed two boat launches and they were filled. The thaw is coming and it's about to get crazy on this street. Mark my word." Mary took her tray and smelled its contents, while letting out a great sigh, "Mmm...mmm."

A couple of people in line chuckled and one playfully swatted for Mary to move out of the line. The faces behind her looked longingly at her tray. Steam rose from the meat pie while she moved aside letting the next customer place his order. Several local businesses, Bayport visitor's center employees, and the local hotel guests had begun to frequent the truck. These patrons supplied Annie with a steady stream of traffic, however, this Saturday was bringing more people out for recreation and shopping.

Cam's nerves heightened when he saw the long line. Annie should be fine on food and service today, but what about the tourist season that was about to be in full swing. She had approximately eight or nine weeks before the first spring break crowd descended on Bayport. "Lord, we're going to need help," prayed Cam.

On cue with his prayer, Cam shrieked and dropped the ladle with Ned's sauce on the floor. "Owwww...I think I burned my hand pretty bad...it really hurrrrts!" yelled Cam. Tears were forming in his lower lids, and he ran to the sink to run water on his palm.

Annie moved to him and grabbed the butter to slather his palm while she blew on the blister forming there. She smiled up sweetly to him and asked, "Want to call it a day, Cam? I can manage the rest...you go on."

The relief on his face was comical, but Annie appeared to stifle her giggle and continued to show her most concerned look while she made an ice pack from a small storage bag.

"Here take this and keep it on the injury for twenty to thirty minutes. That should help with the pain...trust me, I know about burns." Annie winked at him and led him out of the truck before turning quickly back to the window to wait on the next customer.

Cam held the ice pack with his right hand while looking at his left wrist to check the time. 1:25. He almost made it to the end of the shift and now he was standing outside the truck with a throbbing hand. He was not cut out to be a sous chef. He chuckled and peeked around the front. The line was shorter which made him feel a little better about abandoning Annie. He let out a sigh of relief until he also noticed the line was completely covering the entrance to Caldwell Realty.

"Oh, Lord, please don't let this start any trouble. Annie needs this to work and all the help she can get right now," he prayed quietly.

Cam entered the bakery and looked for Hartline. Tony sat behind the counter typing furiously on a laptop perched atop the glass display. As Cam approached, he saw Hartline's blond hair through the double doors. "Hi Tony, are you working on Saturdays now?" Tony looked up from his screen and smiled.

"Oh, Hi Pastor, I'm here now that Ned doesn't need me on the food truck anymore." He raised his eyebrows in a knowing gesture.

"Annie might need you pretty soon too." Cam showed his burned hand and winced.

"That looks about the same size as a Ned's sauce ladle." Tony showed his right palm revealing a long red scar extending across. "I got mine over Christmas break. Yours looks fresh."

"That's been over four weeks." Cam looked pained at the thought of nursing his hand for that long.

Hartline caught Cam's eyes through the small window and pushed through the double doors into the storefront. "Jeremy will be here in a few. Do you want to get a table in the back? I'll bring some drinks over." Hartline motioned for Cam to sit at a table toward the back of the bakery.

Cam sat and placed his throbbing hand on the table letting the ice collect around his palm without too much collecting on the blister.

Hartline came to the table placing a cola, no ice, down in front of Cam. "What happened to your hand?"

"I burned it at the food truck. I don't think I'm going to last as Annie's weekend help." He said the last part loud enough for Tony Glenn to hear him.

"I hear you Pastor Cam…I'll think about it. Right now, I just want to make it through AP Biology." Tony pointed to his laptop that was still sitting perched on the counter.

Hartline sat in front of Cam and exhaled deeply, "I hate to involve you in a situation, but I think it's serious. It's about somebody you know well and the rest of us in town don't."

"Ciara Caldwell. You want to ask me about her. She's driving you crazy with her pampered condescending ways, isn't she?" Cam smirked and folded his arms in front of his chest gingerly lowering his burned hand.

"No, not really. We never really see or hear from her. Bryant Ward has been more visible and has let it be known he is going to fight the food truck being here," said Hartline. Cam's smirk left and was replaced with anger.

"I didn't call a meeting with you and Jeremy to talk about that, though." Hartline furrowed his brow and took a sip of coffee as if delaying the conversation.

"What's up? What do you need me for?" Cam was annoyed and lost his usual pastoral manner. The wrestling with anger toward Ciara and protection for Annie threatened his poise and tried his patience.

"Ciara's in trouble. I think it's probably worse than most people realize." Hartline paused and looked around the room before whispering, "I think she's using."

"Like drugs? You think Ciara Caldwell is an addict?" Cam whispered back quickly while falling against his chair. As he waited on Hartline's reply, he tried to remember any indication from his past that would shed any light on Hartline's accusation.

"She did look very thin and gaunt the last time I saw her, but she has always been on a real health kick with watching her weight," Cam said.

"I'm not saying that I think she's on street drugs. It could be pills or drinking. I just kind of know what the signs are...and they're there, man." Hartline dropped his head and muttered, "I do have some proof...well I don't have it...I just saw it."

Next door at Caldwell Realty, Ciara and Bryant stood with two of the city council members and opened the blinds revealing the food truck line blocking the entrance to the Caldwell business. The two men, John Blevins, and Chuck Neighbors accepted their invitation to meet early for drinks. They didn't seem to notice the line of people.

Ciara watched Bryant waiting for an opportunity to bring the conversation to the people lined up outside. He continued to make small talk about the dining plans for later that evening while Ciara sat behind the reception-ist desk and scrolled through the internet. Ciara didn't want to sound whiny about the food truck neighbors. The city council were aware of the truck and Ciara and Bryant knew some had even visited it.

Ciara's research about the truck did not bring up any loopholes she could find. The only statute she came across was that it was not supposed to be double parked. The truck got away with it because the parking spaces were owned privately by Glenn's Bakery. The street and parking were separated by a very small curb.

Ciara's only hope was for the council members to be-friend Bryant and offer advice. She looked to the two men sipping cocktails and glanced at the Caldwell Re-alty display of recent properties for sale. Most of them were in Florida. Ciara hoped the lack of inventory in Bayport wouldn't be too obvious. They only had the bay side property where she was now living, two pricy loft apartments, and one small inexpensive loft apartment.

The owner of the apartments, who lived out of town, saw the Caldwell advertisement in Orlando and contact-ed Bryant. She was relieved to see some of her market-ing was paying off. She made sure to contact the market-ers and have them add Bayport to the mix before she left Orlando. It was a good thing too because the local word was not bringing in the clients.

Both John and Chuck talked about their latest golf games and rarely strayed to any other topic. Bryant needed to get back on the green fast. Ciara did not want to spend days at the golf course with these guys.

"We at Caldwell are planning a grand opening and would love to host a citywide event." Bryant projected his screen onto the large TV mounted in the reception area displaying the hand-picked and pricey menu for the dinner they would enjoy in a few hours.

Bryant chose the two members most likely to be swayed by his opulent choices. These two were wealthy and stayed on the council because of their family name, not necessarily to manage the city. This could work to Caldwell Realty's advantage. They had generational wealth and could introduce them to the right clients. Ciara understood how important their endorsement would be for the start up in Alabama. Throwing around a name from Orlando would only go so far, now she needed local connections.

Ciara watched as Bryant moved nimbly to the thermostat and pushed it to 79 degrees. Neither of the council members acknowledged his action. The heat kicked on and began to slowly heat the front receiving area of the office space. The doors to Bryant and Ciara's offices were closed, so the heat was trapped in the front. The men's faces turned red, and John Blevins removed his suit coat and dropped it on the expensive Italian leather couch behind.

"Oh, Mr. Blevins let me open this window and get us some fresh air. Our new heating system is working like a charm." Bryant smiled and began rolling out the vintage window that survived the new construction renovation recently completed.

The shop fronts had to keep the outside town charm, but Bryant took liberties to modernize the office space. She watched John and Chuck move toward the window as the sound of chatter on the sidewalk made its way into the room.

"Mr. Ward, how do you get anything done with those people standing out the window? Where are they going?" John Blevins frowned and strained his neck to see down the sidewalk.

"John, it's the little food truck by Glenn's...you know the new business. It's been busy since opening," Chuck Neighbors said this while sipping his drink and moving to the couch.

"Well, I don't think they should be standing out there. This is a respectable business, and it needs the proper space to advertise and greet customers," John said this and looked to Bryant.

Bryant sank casually down on the oversized matching chair and looked up at John. "We've been doing our best. There have been more than a few times we've had to help get our clients through the crowd and into the door," said Bryant. Ciara almost laughed out loud from across the counter. The truth was they never had visitors, but she decided a little white lie wouldn't hurt anything. Besides if they did have clients today, she would have to navigate them through the annoying crowd.

"I'll bring this up in the council meeting next week. I'm sure there's something that can be done." John joined Chuck on the couch and both men looked to one another and nodded in agreement.

"Caldwell Realty could really use the help. We are grateful for anything you do." Bryant casually pulled out his cell and Ciara saw him scroll through the closest golf course while the two men looked on.

"How about some golf next Monday, my treat?" Bryant continued to strategize. The council meetings were on Tuesday and Ciara was glad he was staying close to these guys.

"I see there's a great club close to here," said Bryant.

"That's probably the Bayport Golf Trails...best one around. Monday it is then," said Chuck.

At that declaration, Ciara realized Bryant was making headway with the two men without her help. He would need her tonight with the other council members. She figured he didn't research the ladies in the group as thoroughly as he had the men.

"I need to make my hair appointment. I hate to run out on you guys, but I had to pull a lot of strings to get in this salon." Ciara smiled sweetly as the two men rose. Bryant glanced her way nodding in agreement.

"I hope you feel better Ciara. I know you've been struggling lately. See you Monday." Bryant emphasized the last word as she waved goodbye to him.

"You'll see my friend. You need me," mumbled Ciara as she made her way to her car and pulled out of the lot onto the street. She headed away from the bay.

An hour later, in the resort areas close to the ocean front, Ciara relaxed in the chair while a stylist with a thick southern drawl made small talk.

"Girl, you need to get into my salon more, I'm a miracle worker like I said, but I can't do anything with those split ends if you don't come regular—and those roots, girrlll."

The early afternoon sun was heating up and the wooden blinds had to be drawn in the beautifully decorated salon to keep Ciara from wincing at the glare. The décor was southern with deep antique whites and exquisitely crafted woodwork throughout. She smiled and touched her earpiece to change to the next song on her playlist oblivious to most of what the woman said. She saw the stylist mouthing what looked like a question and she removed the earpiece. She quickly scrolled through her phone finding the cut, color, and overall look she wanted from a posh advertisement she still received from her salon in Orlando.

The stylist, named Trisha, had a small-town accent, but didn't think small town. She understood the style immediately and found the latest colorist book and began mixing the color for Ciara's roots. Trisha texted her understudy to bring out the kits. These were the reserved thousand-dollar packages of beauty products. Ciara was getting the works. All 2,500 dollars' worth.

A few hours later, Ciara could hardly recognize herself. Her long blond hair which had been neglected the past couple of years was cut just below the shoulder. Hair extensions added volume and helped add color and dimension to her hair and hollow face. The face primer, highlights, and false eyelashes brought her brown eyes out boldly while her spray tanned body gave her the color she was missing since her days spent in the office. She looked down and smiled at her nails which had gel extensions and color. She felt more like herself now that she had splurged on the spa treatment.

The expensive, designer store, by-appointment-only, was her next stop. It took some finagling and several phone calls to get a private fitting, but she knew it would be worth it.

"Bryant better not underestimate me...I'm in my element now. I know better than most how to wine and dine clients," she said as she navigated the streets to the boutique.

She extended her company card and quickly texted Jack Junior to let him know she was hosting clients tonight. She name-dropped two of the council members for good measure knowing if Jack Junior researched the two men, he would quickly understand the need to spend lavishly. Bryant would have to corroborate her story because he was her accomplice.

Back at the bakery, Annie walked through the door and caught Hartline's attention first. He looked surprised and spoke her name a little too loudly. Jeremy jumped and turned toward Annie while Cam smiled and moved toward her.

"Am I interrupting something important...I don't want to get in the way...I was just surprised to see Cam in here and then I remembered..." Annie's words trailed off and she looked closely at Cam.

"We were just meeting about a potential client for the rehabilitation clinic. Hartline needed some council and spiritual guidance as well." Cam lowered his gaze and looked to Jeremy and Hartline.

"I think we are just about done. Thanks to both of you for meeting with me. I'll be in touch and keep in mind what you told me. Pastor Cam, will you pray for us?" Hartline relieved the tense moment and held out his hands to join for prayer. Several patrons of the bakery grew quiet and bowed their heads as well.

"I will check on some things on my end. I know we can find resources for the situation." Jeremy smiled and held out his hands too.

"Dear Lord, we are asking You to give Hartline wisdom and understanding to help others who are fighting addiction. Allow him to help with the situation and we ask that you find Your lost children. Thank you for answering our prayer. Amen."

"Amen." Hartline raised his head and looked much lighter since the prayer. However, Cam looked exhausted and overwhelmed despite the prayer.

Jeremy patted Cam on the back and asked about the wedding plans. Jeremy's counseling experience was good for this situation. Cam was torn between concern for someone from his past and honoring Annie. Cam was the only one in town who knew anything about Ciara Caldwell and Hartline didn't know anyone else to contact about the suspected addiction issues.

Cam only knew she had taken anxiety medication on occasion. She never told her parents and asked him to keep it quiet. He didn't feel the liberty to tell them and until now never thought it was important enough for him to intervene. She had obviously gotten worse and was abusing her medication. According to Hartline, it was probably much worse than her taking too much of her prescription. Cam could not tell Annie what they had talked about. Hartline had asked them both to keep it confidential.

Annie smiled and began to give wedding details.

"Hartline's doing the cake...well Glenn's Bakery is... it'll be the specialty cake of course." Annie smiled and looked down at Cam's hand still being held out gingerly on the top of the table. "Honey, is your hand going to be Ok?" The diversion to his hand gave Cam a chance to think on something other than Ciara's issues.

Cam felt a little lighter and chuckled, "Does this mean that I can't be your sous chef any longer?" He smiled sheepishly.

"Why don't you just stick to counseling and pastoring. Looks like you did better here than you could ever do helping me out." Annie rose from the table and rolled her shoulders forward letting out a big sleepy sigh.

"Goodbye all, I got to get this woman home to rest... looks like she's beat," Cam said this while shaking Jeremy's then Hartline's hand. Both men shook hands and rose quickly leaving the meeting with much to research and think about. The food truck and Caldwell Realty neighbors were turning out to be more than just a little issue—now there was a lost soul with a great need in the mix. As Cam and Annie exited the bakery, they both agreed to hang out at Annie's and Mrs. Westin's apartment and get take-out. Both were done with socializing for the day.

CHAPTER 9

That same night down by the bay, Ciara looked several times in the grand mirror left by the Westins. It was antique and too big to move to most houses. It was considered a built-in feature of the grand house. She was delighted the former occupants were down-sizing and had no place to put much of the large pieces of heirloom furniture and fixtures. Ciara felt sorry for the southern lady, Mrs. Westin, leaving behind so many treasures. The rumor was she couldn't afford it any longer.

"Mrs. Westin couldn't bring herself to take the items. These pieces belong with the house," Ciara spoke quietly at her reflection. Ciara was disturbed with the idea of the pain the other woman must have felt. She shook her head to rid the thought and began humming a song she heard from the salon.

"It's better here with me, besides, it would have taken me a ton of time and energy not to mention money that I don't have to furnish this house," Ciara spoke to her reflection while dabbing her lips with a tissue.

Her perusal of her current look boosted her confidence. It was a very regal look, like a politician's wife or the VIP from the local country club. She wore a cream-colored fitted suit with an up-and-coming southern designer's name smartly printed in the seam of her collar. Samantha Shaw knew her fittings. Her fussiness reminded Ciara of a Paris fitting she had one time when she was only fourteen.

Her grandmother thought it would be fun for Ciara

to have it done and it was an experience she would never forget. There was nothing to compare to a tailored fit.

"You will need to be able to breathe, but your tiny little frame will need some help, I'm afraid." Samantha Shaw had frowned and moved through her creations before landing on the cream suit. "Perfect for those big brown doe eyes."

Ciara's figure was accentuated, but not too much in this conservative town. There was no cleavage showing and the skirt was just above the knee. The southern look was a startling contrast to her usual, modern beach vibe that got her through the client list from before. This look made her look like a fixture in the grand bay house. She chuckled at the transformation. What would her friends think? She sipped her hot tea careful not to disturb her freshly colored lips. They were much redder than usual and made her look older.

This house would be a great venue for tonight. If only Bryant wasn't at the helm. They were dining at the Bayport Country Club, but this house would be a strategic place to take one of the most influential council members and acting mayor of Bayport, Mrs. Rita Nelon. She was known for her style. She especially appreciated up-and-coming local designers which directed Ciara's choice of clothing tonight.

Mayor Nelon was also known for her elegance and family values. She attended church regularly and spent much of her time keeping the historic streets of Bayport free from too many modern upgrades. Ciara was glad Bryant hadn't changed the outside of their storefront. He completely modernized the interior but was limited to keeping it much the same on the exterior. That would work to their favor.

Ciara retrieved the keys to her sports car and laughed

at the thought of her current southern form sinking into the modern, little red BMW. Luckily, she could valet park, and no one would know what she drove.

The mother-of-pearl-lined antique handbag sat in the seat beside her. Its only contents were the bright red lipstick, a compact powder given as a special gift to VIP customers of the salon, her company credit card, and one small valium in case the trembling in her hands returned before the night was over. She spaced taking the medication between large protein shakes. The new regimen of medication was working out better since she had extra pills to help with the lack of energy and sleeplessness.

While Ciara drove to the Bayport Country Club, she popped her glove box to retrieve the recent country club members-only print out. It took a rather large charge to the company card to get into the club. Bryant wouldn't need the paper since he was attending with the guests. The recent issue with Bryant prevented her from doing the same.

As she entered the circle drive, Ciara handed her keys to the valet and grabbed the handbag. She tipped the valet handsomely and walked through the great, wooden doors. It took her eyes a full minute to adjust to the dimly lit room. She stood waiting for her eyes to adjust and gave her paperwork and license to the desk.

While standing there she took the time to look for her party. Bryant must have chosen a private room and a special menu. The men in golf attire sitting at the bar wouldn't be close to the party. She smiled sweetly while the man behind the grand, oak counter gushed about the club's amenities. She thought about the best way to get the greeter to give up the location of the VIP party.

Ciara's ears perked up when he mentioned Orlando.

"There's another gentleman here from Orlando. I overheard him telling our very own distinguished mayor that the country club there could not hold a candle to the historic charm of our Bayport."

"Yes, yes...it is most exquisite here. I see you have kept the rich southern hardwoods and updated to kiosks and sharp flat screen monitors at the same time...it's just grand." Ciara grasped her phone and looked through her texts.

"I can't seem to get reception in here...can you lead me to my party? I'm here with Bryant Ward and his party. He's the one you spoke of earlier from Orlando." She dropped her phone back in her handbag and tapped her polished nails on the counter in time to the smooth jazz playing from the inset speakers.

"Oh, that makes sense. I thought so...Come with me. You're in for a treat Miss Caldwell...Mr. Ward works for you at Caldwell Realty, I presume?" He extended his arm and led her to a back room with another set of large, ornate doors and into a beautiful great room.

"That's right, he does work for me." Ciara smiled smugly and celebrated inwardly that her name was Caldwell.

Bryant would be attempting to steer the light conversation to real estate holdings and potential clients; however, he would know to be patient and not look too eager. The right time would surface. It may take some succulent food or several glasses of wine, but she figured he would get there tonight. John Blevins and Chuck Neighbors were golf enthusiasts. Bryant's offer gave them more reason to incessantly go on and on about the Bayport course.

Ciara stood back from the table unnoticed for a while and listened as Bryant put in polite opinions. His eyes darted to Mayor Rita Nelon who was in deep conversation with the other two council members, Nancy McCoy, and young Sara Brown. The other council members were both soft spoken and followed the mayor's lead. Ciara made the right choice coming to the meeting.

"And where is the lovely Miss Caldwell tonight? After your company's glowing recommendation of her, I've been anxious to meet her." Mayor Nelon's southern drawl was heavy, but her piercing eyes were less slow and drawn out.

"She's been having a hard time adapting to the colder climate. Orlando's warmer than Bayport. She's recovering from a cold, I'm afraid." Bryant held the older woman's gaze for a few seconds before Ciara moved closer. The other two men at the table saw Ciara before Bryant did.

"Ciara, what are you doing?" Bryant leaned forward before standing, "You made it...you're better?" Bryant moved quickly from his seat and took her elbow. He coughed and with a grand gesture gave her the seat next to the mayor.

"Well, Bryant. I'm not as fragile as some of you men think. I spent the day at the spa and met a new designer. It's all I needed to get rid of that old..." Ciara waited for Bryant to finish her sentence.

"Colds aren't anything to play with. You're sure you're not still feverish?" Bryant was pleased with his retort to Ciara. He was emboldened by his quick thinking and put his hand to her forehead.

Ciara recoiled and laughed lightly, "I'm fine...no fever. You are so kind to check on your old boss like that." She met his gaze with a threatening stare, and he backed away from her.

"She looks healthy to me." Mayor Nelon looked closer

at Ciara's collar. "How are you dear?"

"I'm just fine and it is very nice to meet you all." Ciara shook each person's hand at the table and nodded to Bryant.

"What's that suit you're wearing? I haven't seen it around the Bayport shops." Mayor Nelon spoke directly to Ciara.

"Samantha Shaw...met her today. Such a fussy person, but well worth it. She fitted me no less than five times before letting me go...you ladies know of her?" Ciara smiled and looked at Nancy McCoy avoiding Mayor Nelon. She didn't want to be too obvious.

"I do know her well. She designed my daughter's bridesmaid dresses before her big break in Southern Shores Magazine. She became a local celebrity overnight. It's such an amazing story of hidden talent being found." A dreamy-eyed Nancy McCoy looked to the mayor and waited for her comment.

"Samantha Shaw is the story of a hard-working woman who defied the odds of being lost in a small town." Mayor Nelon winked at Ciara, Nancy, and Sara before turning to Bryant.

"What do you think of Ciara's suit, Mr. Ward?"

"I think she looks beautiful and very elegant. Heck, I think she could don the cover of Southern Shores Magazine right this moment. Just like she is tonight. My boss lady is such a class act, I think it would behoove us to take a picture of her right now in this very room." Bryant moved for his cell phone and motioned for the mayor to move in toward Ciara.

"Wait a minute, Mr. Ward, I get to choose what dons the cover of Southern Shores Magazine...well not just me, my editor and I actually make that call." Caroline Clay from Southern Shores Magazine had been standing at the table between John Blevins and Chuck Neighbors for a good thirty seconds before the group noticed her presence.

"Ah, our very own Caroline Clay, writer extraordinaire, welcome to our humble table." Mayor Nelon moved to seat Caroline between Bryant and herself.

"Now what's this about the cover of the magazine? Lovely suit, Miss Caldwell, but I don't think I need any more models for Samantha Shaw. She's well on her way to bigger and better magazine covers." Caroline sipped her water and pushed back her long dark chestnut hair. She could have been a model herself. She was very pretty and wore a striking pants suit and heels that made her look sophisticated and capable.

"Can we please change the subject from clothes? I'm starved and have no clue what you ladies are talking about," John Blevins spoke up and motioned for the server, Chuck Neighbors nodded in agreement and looked to Bryant who nodded slowly while looking at Ciara.

Ciara relaxed a bit from the centerstage moment and took Caroline Clay's cue to sip water. It gave her hands something to do and left her off the hook for making small talk for a while. Her mind was whirling, and she attempted to shift from fighting Bryant to assisting him in strategic networking for the company.

Ciara looked up and caught Bryant's gaze. His eyes were steady, but his mouth smiled slightly. He nodded to Ciara and put his thumb up to his chin before turning back to Chuck Neighbors and asking about the golf gear sold at the club.

Ciara took the thumbs up from Bryant as a truce between the two of them. Now she had to focus on building the relationships her company so desperately needed. Jack Junior would expect a profit soon and wouldn't allow her more time before he brought her into the boardroom as a failure. None of the others would see her as legitimate. Her future and lifestyle she grew up with were at stake. Jack Junior wouldn't give her a penny more than she had now.

It would be much harder to convince everyone she could help run the business if Jack Junior succeeded in showing her fail. Jack Junior was waiting on her failure to do something very risky in the company. The rest of the family did not consider her opinion or expertise. She had gleaned as much being in the same office space with him for two years, but he was stopped by her presence at all important board meetings.

The next quarterly meeting was scheduled before summer, and she planned to show up with a profitable extension of Caldwell Realty from Bayport. It gave her the will to keep going. She would not give up or give in. She was the last of the Caldwell family besides Jack Junior still attending meetings.

"At my Bible study, the children of Israel were returning to their land and rebuilding the walls of their beloved city. I take that personally. I want us all to be builders. We got a gem of a city and now new members who bring with them new ideas and possibly a revamping of some of our beloved properties around the bay." Maylor Nelon looked at Ciara and smiled softly. She took her hand and spoke, "You got yourself a beautiful property at the Westin's. Give it some love, honey."

The mayor's reference to the Bible and her motherly tone made Ciara miss her own mother. Ciara's eyes grew moist as the warmth of the older lady's soft hand enveloped her own. The stress of being in the spotlight was getting to her. She did not know how to respond to the sweet and friendly gesture. She locked eyes with

Mayor Nelon.

Ciara did not take any extra medication today and made it through on pure adrenaline. But now, here, with this group she felt exposed and raw. The women reminded her of the church ladies back home at her daddy's church. The real Christians who prayed with you and could council you back to mental health and strength.

"I will," Ciara spoke softly and turned to her soup. The warm liquid coated her throat and didn't quite provide the distraction she was seeking from the tender moment with the mayor. When the server returned, she excused herself to the restroom and stood for two minutes looking at her reflection in the gilded mirror.

Ciara fingered her handbag and thought about the valium she had there, but somehow knew it wouldn't make her stronger. It would probably make her break down like a baby and crawl into the sweet mayor's lap.

"God what's wrong with me?" Ciara whispered. She ran cold water over her hands and grabbed for the towels while leaving the ladies' sitting area.

Ciara exited the bathroom and into the long hall leading to the private room. She spotted Bryant standing in the entrance.

"Ciara, what are you trying to do with this get up? It took me a good long look to find you anywhere in all this...but I got to hand it to you, tearing up a minute ago with the mayor was especially effective. I think it did the trick. She keeps raving about the Westin property." Bryant stopped and looked into Ciara's eyes.

"Bryant, you got no clue how to deal with women... has anyone ever told you that. You need to work on your charm...or might I say lack of it?" Ciara winked at him while walking past. She made her way through the doorway and to the table thankful for Bryant's antagonism.

133

He would keep her focused. If only to outwit him. They both rejoined the party in time to continue the previous conversation.

"I do want to take that picture." Mayor Nelon turned to Caroline. "Could you make a trip to the Westin's property sometime tomorrow after church?"

"Oh, I'm sure I can, what do you say Miss Caldwell? Are you up for a little publicity including your beautiful bayfront property?" Caroline's expression was playful, and she smiled broadly.

"Of course, come on...about what time would that be?" Ciara's mind raced while she considered the magazine displaying her on the Westin property. She wasn't sure how long she could keep this southern belle façade up. This designer suit was all she owned with southern charm, and she wouldn't have time to get back to the designer.

"I'll just snap a picture of you and the mayor here tonight and include it with the bayfront pictures. That way you two don't have to get all dressed up again tomorrow." Caroline softened the blow with this declaration and Ciara relaxed while enjoying the main course.

Bryant smiled at Ciara and raised his brows. "Let's get that photo here in the great room by the massive chandelier. Miss Caldwell and I would love for our clients to understand we value beauty and heritage." Bryant rose to find the perfect spot for the photo while the other two men ordered dessert.

Ciara smiled broadly under the soft glow of the fifty-year-old chandelier. She played her role well. She created the aura of a beautiful woman flanked by a smart, well-respected mayor of Bayport. It was meant to be the major break for Ciara, but somehow it felt hollow. Something awakened inside of her she had suppressed for many years.

The awareness of her need for a relationship threatened to expose her true vulnerability and lower the protective façade she had worn since childhood. She left that night with a crack in her hardened heart, but knew she still possessed the very pills that could help her slip back into the familiar clutches of her addiction and ultimately back into her stone-cold life.

Part Two

But whenever someone turns to the Lord, the veil is taken away. 2 Corinthians 3:16 (NLT)

Chapter 10

Ciara opened one eye and glanced at the digital clock. 7:02. It was time for her to wake and dress before hosting Mayor Nelon and Caroline Clay. She rolled to face the wall and practiced taking deep breaths. It was something the doctor recommended for anxiety and Ciara watched her dad do the same from time to time when he had dealt with real estate problems.

She and her dad were similar in temperament. She grabbed for a photo of her parents and carefully looked at the image of her mother and father. How could they be happy in Honduras? The photo and Ciara's own clothing were the only personal items in the grand house. Otherwise, the furniture and décor were completely original to the Westin family.

Ciara was glad the contents were in the purchase agreement. The new roof, window repairs, floor refinishing, and central heating and cooling were the only additions so far. That suited the present need for Caldwell Realty in ways Ciara could never have planned.

Ciara sighed deeply while moving to her stomach. Looking up she caught sight of herself in the wall-length mirror. Remaining in the slip and make-up from last night was a bad decision. It would take a full hour just to cleanse away the thick foundation and comb the tease out of her hair.

Her usual blow-dry-and-go routine was not going to happen today. She grimaced at her reflection. She needed to get started soon to be presentable for her company. Her instincts led her to keep things simple. Focus on the property and keep the conversation flowing away from anything personal.

About two hours later, the grandfather clock chimed 9:00 as Ciara applied a thin coat of lip gloss. The hair extensions and false lashes remained giving her a fuller, healthier appearance. She took time to hang the designer dress and avoided getting it soiled or wrinkled. It hung on the outside of the ornate, wood-carved bureau.

"You look like a work of art on display. I'll just leave you there," said Ciara.

While she admired the dress, her cell phone chirped with a text message. She reached for her phone. "This is Rita Nelon. My family and I would love to have you with us at church this morning before we meet for lunch."

"Oh no, I'm not up for that," Ciara shouted to the walls. Her mind whirled while her eyes darted around the room.

Ciara called Bryant while fishing for her valium at the bottom of her oversized handbag. Her heart pounded while she searched and calmed only after she felt the lid of the prescription bottle. She pulled it up and grabbed for two pills while relaying the text to Bryant.

"Go to church, Ciara." Bryant's voice was calm and assertive as he spoke.

"I just can't, Bryant. I draw the line at mingling my personal life with business. I've been taught better. You don't go to church to impress clients. I haven't been to church since my dad stopped pastoring." Her voice trailed off and the tremble revealed more vulnerability than she liked to show. She breathed deeply and waited on Bryant.

"I'll go too. We'll go together...I will sit with you, and

you can explain it all to me. I'm not religious and I've only been in a church a couple of times or so."

Ciara paused before replying, "Ok, I'll go, but you better hurry. I think the worship service will begin at 10:30 and her church is in Mobile. It'll take a good half hour to get there from Bayport. Pick me up here?" Ciara scrambled through her closet replacing the slacks for a tasteful full-length skirt. She wasn't sure how traditional the church might be, but she wasn't taking chances on being underdressed.

As Bryant's sedan pulled into the freshly manicured circle drive, Ciara began calming. The valium was taking effect. She walked to the kitchen and reached for juice adding protein powder to fill her stomach. It would taste disgusting, but she didn't want to have her stomach growl during service. She added some caffeine powder for good measure, took a second glance in the ornate mirror in the foyer, and scrambled to the car.

"You look...you look different, Ciara." Bryant turned to Ciara sitting next to him. Her shoulder length blond hair now thicker with extensions fell behind in soft tendrils. Her face was clean and natural. The white skirt and lacy shirt gave her an angelic look. "You should have gone into acting. I've never seen anyone who could imitate different groups of people so well."

"Hmmm?" Ciara looked out the passenger window and rattled off the address to the church. She drank deep from the juice concoction while humming quietly. A few times on the ride she mumbled a prayer; ending each time with, "Thank You, Lord."

As Ciara and Bryant parked outside the large, traditional church the sun was peeking over the large steeple. They walked to the front doors and across the foyer. They shook hands with two greeters and made their way into the large sanctuary.

Ciara and Bryant stood under a balcony looking for a place to sit. Rita Nelon sat second row on the right side of the beautifully carpeted sanctuary. The teals, purples, and reds were brilliantly accented with recessed lighting projecting on each wall. A small orchestra pit exuded soft music while a large choir sat poised to sing. Ciara spotted the mayor and motioned for Bryant to follow her on the long aisle.

She made it to the end of the wooden pew before Rita Nelon spotted her. The mayor rose to her feet and reached past Ciara's outstretched hand and enveloped her in a warm hug. Rita Nelon wasn't a large woman and most people thought of her as average height and size, but she was almost twice the size of Ciara, whose frame was petite and recently impoverished by her small appetite.

Bryant extended his hand while Mayor Nelon motioned for Ciara to sit beside her at the end of the pew. The mayor shook his hand quickly while filling the seat beside Ciara and in the process took the only available seat on her row. Bryant looked around and contemplated squeezing in the church pew beside Ciara.

Ciara caught his eyes and shook her head, no, while pointing to an open space on the front row. Bryant took the cue and sank into the cushioned navy-blue seat. He turned to Ciara and mouthed, "I like it up here, I'll be able to see the show so well from this vantage point." He smiled at the silver-haired man beside him while reading aloud the little pin prominently displayed on his lapel, "Usher." Bryant pointed to the lapel and said, "And look I'm in good hands if I need to find the bathroom when the lights dim."

Ciara closed her eyes and suppressed a giggle.

Bryant had no clue about church. He thought he was at a Broadway show. She looked down at her tasteful designer pumps her mother purchased over five years ago. They weren't her usual style but served her well in this environment. The worship music began, and the choir sang out strong.

Ciara swayed slightly as the choir sang. Tiny hairs stood up on her arms and the back of her neck. "I praise you, Lord. I remember all the times You met me like this," she whispered as the music continued. She stood and sang quietly with the choir. The words were displayed on the projection above the baptistry, but she didn't have to glance at them.

For an hour Ciara forgot about her surroundings and relaxed. Mayor Nelon smiled sweetly at Ciara and winked. "You look like you belong here in this place. Even more than the country club last night."

Ciara smiled back and nodded her head in agreement. The pastor approached the podium and began to read scripture. The familiar passage in John 15 read like a dog-eared, classic novel and Ciara could quote it well.

"Jesus said, I am the vine, and you are the branches," the pastor spoke clearly.

"Why do I feel like I need to go home? I no longer have a home to go to. My parents are so far away, and Honduras might as well be on Mars," Ciara leaned forward and whispered to Bryant.

"Is this reminding you of your parents? I guess this kind of thing would." Bryant turned his head slightly to hear her better.

"Why would they leave me?" Ciara whispered to herself and sat back from Bryant hoping he did not hear.

As if on cue a father and daughter sitting to Ciara's left caught her attention. It could have been her and her

143

dad years ago. She remembered before he became pastor, and she was first able to attend "big church." She sat beside him like the young girl in the adjoining aisle.

Ciara did not listen to the rest of the sermon. She wanted it all to end. A dull headache began forming and she contemplated excusing herself to the bathroom and taking a pain pill. She wanted to be numb. She felt out of control. Ciara concentrated on the back of Bryant's head. He listened intently and didn't even move a muscle when Ciara leaned forward and cleared her throat hoping to get his attention again.

"We're getting out of here as soon as we can. I need some time to get my wits together before Mayor Nelon and Caroline Clay meet at the property," Ciara whispered.

Bryant didn't respond, and Ciara almost missed the invitation for everyone to stand. The pastor invited people to come down to the front. Ciara stood beside Mayor Nelon and smiled sweetly. She was very accustomed to this part of the service. She prided herself at how many times she resisted the call to come forward.

Ciara didn't want to go to the front. Her father asked her a couple of years ago why she never responded. Her dad's sad face caused her to reassure him that she talked to God in her own way.

Ciara reached for Bryant's arm as he moved forward to the front of the church. She moved back to her seat when he shrugged her hand away. Bryant moved to the aisle and stood with several others who came forward. A pretty melody played softly on a single instrument while Bryant joined several other men and women and two small children.

They stood praying in front of the ushers. Bryant's head lowered as he held the silver-haired usher's hands.

His head bobbed up and down while listening intently to the older man's words. Ciara saw him wipe at his eyes with one hand and raise the other one. His fingertips were pointing to the tall ceiling of the large building.

"You are taking this to the next level, Bryant. You don't have to pretend to accept Christ," Ciara whispered under her breath looking to her side.

Bryant turned around facing Ciara. The change in his tear-soaked face was undeniable. He rushed to her and hugged her tight. "Ciara, this thing is real. Jesus is real. Why didn't you tell me more about this?"

She patted his back and looked at Mayor Nelon. She felt the heat rush to her cheeks at Bryant's display. Ciara searched the older woman's expression looking for her disapproval but didn't find it. As Bryant pulled back and shook the mayor's hand, Ciara took it as a chance to distance herself from the second row of the church. She made her way to the foyer and to the ladies' room. Finding a stall and breathing deeply didn't calm her. She moved out of the restroom to locate Bryant and get home as soon as possible.

As she emerged from the door and to the foyer, she caught sight of Bryant talking to the usher. He was animated in his expressions and his hands flitted about him wildly.

Bryant walked to her in three large steps. He grabbed her arm and spoke loudly, "Ciara, it's amazing how great I feel."

Ciara smiled and quickly said, "Bryant, I think I need to get home. Can we go now? I'd like to get home before I have company." She smiled at the regal elderly gentleman flanking Bryant.

"Come back next week, son. You need a church family to help you grow in the Lord." The man closest to

Bryant shook his hand and smiled broadly at Ciara.

"I'll be sure to come back, and I really appreciate this Bible. I admit I don't know anything about it, but I'm going to start reading it immediately. I can probably finish it by next Sunday." Bryant held the leather-bound Bible in his right hand and grabbed for Ciara in his left pulling her toward the double glass doors leading outside into blinding sunlight. She winced at the light and followed Bryant to his car.

"You're not pretending. You're serious about this," Ciara said.

She looked through her over-sized handbag for her sunglasses while trying to think of how to maneuver the new Bryant. She had been around new converts before. Smile and agree with him. She looked over at a grinning Bryant and listened as he dialed his father's phone. He took it off Bluetooth and talked through his receiver privately.

"Dad, I went to church, and it was amazing." He paused a few minutes listening to the deep male voice on the line.

Ciara was relieved Bryant called his dad. This gave her time to regain her composure. She half-listened while Bryant described the service and his experience. She mentally took stock of the text she needed to make for the catering and flowers being delivered in the next half hour.

She scrambled to find someone on short notice but was relieved to find a tearoom who could do both on the same day if she kept it very simple and went with the already prepared menu for the Sunday crowd. They were cutting it close, but she would be home to accept the delivery before Mayor Nelon, and Caroline arrived.

As they exited I-10 driving to Bayport, Ciara caught

sight of a full-sized pickup truck at the intersection of Bayport Drive. As she looked closer, her eyes locked on Cameron Shivers and Annie Westin. Her pulse raced, and she looked away from them. Bryant disconnected his call with his father and looked at Ciara.

"Bryant, can I talk to you for a minute?"

"What's up Ciara?" Bryant turned his head to face her as the pickup truck turned on the road in front of Bryant's sedan. He turned in the same direction and followed the truck closely. Ciara could see Cameron's eyes reflected in his rear-view mirror. His steady demeanor and quiet spirit created a longing in Ciara that had been dormant for the past two years. The homesick feeling resurfaced, and she closed her eyes tightly.

"I'm not feeling so well. I'm going to need to stop at this next service station and get some water." She reached in her handbag and grabbed the oversized bottle of pain medicine. She pulled it out and sat it between the seat and the passenger door. Bryant pulled over and walked into the store.

He returned and handed her the water. She discreetly put her hand to her mouth depositing the pill and drank deep. She reached for the prescription bottle to place it in her purse again. Her hands frantically moved about the seat searching for the bottle. She leapt from the vehicle and began looking in the floorboard of the car.

"Ciara, the bottle is right here." Bryant held it in his right hand and his lips contorted into a slight frown. His eyes narrowed, and Ciara hated his pitiful expression. His usual smugness was different now since church this morning.

"Thanks Bryant." She calmly reached for the bottle and was surprised when he moved it out of her reach.

"I don't think I can be a part of this any longer. You

need to get clean and not abuse these pills. I...I...know I've played a big part in you getting your hands on these. I'm sorry...I don't know why I did it, but I know it's wrong." He looked into her eyes, but only succeeded in getting a glimpse before she lowered her head.

"Just give me that bottle and as soon as it's gone...it's gone. No more." Ciara looked up and into Bryant's sad eyes. "I don't blame you for anything. It's not that big of a deal. There's still half a bottle left, and I have used them sparingly." Her eyes were no longer drooping, but her pupils were now constricting. All the muscles in her face were relaxing and she was unusually calm and energized at the same time.

Bryant shook his head, no, and stepped out of the car. He made his way to the storm drain close to the highway but still in the service station parking. He unscrewed the lid and poured the contents of the bottle into the storm drain. He held the bottle and Ciara looked on as he stared for a few seconds at the label.

Ciara sat in the car stewing while Bryant drove to the Westin house. The beautiful spring day was picture perfect, and the bay water glistened in the early afternoon sun. Everyone would be arriving in thirty minutes. What was the best way to hide she had just taken Oxycontin? She felt elated and relaxed, but also knew it came at a price. She was not in control and would need to navigate lunch before she could be in the clear to process the Bryant situation.

She considered contacting Jack Junior but thought better of it. What was she going to say? Bryant found religion. Jack Junior wouldn't care. He would probably use it to his advantage. He would exploit Bryant's new weakness—honesty.

Caroline Clay's sedan followed by a large black

Cadillac pulled into the circular driveway as Ciara placed the last flower arrangement. The smell of the Cape Jasmine blooms was biting to her heightened senses. She moved from them and looked out the lacy, white, full-length drape covering the foyer window. Bryant helped both women out of their cars and walked them to the door. She opened the door avoiding eye-contact and welcomed the two women. She was thankful the bright sunlight gave her a reason to look away.

"Ciara, this house, this day, and your company is just perfect." Mayor Rita Nelon smiled warmly while looking around the foyer and beyond to the great room. Caroline looked at Ciara and extended her hand. Ciara took it and began rattling off the research she had done for the Westin property.

"We at Caldwell want to keep the integrity of the house while updating the necessary things." Her rehearsed statements hung in the air as both women walked around talking with one another about photo ops and plans for an article. Neither woman paid attention to Ciara. She excused herself to check on lunch preparations. She walked to Bryant and stood beside him.

"I may need to talk to them at lunch. You seem a little out of touch. Your speech is slightly slurred and I'm afraid they will discover that you are on something." Bryant gave a brotherly look and lowered his eyes.

"Bryant, let me handle this. Since you've found 'Jesus' I don't want your new conscience to fumble the basketball right now." Ciara swayed slightly. Bryant was right. She took the Oxycontin on an empty stomach after she had taken two valiums earlier. "I got a pl.. pl.. plan."

Ciara made her way into the sunroom where Caroline took a picture of the bay and Mayor Nelon sat regally at one of the settees. "Mayor Nelon and Mrs. Clay I must apologize. I have taken some allergy medication. Silly me ordered southern flower arrangements not realizing the arrangements would contain Cape Jasmine blooms. I am terribly allergic."

"Oh, Ms. Caldwell, you need to lie down. Allergy medicine is the worst." Caroline gave a sympathetic pat on Ciara's back. Both Caroline and Mayor Nelon flanked Ciara and began giving motherly advice.

"I think I will go lie down. You've already taken pictures there. Bryant can keep you company for lunch. Please enjoy." Ciara laid it on thick and nodded at Bryant.

"If you will take the arrangements to the porch and allow these women to have lunch, I would appreciate it." She motioned to Bryant who narrowed his eyes and began retrieving vases.

She looked back to the two concerned faces, "I am so embarrassed to leave you two in my home."

"Don't you worry, we will be fine. Go get some rest and get away from these arrangements." Mayor Nelon swatted at one of the vases in Bryant's hands and motioned him to the porch.

Ciara excused herself and went to the bedroom closest to the kitchen. She left the door cracked to have access to the lunch conversation. She was thankful for the protein bars she stuffed in her large handbag and began nibbling on a peanut cluster bar as she watched Bryant pass out freshly prepared plates of chicken salad, pasta, and fruit from the local tearoom.

She could see him facing the bedroom, while the two ladies sat facing Bryant. Ciara tucked her feet under her long skirt and draped a blanket over her shoulders. She was surprised when he walked through the small hall and rapped on the half-opened door. He handed her a plate piled with chicken salad.

"You should eat."

She ignored his questioning eyes and worried expression. She took the plate and pulled the door between them leaving him standing at the other side of the large, mahogany door. When she heard his retreating footsteps, she cracked the door again. Bryant returned to the table and sat leaning into the conversation with Mayor Nelon.

His face softened, and Ciara thought she saw a tear escape down his face while he ate and listened. Ciara could hear most of the conversation and became bored with the incessant talk about the morning church service. She learned Caroline had been at the church too. However, she had been in the nursery this morning with her two children.

"I want to go back next week. I don't know much about church or God or Jesus." Bryant admitted to the two ladies. "The last time I was in church my little nephew was getting Christened." He put his fork down and smiled broadly. "I showed up in time for the priest to pour water and excused myself after the family photo."

"Bryant, you will be surrounded by good, godly people who can help you. Come back to church and sit with me." Mayor Nelon reached for his hand in a motherly fashion and shook her head as if all was decided.

"I'm going to kill Bryant! He's making my connection. I'm supposed to have that invitation," Ciara whispered through clenched teeth.

She stood quickly and stumbled to her right dropping the blanket from her shoulders to the floor. She was trapped in the bedroom while Bryant formed relationships, and she did it all to herself. She paced the room and was relieved when the ladies walked out the double front doors and said their goodbyes. Ciara bounded from the room when she saw both sets of taillights turn right from her drive.

What she didn't expect was Bryant's taillights soon following theirs. She watched as he exited her drive and turned left. She attempted to call him five times before giving up on reaching him.

"Why did you leave so early? I need to talk to you, now!" she yelled into her cell phone while leaving a voice-mail. Three hours later, Ciara collapsed into a heap on her bed and slept fitfully. She dreamed of Bryant smiling and holding Mayor Nelon's hand. Her anger was growing leaps and bounds while she slept.

That night, Cam woke at 3:00 am with an image of Ciara stuck in his mind. In his dream, she reached out for him and then disappeared into a fog. Her eyes were child-like, and she mouthed, "Help me," over and over. She was dressed in all white and her hair was brushed back. She was not in the car he spotted yesterday. Instead, she stood outside of a large church building barefoot with her small hands clenched at her side. He sat up in his bed trembling.

His t-shirt was wet with sweat, and he was thankful for his pajama pants. It was cold despite the approaching spring. Yesterday had crept to the high seventies, but the night had fallen into the forties. He did not switch his heating system on before bed and regretted it now that he was covered in sweat.

"Oh Lord, please help Ciara." He moved to his knees and began to pray for her. His hands raked through his hair leaving it standing up at his forehead. At last, after about thirty minutes, he felt the heavy moment lift and he crawled back into bed hoping to go back to sleep without a recurring dream. He finally dozed around 5:00 am and slept deeply.

The alarm sounded loud and clear at 6:15 waking him mid-sleep cycle. He rolled over pressing snooze. He would take an additional fifteen minutes today since Annie didn't need his help at the food truck. They were meeting after he was done at the church. He smiled when he thought of Annie. They would be married in a few short weeks and his new life with her would finally begin.

Two weeks later, Ciara pulled into the parking space in front of Caldwell Realty. She lifted her visor in time to see Hartline exiting the bakery holding one end of a large box. He was dressed in a grey suit and his shoes were shiny, brown, and looked like they pinched his toes.

The other end was balanced by Tony Glenn and another teenage boy also dressed in shiny brown shoes. She took inventory of the day and tried to think of any special occasion for March 21st. It was spring, but other than that she couldn't think of a holiday. Her brows furrowed as she sat in her car.

"Hartline, we may need to put the cake in the church's fridge before the wedding." Tony grunted while holding his end. Ciara cracked her window and overheard them as they walked to Glenn Bakery's only delivery truck. It was rusted in spots and the pin-striped lettering was peeling. Ciara never saw it go anywhere and assumed it would always stay parked in the back.

"Pastor Cam will know a place to store it. I'm not sure the church's fridge can handle a cake this size. Annie will love this." Hartline opened the back of the truck as the two young men got in to hold the cake steady. As the threesome drove away, Ciara felt a lump growing in her throat. Cameron was getting married today. She felt the urge to vomit, and tears formed in her lids before she could make her way to the office. To her relief Bryant was on a call and didn't glance her way when she walked past his door.

Ciara closed the door and lowered herself into her plush office chair. She let the tears fall and wiped at her face briskly. She sat a full two minutes before opening her eyes and reached for her computer mouse. The screen to her desktop computer clicked on revealing her screensaver. It was a picture of the latest BMW sports car. It's chrome finish and tan leather interior were visible in the photoshopped image. She needed to think about a new car. The business expansion was doing well, and she would soon be able to leave with her head held high.

Her left hand fell on her desk, and she noticed paperwork with a red arrow post it pointing at a signature line. Ciara's eyes widened at the Westin house offer before her. She stood suddenly and looked again. It was twice the original purchase price even after she deducted the repairs Caldwell Realty had made. Her heart leapt in her chest. Bryant wouldn't have left this for her to sign if he didn't think it was the best deal.

What would Jack Junior think now? The profit was dazzling and there were several more clients on her list since Mayor Nelon visited her home. She needed to stay focused and not lose sight of her goal. She dialed the number from one of the potential clients on Bryant's list. The clients were young and wealthy. They both wanted to find beachfront property, and they were willing to spend a lot of money. She would do this deal alone. Minus Bryant.

Bryant made all the connections so far and his recent relationship with Mayor Nelon bothered Ciara. He was gaining Mayor Nelon's trust while she was drifting far from her. She would meet the new clients herself and the sooner the better. She felt a raging need to be busy tonight. She signed then took a quick photo of the proposal in front of her. She quickly sent the photo to Jack Junior.

"Read it and weep big brother," Ciara mumbled to her phone.

At Bayport Community Church the weather was playing tricks on the Shivers and Westin wedding party. The latest forecast was for rain in the afternoon, followed by a cold front. The first day of spring, March 21st, fell on a Saturday. A perfect day for a wedding.

Unfortunately, the season temperatures could fluctuate wildly between mock summer days and cold, wet winter ones. Annie stood in the nursery-turned-bridal-suite of the church looking out the long tinted rectangular slit. The window was allowing her a small view of the clouds gathering to the west at the edge of the parking lot.

"I guess we can move indoors to the fellowship hall if it rains too hard." Annie nervously gnawed on her manicured nail while her mother fussed with her lace veil. It was the only thing Annie wore of her mother's. Mrs. Westin's full-length ballroom wedding dress did not fit Annie's tall slender body nor her simpler taste.

She chose a simple stark-white dress that fit her well. The neckline was tasteful, and the train was beautiful. The train was the only accented or adorned part of the whole ensemble. Little faux diamonds and pearls outlined the edges. She wore strappy shoes that clasped her elegant feet. The auburn hair and crystal blue eyes added beauty to Annie's whole look. She opted to wear her hair up with large tendrils falling on both sides of her face.

Caroline Clay offered their studio photographer from Southern Shores Magazine and the young woman was great at capturing sweet, candid photos of the bridal party. Mary moved between the two rooms for the bride and groom, but soon decided to stay with Annie.

Cam stood with his dad at the front of the church and nervously fiddled with the white rose in the lapel of his tuxedo. His dad gave him a wink and stilled his hand, moving it to Cam's side. Cam responded with a deep sigh and focused on not locking his knees. Mary made him promise to remember this advice. He was grateful the pastor from Mobile Community Church agreed to do the ceremony. He was older and helped calm Cam's nerves at rehearsal.

The church was packed with friends and family. Many were chatting while a violin played from the choir seats. His mother was escorted and sat a few feet from him. She smiled through large crocodile tears and commented on how handsome he looked. He smiled at her and his heart raced when he heard the music change indicating that bridesmaids were now walking down the aisle.

He craned his neck to get a glimpse of Annie behind them and found her flanked by Mary and Mrs. Westin. Both ladies walked her down the aisle and Cam strained to see Annie's face through the veil. What he could see made his heart leap again. She was gorgeous. He knew she would look dazzling in white and anticipated her elegant form being clad with silk and lace, but her image was more than he could have imagined.

Cam had performed a couple of weddings since being senior pastor at the church, but those brides paled in comparison to the tall, elegant Annie. The transformation was startling, and he noticed everyone staring at her. She did not have to worry about sharing her wedding day with any other soul present or not present. All eyes were fixed on her.

The ceremony began, and Cam anxiously waited to push the veil aside and see Annie's face fully. When the time came for him to face her without the veil and recite the marriage vows, he felt intoxicated. She smiled sweetly and swatted a tear from her cheek while he retrieved the ring from his father and put it on her finger. She held his hand tightly and did the same with his ring.

Before Cam and Annie knew it, it was time to kiss. Cam held her close and kissed her fully before Mary let out a loud "Woo-hoo!" The wedding party laughed heartily and walked back down the aisle and out to the white tables donned with scrumptious wedding food, a beautiful Glenn's Bakery cake, and white foldable chairs.

The threatening sky stayed west of the church for a full three hours before moving in. Cam and Annie were about to ride off in his recently waxed and shined pickup truck when small drops of water began to fall. Annie quickly threw her white-rose bouquet behind her and laughed till she cried when Mary caught it.

"Oh, Lord no. I'm not the next bride." Mary offered the bouquet to several ladies standing by her to no avail. She finally just lifted it in the air and laughed with everyone else.

They both looked out the rear window watching their friends and family wave them on while the sun set through the clouds. A full, double rainbow appeared, and the photographer was able to capture both Cam and Annie's face through the window lit by the rainbow. It was the photo of the year for the small town of Bayport and the young photographer was giddy while showing it off to everyone who would give her the chance.

Cam turned toward Gulf Shores to take Annie to the beachside bed and breakfast his parents found while visiting during Christmas. They spared no expense and Cam knew this place would be an amazing start to his new life. He took Annie's hand and kissed it softly. "Annie, you're going to love this place Mom and Dad picked out."

"I can't wait to see it. Her eyes danced playfully. Does it have a kitchen? I know I don't need to cook tonight..." Annie felt heat rise to her cheeks at the thought of their wedding night and giggled lightly.

"No cooking, you'll be too busy tonight." Cam smiled and raised his eyebrows.

"Cam, I realize that, but you got to eat a good meal sometime." She swatted his arm and smiled broadly. Cam's stomach flopped as Annie snuggled close to him. Annie had shied away from guys, not understanding their language after her father died. But now, here with Cam, things were different.

They pulled into the beautiful cottage flanked with soft, white lights. The interior was lit with a glowing tiffany lamp. The white fireplace burned bright and gave warmth to the cool night air. Cam reached out and picked Annie up in his arms. His thin but muscular frame completely supported her. He walked across the threshold and slowly let her down in front of the fireplace on the seashell printed rug. He pulled her into his arms quickly and kissed her full and deep.

"Thank you for being my wife, beautiful and talented Annie."

She exhaled and smiled before he kissed her again. Each time he closed his eyes, he saw bouquets of white roses and the beautiful smells from the vanilla candles in the cottage made him smile; but when he kissed Annie this deeply a strong feeling emerged. She trembled in his arms. This was what he waited for all those years when friends were playing at love and giving themselves away to passion and lust. Cam and Annie now had the chance to drink deeply of love and know that it was the right thing to do before God, their family, and their church.

Back in Bayport, Ciara sat at the bar of the Bayport Country Club. She agreed to meet her new clients for drinks. They were young brothers with plenty of discretionary cash and had recently heard of Caldwell Realty.

"Pastor Cameron Shivers is crazy to stay in this small town and I'm glad he found a local girl who could put up with this boring place," Ciara said. She sat across from two men who inched closer to the emaciated but beautiful Ciara Caldwell.

"Isn't he getting married today? I thought I heard Pop talking about it while golfing." The youngest client, Brent Lightsey, sat totally enthralled by Ciara. She was from Orlando and her halter top and tight slacks were not the usual dress for the southern country club ladies. He touched her smooth back and moved in closer while his older brother ordered more drinks.

When the shot glass was deposited in front of Ciara, she drank quickly, wincing at the taste. Out of her shaky peripheral vision she caught sight of a nicely dressed dark-haired man. He stood close and stared at the three of them. She willed her eyes to focus on the figure approaching her. Her curiosity gave way to shock when she realized it was Bryant.

"Ciara, I need to talk to you." Bryant pushed young Brent away while grabbing for Ciara's right hand. He laced his fingers in hers and attempted to walk her off the barstool.

"Bryant, what are you doing here?" Ciara looked him in the eyes and smiled, "Sit down, partner, I found us two new clients, meet Brent and Brian Lightsey. You guys can be three B's with a bod." She giggled and scrunched up her nose. Her head swayed and bobbed.

Bryant ignored the outstretched hands of Brent and Brian and spoke into Ciara's ear, "Let's go, I'll make an appointment in the morning for these two."

Ciara stumbled to Bryant's arm and held on tight. Her head was spinning, and she felt like she might faint. The fourth shot of vodka sat empty in front of her seat. Brent's and Brian's were mostly untouched.

"Bryant, did you see the magazine article today about Caldwell Realty?" She pointed to the front cover which displayed her picture in the left corner and the Westin House in the background. "We did it, friend." Bryant looked around. Most of the patrons in the dining area were now watching them.

"Yes, Ciara. Now we need to leave so we can celebrate." He motioned to the door. She smiled at him and followed Bryant out the huge double doors before grabbing for him and collapsing in his arms. He quickly strapped her into the passenger seat of his car. As he drove, her head began to bobble, and her breathing became shallow.

"Ciara, wake up. What did you take? Speak to me!" Bryant shook Ciara's shoulder while driving. He dialed his father quickly and left a message for him to call soon when his voicemail picked up. He pulled over at the Bayport Rehabilitation Clinic and ran to the door. He was greeted by a young man a little older than himself. He was dressed in slacks and looked clean cut.

Ciara slept for an hour before waking to two men standing over her. One was Bryant and the other was a man she had never met but remembered seeing at Glenn's Bakery and the food truck. "Where am I?"

She tried to sit up but couldn't. She was in a small office building with a receptionist desk. She felt the overstuffed brown couch before she looked down at where she lay. Her head hurt, and she coughed when taking a sip from a water bottle the other man offered.

Beside the couch a blood pressure cuff and thermometer lay on a small table strewn with pamphlets. "Where am I Bryant?"

"Ciara, this is Jeremy Clay, director of Bayport Rehabilitation Clinic and I'd like for you to talk with him. Thankfully he stopped by here after attending a wedding to do some last-minute things or I wouldn't have known what to do." Bryant pointed to the other man who sat on the table beside her. He was wearing a suit and his crisp white button-down shirt was unbuttoned at the top.

"Why do I need to talk to him?" Ciara closed her eyes tightly. She looked at Jeremy Clay and saw the concern in his eyes.

"Wait a minute. You brought me to a rehab? I've got to get out of here." Ciara tried again to sit.

"Ciara, you need help." Bryant put his hands on her shoulders and helped her sit with her head against the back of the over-sized couch.

"Bryant, I just want to go home. I'll talk to this guy another time. Can you take me home, please? I'll get my car from the club later." She fought the urge to vomit and leaned on her knees.

"I think she's right, Mr. Ward. You should take her home and have her give me a call when she's able to talk." He patted Bryant on the back and smiled at Ciara. "I am here when you want to talk, Ciara."

"Thank you, I will call when I need help." Ciara fought to keep her composure and glared at Bryant.

"I'll take you home, but you've got to promise me you

won't do this again. I'm serious. You scared me half to death. Jack Junior and your family may need to help you." Ciara noticed Bryant's frown.

"I'll call my mom and dad and have a long conversation about my little indiscretion last night. It'll be fine. I just got carried away and had too many drinks. Never again, scouts honor." She smiled at Bryant and rose to her feet still swaying from the vodka. Jeremy held her elbow while Bryant brought his car to the front awning of the building.

"Ciara, you are not alone. No one's judging you. When you really want help, don't forget that you have people who care." Jeremy nodded at Bryant and held the passenger door until Ciara buckled in and sat securely beside Bryant. Ciara waved at Jeremy and plastered her head against the headrest of Bryant's car. The spinning remained, but she was not nauseated.

Neither of them talked as Bryant navigated the streets to Ciara's house. Earlier that afternoon she signed to accept the sizable offer that came in since the recent article and it was just a matter of time before Ciara would be moving. Jack Junior deposited a commission check for Ciara to use as a deposit for rent. He was being generous, and she worried he was still trying to buy her. She would take the commission. She earned it, but his generosity didn't come without a price.

Ciara studied Bryant. Why didn't he tell Jack Junior about her recent problems? He knew about the pills and now she was drinking. He was sincere in his new-found faith. She watched as he read his Bible each day and he hadn't missed a single church service or event in three weeks. It was paying off for the business since he was getting to know the locals, but he didn't seem to care about the success he was having.

"How did you find me?" Ciara asked.

"The Lightsey brothers' dad called me. He mentioned where you were meeting and wanted to make sure we didn't take advantage of his sons." Bryant said.

He pulled into Ciara's drive and turned the key. "I'm worried. You are making careless mistakes and now you're living recklessly. I can't make you care or behave. You're not a child. I am telling you this as your friend."

"Friend? Bryant Ward you and I both know the arrangement is you scratch my back and I scratch yours. There's no true friendship. This new Bryant who is now Christ's man is driving me crazy." Ciara huffed loudly and opened her door. As she looked back at Bryant, she was surprised to see his nostrils flaring and his eyes narrowing.

"I'm sorry, Ciara, but if you think for a minute, you may find I'm the only friend you have left." Bryant grabbed the steering wheel and looked at Ciara, "Get it together or I will be forced to say something to Jack Junior. I don't want to be caught between you two any longer, and know this Ciara Caldwell, I will not lie for you ever again. Understood?"

Ciara recoiled and slammed the car door. Bryant skidded out of the drive leaving her looking on shocked at his outburst. She turned and collapsed in a giant heap on the steps before the grand entrance to the Westin property. The bay water lapped loudly in the background after being stirred by yesterday's rainstorm. Ciara sat sulking while the morning sun made its way up in the east and over the water in soft glows leaving the beautiful property washed in light.

She strained to pull herself to her feet and through the grand doors. "I will be so glad to be rid of you, stupid house."

At that declaration, she slammed the doors and walked quickly to her bedroom to pack. She methodically dialed Jack Junior's phone while she filled her designer luggage to the brim with as many clothing and toiletry items as she could fit. She frowned when his phone rang to voicemail but decided to leave a message. "I'm coming home for a while. I need to take care of some things in Orlando."

CHAPTER 12

Cam drove through the narrow streets to Bayport Community Church. He felt much different since his week-long honeymoon. It was the longest absence from his post as pastor since he arrived almost three years earlier. It was difficult to watch Annie dress for work at the crack of dawn and kiss him goodbye for the day, but he was also anxious to get back to the church.

The parking lot to the church was empty except for Hartline's rusted pickup truck at the edge of the palm trees. One light was illuminating the stained glass and Cam parked at the side door closest to the hall leading to the sanctuary. Cam entered the sanctuary and knelt in the altar opposite Hartline, who slowly paced the back row of the church. He tried not to eavesdrop on his church member's prayer but couldn't help hearing two names being mentioned in the spoken prayer.

"Heavenly Father, I pray that you help Bryant and Ciara. You know the need and that things are desperate. Give me wisdom to talk to Bryant and help Ciara get the help she needs." Hartline stopped pacing and Cam turned to face him.

"I didn't mean to interrupt you, man." Cam grimaced and walked toward Hartline. He noticed Hartline's expression change from surprise to sadness. Cam sat in the back row in front of Hartline and motioned for him to sit too. Hartline sat and looked down at his hands.

"I guess you heard my prayer. I think she's using

those pills I saw when she spilled her purse. I don't want to ruin things for you and Annie right now. I asked the Lord earlier this year to let me help other addicts and now I believe I have one right next door every day of the week." Hartline looked intently at the cloth-covered seating in front of him.

"I prayed the same prayer never thinking my ex-fiancé would reenter my life and start popping pills." Cam sighed and rubbed his hands together. Both men sat in silence while Cam prayed under his breath. The morning sun began pouring through and warming the room. The air conditioning kicked on and the low hum broke the silence as Hartline looked at his watch.

Hartline rose to his feet and extended his hand to Cam. Cam shook his hand and followed Hartline down the aisle and to the foyer of the small church. "You're not ruining things for Annie and me. We had a great honeymoon and now it's time for us to be back. We are ready to get back to our lives. I am praying for Ciara."

"I know, Pastor Cam, so am I." Hartline nodded to Cam and exited through the double-glass front doors. Cam turned and walked through the narrow hall to his back office relieved to be faced with the mundane tasks a Monday morning brings. He would have some time to get reacclimated to the business of the church before working on his next sermon. He was glad to see the framed photo of Annie sitting prominently on his desk. He picked it up and smiled broadly. "I'm a married man," he whispered.

In Orlando, morning sun was pouring on Ciara as she approached Caldwell Realty's front entrance. She arrived at the office before Jack Junior. She only saw the security guard's vehicle in the parking deck and raced to the glass door. She pounded on the door until the guard looked in her direction. The young Hispanic man turned and pulled on his keyring. He smiled and rushed to the door to let her in.

"Gracias, Manuel." She smiled at him and ignored his surprised expression while passing the hall leading to Jack Junior's office. She walked to her little abandoned office and was surprised to see her brother had left it completely intact. It was as if she had just left for the weekend. Her computer, her desk calendar, and her picture of their parents in Honduras was still where she left them.

She smirked at the desk calendar still showing November of last year. A lot had happened since then. Cam was married to another woman; Ciara was homeless, and Bryant found Jesus.

"We really need to catch up 'ye 'ol desk calendar," Ciara said.

She grimaced and turned on her desk lamp. She didn't bother with the main fluorescent light. The morning sun and her lamp were more than enough for the small room.

Thirty minutes later she clicked off her computer search for BMW's. Jack Junior should be coming down the hall any minute. She adjusted her cream suit jacket and drank deeply of the single serve coffee she made herself from the machine behind the receptionist's desks. The warm liquid made her cheeks redden and her breathing relax.

Her heart skipped as she heard footsteps clicking down the tiled hallway toward her office. Ciara didn't relish the thought of negotiating with her brother in his large office or in the conference room over the large cherry wood table. She hoped he would come to her office. It would be better in this small space where she was more comfortable.

"Hello Ciara, did you forget where your office is in Bayport?" Jack Junior's eyes narrowed as he stood in the small doorway. He smiled slightly and crossed his arms in front of his chest.

"Sit down Junior, we need to talk." Ciara couldn't believe her own voice. It was strong and emotionless despite the fluttering in her stomach. She relaxed a bit when he slowly moved from the door and sat in the chair across from her. She didn't let her guard down, but she did change her stoic expression into a slight smile.

"I'm ready to come back to Orlando. The big deal on the Westin property is done and there is a steady stream of clients to keep Bryant busy for a while. He's got it under control and I am ready to be here." Ciara sat back in her chair and crossed her arms. She learned this determined pose from Jack Junior and silently congratulated herself on how bold she sounded to her own ears.

"Little sis, I don't think that would be wise. I spoke with Bryant when I got your text about coming here. It seems he also wants to come back to Orlando." Jack Junior paused for dramatic effect and studied Ciara's eyes.

"What? He can't leave Bayport. He's got a lot of work to finish and he's not leaving it to me to do by myself." Her arms flew to her side, and she reached for her phone scrolling through to see if she missed reading any texts from Bryant. Jack Junior sat silently watching Ciara. His expression was controlled, and he sat back in the chair.

Bryant wasn't going to text or call her. She hoped Bryant didn't tell Jack Junior about the pills and drinking. Her hands trembled slightly, and she lowered them to her desk.

"I gave Bryant the go ahead to leave Bayport. He was never supposed to stay past the Westin deal. Remember,

Ciara? He was there to handle the deal and get the company up and going. Considering recent business transactions, I'd say he did a pretty good job. Wouldn't you?" Jack Junior measured each word as if talking to a disgruntled child.

Ciara lifted her gaze to Jack Junior. Nothing she said would change his mind. Instead, she fingered the desk calendar and wriggled the computer mouse. The nearest car dealership came into view, and she started scrolling to the latest model sports cars.

Jack Junior rose from his seat. He stood facing Ciara and spoke in a hushed tone, "Ciara, do you need to tell me something. Are you ready to close the Bayport office and take the deal I offered last year?"

Ciara looked directly into her brother's eyes. She studied his expression and was perplexed at what she saw there. Did he pity her? She mustered her pride and spoke clear and concise words, "I will return to Bayport myself and finish up what needs to be done there. Let Bryant come back here. No, I don't have anything to tell you and, no, I'm not ready to make any deals."

She rose from her desk chair and walked past Jack Junior. As she navigated the steps to the front door, she felt her body begin to shake. The desire for more pills came as a flood and she took one while driving to the nearest liquor store. Her bottle of valium would not be enough.

She stuffed the pill bottle and the fifth of vodka in her oversized purse. Before she decided to drink any of the liquor, she drove ten miles to the luxury car dealership close to Caldwell Realty. Her sizable commission check would be enough for a down payment, and she could probably finance the rest of the car. It was time to upgrade her car and travel back to Bayport in style. She would not be able to use it for a place to rent, but now she didn't care.

Ciara smiled in her rearview mirror as she pulled out of the car dealership just after three o'clock eastern time, she would gain an hour driving back to Bayport. The new leather interior held the familiar new car smell and she felt giddy making the trip back to Bayport in this new upgrade.

Ciara saved the vodka for later. She didn't want to make the trip back with alcohol in her system. The bottle could wait until then. She called ahead and checked on a small apartment close to Caldwell Realty. The owner agreed to let Ciara lease it for the next few months since Caldwell Realty was grooming the property to sell.

"I won't have to go back to that stupid big southern house ever again," Ciara mumbled.

She was starting over in the apartment and was ready to drive into Bayport and pour herself a drink. She hadn't seen the apartment, but it was all she could afford now.

She ran several stoplights and went over the speed limit on Interstate 10, but somehow, Ciara made the seven and half hour trip without any trouble. She pulled into the small apartment's street side parking at eleven pm sharp. She grabbed her purse, one piece of luggage and struggled at the key box on the door of the rental house. When she finally opened the door, Ciara clicked on the small light beside the couch and collapsed.

The next time she roused she felt a pounding in her chest and woke on the plush, white-leather sofa pushed against the only window in the small apartment. She saw a small kitchenette, flanked by a door leading to a minimally furnished bedroom with a small three-piece bathroom. It was pitiful. The place could fit twenty times in the house Ciara grew up in and at least ten times in the Westin House. Ciara felt tears on her cheeks, and she rose to her feet.

As she stood, her foot kicked her purse, and she heard the thud of the glass bottle against the wooden couch leg. She methodically reached for the vodka bottle and walked to the kitchenette fishing out a juice glass. She poured herself a full shot and winced at the burning liquid coating her throat. That was the last thing she remembered about her first night back in Bayport and her new little apartment.

The next morning in Bayport, Cam lowered the sun visor blocking the startling, morning sun. He turned into the church parking lot. He planned to surprise Annie at the food truck for lunch. His mouth watered at the thought of biting into a steamy pie. His coffee with extra creamer was not enough to stave off his hunger as he thought of the food.

Cam chuckled and made his way through the small hallway leading to his office. A slight headache began forming and he rubbed his eye, dislodging one of his contacts. He riffled through his desk drawer before finally finding his contact solution and Ibuprofen. A nagging feeling kept coming upon him until he finally left his study notes and walked to the sanctuary to pray.

He knelt at the podium where he would deliver his next message in a couple of days. He struggled to stay focused and shed the feeling of foreboding he felt heavy on his shoulders. His thoughts drifted to the last time he spoke to Hartline.

"I don't know how to pray for Ciara. I want her to disappear and leave me alone," Cam spoke loudly.

He opened his eyes and understood the foreboding and burden he carried for the last week. "Lord, I still feel responsible for her, but I can't dishonor Annie. I feel lost about how to help Ciara." Cam lowered his head and waited for a few minutes before walking back to his office.

He sat in his office chair and began reading aloud, "Wine is a mocker, and strong drink a brawler. He who is led astray by it is not wise." As he heard the words, he realized the pressure he felt was because Ciara was alone in her addiction. Cam wasn't feeling responsible for her because he still had feelings for her. Instead, he was feeling like he was supposed to intervene in some way.

He needed to call Jack Caldwell. He should let him know. The weight lifted. It was very unlikely Ciara's family knew anything about her addiction.

As Cam dialed the church number in Orlando, his legs bounced nervously under his desk. When the familiar voice of the secretary came on the line, he almost hung up before asking for Jack's email address. He knew Jack Caldwell was in Honduras. The email would be the best way to get in touch with his old pastor. The friendly voice of the secretary rattled off the email address and made small talk with Cam until he interrupted and told her he needed to go.

Cam wrote and retracted the email so many times he almost missed his lunch with Annie. He finally settled on a short phrase, "Call as soon as you can."

He didn't want to scare the man, but he also felt that he would lose his courage to tell him what he knew if Jack delayed calling him.

Cam rose and placed his phone in his jacket pocket while walking out the side door. Before he reached his truck, his phone vibrated. His stomach turned at the site of the international phone number sprawled across his phone.

"Hello Cam, I was in prayer when I got your email. Is anything wrong?"

"I...I...I really need to talk to you about Ciara." Cam paused trying to find the right words. How could he tell his old pastor that his daughter is an addict?

"Is she Ok? Has anything happened to her?" Cam heard the fear in Jack's voice and almost lost his courage.

"No sir, I don't think anything has happened to her. It's just I have good reason to believe she is involved in some pretty risky behaviors." Cam exhaled and waited for a barrage of questions. Instead, there was only silence.

"Are you still there, Jack?"

"Yes, Cameron, I think you need to tell me what's going on," said Jack.

"I have reason to believe she is abusing medication and taking pills that aren't prescribed to her. It's gone around town here and a few people have noticed some erratic behavior from Ciara." Cam waited for a painful moment for Jack's reply.

"Are you sure, Cameron? It's not like you to be a part of idle gossip." Jack's voice trembled, and he cleared his throat.

"Sir, I would not have contacted you if I wanted to be a part of a gossip ring." Cam shifted in the driver's seat.

"I believe you, Cam. I don't want to believe you...I would rather believe you are just bitter...but I believe you." Jack's voice trembled and trailed off.

"If you need me to do anything."

Jack spoke, "Cam, it's not your place. I will fly back soon and try to get her help. Thanks for contacting me."

"I'm praying." Cam waited.

"I better go and make arrangements."

"Yes, sir. Bye." Cam dropped his phone in the passenger seat and turned his key. He drove the short distance to the food truck and parked behind Glenn's Bakery. He looked at the brick wall and the rear entrances to the storefronts. He didn't have much of an appetite, but he didn't want to leave Annie in the dark about his last conversation with Jack Caldwell.

At that moment, Ciara stumbled to her office chair attempting to grab the office phone before it stopped ringing. "Hello, Caldwell Realty, Ciara speaking." Her words were breathy, and she pushed at her temple trying to stop the hangover headache. "Hello?" She was too late. She should have left her apartment sooner. She missed two appointments to show properties. Bryant's neat handwriting filled each day on her desk calendar and made her swear under her breath at the thought of him.

"You should be here with me Bryant," Ciara spoke through clenched teeth.

Ciara calmed herself and decided to make some coffee before she called clients to make apologies. She walked slowly to the reception area and wished she had the money to hire a receptionist. She riffled through the coffee cabinet for several minutes before realizing she drank the last single serve cup last week.

"What to do, what to do? I could walk to the coffee shop," she said. Ciara decided against the idea and went next door to Glenn's Bakery.

Ciara walked out the front door and averted her eyes from the large food truck parked prominently in the parking area. Anger rose when she passed the long line forming at the open window. She pushed past two teenagers and jerked open the bakery door. She looked around wildly and caught sight of Hartline on the other side of the display counter. "I need some coffee, you got coffee, right?"

Hartline's eyes widened as he finished closing the display case. She waited while he looked to her hands and feet and then back to her face. Ciara did not put on her usual make-up, and she opted to wear the same clothes she wore the day before. She did not have time to unpack and woke up after passing out from the vodka and valium too late to do much more than shower and pull on the same clothes.

"Ciara, are you alright? You look...you look." Hartline reached for the coffee pot behind the counter and held the glass container with black liquid in his right hand while reaching for the paper cups stacked neatly on the back counter.

"Well, Ok...I know I didn't take time to put my make-up on...but goodness I didn't think I needed it that much." Ciara's voice quivered while she sniffed loudly.

The bakery door opened, and Ciara watched as Hartline's eyebrows raised. He cleared his throat, "Pastor Cam, how's it going?"

Ciara turned around to see Cameron standing in the entrance. His right hand was on the glass door. She looked into his eyes and swayed on her heels. She felt nauseous and decided to sit in the nearest metal chair. As she reached for the chair, she stumbled knocking over the napkin dispenser. It crashed to the floor a few seconds before she could catch it. She doubled over and began to vomit.

Hartline stood beside her while Cam held her arm. His strong hand was keeping her from falling backward on her heels. She started dry heaving and finally sat back full on the floor. She missed sitting in the vomit by inches and felt heat rise to her face when she saw the auburn-haired Annie come through the door.

"Ciara, you look terrible. What's going on? What have you been doing?" Cameron locked his gaze on Ciara while Hartline hurried to retrieve a mop bucket. Several food truck customers came to the bakery entrance, but they did not enter. Two men stared through the bakery storefront window, while Ciara sat.

"Oh God, what is going on? I just want a cup of coffee. Why are you people all staring at me?" Ciara questioned.

She looked from Cam's face to Annie's. Her eyes rested on the golden band on Cameron's finger. She rocked forward and rose to her knees, but her head started spinning, and she sat back down. Hartline cleaned the vomit from the floor while Annie brought Ciara a cup of water and knelt beside her.

"Here, drink this."

Everyone was concerned about Ciara. Her mind raced at what they must all be thinking. She quickly pushed the water away, spilling some of it on Annie as she rose to her feet. She focused on Cam and said, "What do you mean, what have I been doing? I've been building my father's company here in Bayport despite all the crazy distractions and crazy food trucks in the way."

Cam flinched at Ciara's words and felt anger rising. "Annie's food truck is not your problem. You have other problems."

Ciara eyed Hartline shaking his head, no. They had been talking about her. "What, do you think something is wrong with me? You all are the crazy ones. Putting a food truck in front of respectable businesses and just to spite me."

"Ciara, you've got to stop the pills and come clean. We all know you need help. Professional help..." Cam's voice trailed off.

"What...what...what are you talking about? My medicine?" Ciara squared her shoulders and stood with her hands on her hips.

"It's over Ciara, I called your father and he's coming here." Cam's eyes softened, and he took Annie's hand. "We are praying for you and believe you can get the help you need."

Ciara turned on her heels and pushed past Hartline to the bakery entrance. She exited and scrambled to her office. She methodically walked to her office and picked up her cell phone. Three missed calls. Two from her father and one from Jack Junior.

"It's over...huh. I will fight this," she yelled to the office walls.

Ciara grabbed her purse retrieving her keys. Her hands shook violently. She made her way to her new BMW parked in front of Caldwell Realty. Her pulse quickened. She watched as Annie returned to the food truck and the crowd in front of the bakery was mostly gone. Cam stood at the food truck window.

Anger threatened again. She cranked the car and stepped on the gas intending to leave the parking area. She peeled out in reverse and switched to drive. She made one circle in the parking lot and then stepped on the gas. The power of the new sports car surprised her. The car lurched forward before she thought to let off the accelerator.

As Ciara braced for an impact, the front of her car crunched into the side of the food truck. The food truck rocked toward the sidewalk as its back tire jumped the curb. The last thing Ciara saw was a white balloon object leap from her steering column and strike her hard on her right cheek and then everything went black.

CHAPTER 13

C am felt the full impact of the large metal window as it flew forward and ripped from its right hinge. It struck his left arm and sent him backward onto the paved sidewalk between the food truck and Glenn's Bakery glass storefront window. His body collapsed on the concrete with his head striking fully the edge of the brick wall of the bakery just under the window. He sat stunned with his ears ringing as a flurry of hands and feet moved frantically around him. He turned his head right and then left before he attempted to sit up.

He moved up on his right arm, regretting the movement. His left arm screamed in pain and blood was pooling on his shirt. He watched his left arm fall beside him and decided against trying to move it again. Tony came to his side and pulled him to a sitting position.

"I'm calling 911...don't move anymore Pastor."

He sat up watching the food truck as Hartline raised the broken metal window and yelled for Annie.

"Annie? Is she hurt?"

Cam pushed up again and thought better of it when his left arm throbbed again reminding him of the large amounts of blood flowing from his forearm. He looked at the wound and could see the bone. He felt vomit rise and he focused on pulling his arm to his stomach and covered the wound with his shirt tail.

As Cam moved his attention from his arm, he watched Hartline help Annie out of the rear door of the truck. She quickly ran to his side while Hartline moved around the back of the truck. A caustic smell of burning rubber and transmission fluid filled the air while Annie knelt beside Cam looking closely into his eyes. A large bruise was forming on her forehead and her hands were covered in blood.

"Annie, are you Ok?" Cam moaned and moved his right hand to her forehead.

"I'm fine...just a few bumps and bruises...wha...wha... are you feeling? Are you in a lot of pain?" She looked at the blood-soaked shirt and back to his face.

"I think my arm is broken and my head is pounding, but I think I'm Ok." Cam shifted slightly and winced.

The blare of sirens filled the street while lights flashed first from the local fire department and then from two ambulances pulling into the cluttered parking area. They stopped in the street and Cam watched as two men walked to the back of the food truck.

"I'm over here. Not back there," he whispered.

Annie stood and motioned a young man in a white paramedic's shirt over to Cam and stepped aside while the man knelt. "Can you tell me your name and the extent of your injuries?"

Cam winced again pointing to his left arm. He watched intently as the man unwrapped his forearm and examined the wound. He called his partner over and they began placing gauze while the older man listened for his pulse and put an oxygen sensor on his right index finger. As the two men worked on Cam, he began to relax his other muscles. They helped him onto a stretcher and into the back of the ambulance. Annie joined him and pushed off any attempts to be examined.

As the ambulance driver left the back and stepped down to close the double doors, Cam saw for the first time the small, silver car that smashed into the side of

Annie's food truck. His eyes widened as he looked over at Annie.

"Who did this? What is this madness about?"

At that moment he watched as another stretcher was lifted on its wheels and a small, blond figure lay unconscious strapped to the padding. The blond tendrils pooled on both sides and the head was strapped tightly to the stretcher. He watched as Hartline moved beside the stretcher and recognition of the petite woman on the stretcher flooded into his mind. Cam's face contorted and he half-breathed out through clenched teeth, "Ciara."

Two hours later at the Bayport Community Medical Center Emergency department, Ciara slowly opened her eyes. Her vision was blurred, and she blinked several times before squeezing her eyes closed. She opened them again and stared at the white, tiled ceiling above her. "Where am I? Why can't I move my head?" she said.

She felt her heart race and tried again to raise her head. A tear escaped her right eye as she moistened her lips and cried out, "Help me."

"Ciara, you're awake? Don't try to move. The nurse says they are going to X-ray your neck before you can get up." Hartline moved to stand over Ciara and stared into her eyes. "You had an accident, and you were unconscious, and it looks like your little sports car crushed into your leg. It took them twenty minutes just to get you out of the car."

"I don...on...'t remember. My car's Ok?" Ciara moved her fingers and wiggled her toes.

"You lay still. I think the X-Ray is a precaution. Your leg seems to be the worst injury. At least that's what the nurse told me." Hartline shifted his feet and patted Ciara on the shoulder.

"I...I...don't know." Ciara felt numb and tingly, and a deep throbbing pain was beginning to rise from her left leg. "My leg hurts."

"I called Bryant. His was the only number I had for you. I thought about calling Caldwell Realty in Orlando, but I couldn't remember what you said your brother's name is. Anyway, Bryant answered right away and is letting your family know about the accident." Hartline moved back a fraction and sighed deeply.

"Oh Ok...Momma and Daddy won't be here. They are in Honduras...and Jack Junior can't leave Orlando...Jan and Luke are in Vero Beach...I don't know who besides Bryant..." Ciara followed Hartline with her eyes and scrunched up her nose, "I'm alone...pretty much." Her voice trembled, and another tear escaped while she closed her eyes tight. When she opened them again Hartline moved out of her sight while a young nurse in purple scrubs moved over her and smiled.

"Ciara, we are going to take good care of you. I'm taking you for an X-ray and I'll bring you back to your handsome boyfriend in a quick minute." Her brown ponytail moved to the other side of her shoulder as she moved the bed out of the small room.

"He's not my boyfriend," Ciara said this matter-of-factly and counted the light-to-tile-ratio above her head as the bed was wheeled down two halls and through large double wooden doors.

"What Ciara, did you say something?" The young nurse smiled and patted her shoulder in the same manner Hartline had done earlier.

"Nothing, nothing." Ciara attempted to find her resolve. She knew she was in bad shape and none of the attempts by Hartline or this nurse were giving her any comfort.

Down the hall, Cam sat in the emergency room triage watching the digital readout measuring his pulse rate. Several doctors examined the gaping wound. "Can I now have something for pain?" He looked to the man closest to him and lowered his head to catch his gaze.

"We can't give you anything stronger until we determine next steps. Mr. Shivers, you may be in surgery tonight if we can get the right X-Ray and the surgeon decides to go ahead."

Cam grimaced and lay his head on the pillow. Annie walked back into the room placing her phone into the back pocket of her jeans. She was still covered in blood and had a butterfly band aid on her forehead and a bandage on her right hand. She walked to the bed looking from doctor to doctor waiting for either of them to speak.

"Mrs. Shivers, we are ordering an X-Ray and believe surgery is the best option. We will prep him soon and it should take about an hour to complete. He will be in recovery for about an hour. If you want to wait in the ER waiting that would be best since we don't know where he will be for recovery." The doctor smiled reassuringly and motioned for the X-Ray tech to enter the room.

"Cam, I'll be right here. Don't worry, honey. They are going to help you." Annie kissed his forehead and squeezed his right hand.

"Annie, I love you. Thanks for being here for me. I got to get some relief from this pain." He grimaced and tried to wink. Annie walked out of the room.

Down the halls and in the trauma triage, Ciara was surprised to see Hartline still standing by the curtain of the room. A new older nurse with gray hair in her temples, wheeled Ciara into the room and began telling Hartline her current condition.

"They can take the neck brace off...that'll make you

feel better, I'm sure." He smiled at her and nodded.

"Thank Godddd...I want to turn my neck so much." Ciara grinned as the nurse unlatched the plastic neck brace and then raised her head. The pounding began as soon as her head touched the pillow, but she was able to see more than the ceiling and people standing over her.

Hartline moved to her side and touched her arm. "Can I pray for you, Ciara? They are going to examine your leg further and probably do surgery. I know you don't have family here yet and I don't want you to face this alone." He looked into her eyes and waited.

"I really appreciate it, Hartline. I know I'm a lot of trouble all the time. Yes, pray. I need it," said Ciara as she looked at her leg lying still uncovered and strapped to a board.

Hartline lowered his head and put one hand on Ciara's shoulder. "Dear Lord, Ciara needs you. Please help her with the pain and guide the doctor's hand. Amen."

He stood beside Ciara and waited in the small, curtained room. She closed her eyes tightly, wanting desperately for the pounding in her head and the pain in her leg to subside. She pushed with her hands against the metal rails. Her left leg brushed the side of the hospital bed and sharp pain coursed through her body.

Hartline walked out of the area and winced as a nurse with needles in tow entered behind the curtain. The nurse prepared her for surgery and smiled, "When you wake, you will be in a room with your boyfriend again."

That was Ciara's last thought before she drifted into sleep.

The next morning Cam watched closely as Annie pushed the nurse's button, "Honey, I'm not sure if they want to bring me another pillow right now."

"Cam, they will bring you one. You've got to keep that arm elevated, and I can tell it's not up as much as the doctor said." She pursed her lips and kissed the top of his head.

"Did you talk to Hartline this morning? Did Ciara accidentally ram the food truck?" Cam watched Annie's face turn dark and a scow replaced her usually relaxed features.

"Cam, I don't want to disturb you now while you are trying to recover...I think we should talk about it later." Annie moved to the chair beside his bed.

"I don't need time to recover, I want to get to the bottom of this." Cam raised his voice and shook his head. He looked intently at Annie and raised his brows.

"OK, Cam, I think she did it on purpose. There I said it...I've been stewing all night. Hartline thinks it too. He just didn't think we should talk to you about it until you recover." Annie leaned back and rubbed her temples.

"You think she did it on purpose? I think so too. She needs to pay for all of this." Cam clenched his teeth and breathed out in quick breaths.

"Cam, I'm mad too, but we don't have all the facts and even though we are very upset, I don't think we need to get emotional right now. Hartline helped me pray and Mary is coming at lunchtime today. She will be able to help us." Annie attempted to pat Cam into a calmer position on his pillow. She gently pushed his right shoulder back down and looked relieved when the young nurse came in with another pillow.

Down the hall, Ciara raised the top of her hospital bed and watched as Hartline shook hands with Jack Junior. He was flanked by Bryant who stood talking to Hartline while Jack Junior made his way to Ciara's side. Jack Junior looked out of place with his shirt unbuttoned at the top and his sleeves rolled up. His clothes were wrinkled, and his face looked unshaven.

"Mom and Dad are flying in this afternoon. I will be here, and Bryant is going to the storefront to figure out how to handle things there...are you OK sis? You look... you look...really messed up." Jack Junior looked sympathetically at her leg held in traction above the bed. Ciara noticed Hartline walk out the door and turn to give a wave goodbye.

She waved back slowly and fought the urge to call him back. She sighed instead and focused on Jack Junior. "Mom and Dad? What? How did they get flights so soon? I'm fine. I'll b..b..be fine just as soon as I get out of this traction in four weeks, I think." Her voice was high pitched, and she moistened her lips.

"Ciara, you're not fine and I am here to help you." Jack Junior looked over to Bryant who slowly moved toward the foot of the hospital bed. Ciara couldn't read his expression. He was dressed in the same manner as Jack Junior.

"Ciara, I am here to help too. You don't have to get through this alone." Bryant looked concerned and patted her good foot covered with a thin sheet. The warmth of his hand was comforting, and she was confused at her response to his kindness after their last encounter at the Westin house.

"Bryant, I don't know what you are going to do to help." Ciara tried to sound smug, but her thin trembling voice didn't cooperate.

"Bryant's going to pick up the accident report and get to the bottom of the accident. Now that we know you will recover, we need to do damage control for the business." Jack Junior changed his brotherly expression for the familiar business partner she knew well.

"Junior, I am tired, and my head is pounding. Can we talk about business later?" Ciara couldn't believe her own thin voice. She was done. She didn't have the energy to go toe-to-toe with her brother right now. She just wanted her mom and dad and some rest.

She lowered her head and watched as Bryant and Jack Junior whispered quietly in the chairs by the only window in the room. Rain splattered the window and Ciara watched the rhythm until her eyelids drooped. She heard Bryant say in a low tone, "They say the report indicates several substances in her bloodstream."

Down the hall a uniformed police sergeant stood at Cam's bed taking the eye-witness account. Hartline stood at the foot of his bed and nodded as he explained what he saw. "I heard screeching tires and a loud crash. When I ran outside the front door of the bakery, I saw Cam on the sidewalk and the food truck up on the curb with its large serving window swinging from the hinge." Hartline continued telling what Cam already knew.

"She did it on purpose and she was high on drugs." Cam couldn't believe his own voice. Cam closed his eyes tight as Annie held his hand, "I think Cam needs to rest. Can you come back another day, officer?"

"Yes, Mrs. Shivers, I will use Hartline's statement for now. I am very sorry for this, and I want Pastor Cam and you to know that we will get to the bottom of this." He gave a sympathetic nod and walked out the room door.

"Cam, I agree with you. I think Ciara was high and she might have done it on purpose." Hartline looked very upset. "I just hate to think about what is going to happen to her now...that the police are involved."

"I agree, Hartline. I am worried about what will happen to her. I kind of feel sorry for her." Annie's voice trailed off and a tear rolled down her cheek. "It's just all so awful and I don't know how to even talk to God about this."

"Annie, I'm sorry I am so bitter. We are going to be Ok. I just can't forgive her right now. I must forgive her...I just can't stop thinking about what she did and the pain in my arm and the bruise on your head." Cam gripped Annie's hand.

"She's really battered. The last time I saw her, her left leg was in traction, and she looked like a little ghost lying in the hospital bed." Hartline looked down at his feet. "Pastor, can I let the congregation come and visit now? I think it might be time for us all to help you. You are always there for us in times like this...it's your time now."

Cam was glad for the change of subject and thought fondly about his congregation, "Sure, bring on the visitors. Maybe they will give my sweet Annie a break. She's been here for 24 hours and won't leave for anything."

"I do probably need to go home and get out of these bloody clothes." Annie giggled and smiled when she saw Cam's eyes brighten.

At that moment, Mary's full-figured frame filled the hospital room door. As if on cue, she let out a "Ooooweee... you look terrible Pastor Cam."

Cam looked at his friend and smiled broadly, "Thanks, Ms. Mary. I can always count on you to tell me the truth." He was delighted to see his friend and the visit from the officer left his mind for the next two days. The next time he thought about the possible criminal charges came when one of his deacons let it slip that the police found several substances in Ciara's system.

CHAPTER 14

C iara watched as first her mother and then her father started crying at the news Ciara could be facing criminal charges. She was still in the hospital and was in her third room in two weeks. In two more weeks, she would be able to get out of traction and start therapy. Her parents, who flew in on day two of her crisis, were staying in her small apartment while taking turns staying with her in the hospital.

The last doctor's visit brought good news and was an answer to prayer. Ciara would be able to use her leg again after extensive therapy. The bad news for Ciara was that the hospital was aware of her pill addiction and wouldn't give her any strong pain or anxiety medicine. Her request to the doctor had resulted in daily substance abuse counseling by the hospital.

Ciara looked out of the window while the officer dropped the paper on her bedside table. "Where do I sign?" she asked matter of fact. She watched as the officer pointed and she methodically signed in two places. The officer left the room and her mother sat in the chair beside the hospital bed.

"Ciara, we are going to get you a lawyer, but we need to know the truth. What have you been doing and why did you hit Cam's food truck?" Jack stood over Ciara and touched her arm while looking into her eyes.

"Daddy, I have been taking my medicine and maybe a few other things and I did drink some," Ciara said softly.

"Ciara, you can't lie to your mother and me. We can't help you unless you are truthful. You could go to jail for this." Jack sighed deeply and frowned. His patience was thin, and Ciara could see the anger and fear in his eyes.

"I know, Daddy. I am telling the truth. I have been taking too much medicine and other people's prescription and I drank a fifth of vodka the night before I rammed the food truck." Ciara huffed and moved up until her leg swung in protest. The pain shot through her whole body, and she winced.

"Ciara, are you alright? It's Ok. We are here to help you. Somehow, we will help you." Ciara watched as her mother moved beside her dad. She took his arm and pulled him back.

"No Mom, Dad's right. I should go to jail for this." Ciara began to sob. The three of them cried for a full two minutes before they looked up and noticed a full-figured person standing at the large wooden door. Her eyes peaked through the opening from the hallway.

"I'm Mary Jolly and I am here to talk to Ciara," Mary said while opening the door. She made her way into the room. Ciara watched as the woman shook hands with both of her parents and came to the side of Ciara's hospital bed.

"Ciara Caldwell, you remember me, right?"

"I know you're Cam and Annie's and Hartline's loud friend at the bakery." Ciara looked full into the older woman's eyes. She watched as she winked and said, "It seems you know something about me, but what you don't know is that I'm going to help you."

"Oh, is that so, how can you help a crippled criminal...you got some pills for me or maybe a drink...I'd like that. Mom and Dad have lawyers, but I want a fix right now." Ciara regretted her words the moment she saw the pain in her mother's eyes.

"No ma'am, that's not what you need...well, maybe a lawyer...yeah that would help...what you need most though is help to get off those pills. Girrlll, you don't even have a clue how much you need that." Mary's eyes softened as she took Ciara's small hand. It disappeared into her larger one and immediately Ciara felt the warmth. She wanted to pull away, but she couldn't find the energy.

Mary began a prayer loud and strong while Mr. and Mrs. Caldwell lowered their heads in agreement. Ciara watched the top of Mary's head and looked around the room wondering how she could escape.

Mary pushed her card into Jack Caldwell's hand and Ciara heard her loud and clear, "Your daughter needs rehabilitation. We are here in Bayport if you need us."

"We will be getting in touch with you. Thank you for visiting." Jack Caldwell shook Mary's hand again and turned back to Ciara. "Ciara, you are going to do this. One way or another, we are getting you help. Not helping you go back to your secret lifestyle. We won't be a part of that ever again. You are going to get help to get off the pills." His face softened, and he looked at her closely.

"Tell me truthfully, did you hit that truck on purpose? I need to know." Jack's eyes searched Ciara's face. Ciara racked her brain trying to remember. She just couldn't recall anything after getting in her car.

"Daddy, I don't remember. I don't think I meant to hit the truck exactly. I was mad and upset and my head was spinning, but I don't remember thinking I should hit it...I just can't remember exactly." Ciara looked between both of her parents and was relieved to see their expressions relax.

"Then it's settled, we will help you fight to stay out of

jail. You will still have to pay the damages and you will have to get help for your addiction, but I think you can at least not have to go to jail." Jack pursed his lips and began to pray, "Dear Lord, provide a way for Ciara to get the help she needs. If it's Mary Jolly, then we accept her help. Amen."

Two days later, Cam watched the sunrise from his hospital room. Annie was picking him up at 9:00 am and he had been waiting since he woke in the early hours. Just before daybreak he waited as the shadows were replaced by first a small sliver of light and then a full sunsoak illuminating the floor beside his bed.

He sat in the middle of the bed anxiously waiting. He re-strapped his arm tightly beside his abdomen. The morning nurse had been in once and checked his vitals just before a breakfast of eggs, ham, and fruit was delivered. The tray sat barely touched.

He knew Annie would make him an early lunch and he could almost imagine her in their little apartment getting her ingredients together while pushing her auburn tendrils behind her ears. He could almost smell her meat pies baking in the little oven. The small kitchen bar would have steamed vegetables resting on a platter and fresh juice would be squeezed and waiting.

He smiled for the first time in two weeks, realizing he needed home and Annie and his church just to feel any comfort in this world. He was ready to get back. Physical therapy would be long, but he could do it. Especially now that he had the hope of his normal life back.

Cam leaned back on the raised bed and breathed deeply. He opened his Bible app and listened to the book of Psalms while waiting on Annie's arrival. He felt his breath slow and felt his eyelids droop. The next thing he knew he felt strong small hands on his shoulders and smelled Annie's freshly shampooed hair as he opened his eyes and blinked.

"Hey, handsome. You got tired of waiting on me?" Annie winked and kissed him on his lips.

"I waited as long as I could, sweetie, I watched the sunrise and realized it would be three full hours before you'd be here, and they'd let me out of this place." Cam stood too quickly and reeled slightly on the balls of his feet while grabbing the side table to steady himself. He saw Annie's concerned expression and noticed for the first time the dark circles under her eyes.

"I'm fine Annie, don't look so worried. I need my sea legs back. The infection is almost clear, and my bone is on the mend. It won't be long until I'm back in full swing." He embraced her with his good arm and kissed the top of her head.

The tender moment was interrupted by the discharge nurse. After another grueling examination and countless prescription and cleaning instructions, Cam was carried by wheelchair to Annie's small car. He felt ridiculous riding in the chair since his legs were fine, but he didn't want to delay leaving any longer and dutifully sat in the chair.

As he took in the outside surroundings for the first time in two weeks, his heart felt lighter. He drank in the warmth of the sun and broke out in a sweat despite Annie's air-conditioner. The spring weather was changing to summer and Cam knew it wouldn't be long until the heat was unbearable. His mind switched to thinking about his church. He had assistants filling in for him, but he was very anxious to get back to his office.

"I'd like to go to the church first thing in the morning before my therapy appointment." Cam fumbled with the air vent with his right hand. He opened the vent further and pointed it directly at his face.

"I agree, I think it would be good. I'd like to go with you to pray. I'm not going to get the money from the insurance for another full week. The food truck is at the shop." Annie smiled and breathed out a sigh of relief.

"When is the court date? Have you thought about whether we should press charges?" Cam felt so conflicted about how to proceed with the Ciara situation. He purposefully avoided talking about the accident and hadn't really prayed or had any meaningful devotion since. His heart was jumbled with so many mixed emotions it was becoming almost impossible to make heads or tails of anything.

"Sweetie, that's why I want to go pray. I guess I'm glad the food truck will get all necessary repairs and it won't be long until I am back cooking. It should be ready a month before for the 4th of July weekend."

"4th of July huh? You're going to need extra hands... too bad your sous chef will only have one in operation at that time. I guess our delightful storefront neighbor saw to that and she needs to get what's coming to her." Cam felt anger rising.

"I don't want us to press criminal charges, Cam. I don't need money from Ciara Caldwell, and I don't want anything more than the insurance to replace our losses and pay our hospital bills...it just doesn't feel right to take more." She sighed and pulled onto the highway leading home.

"I don't want her money. I want her to understand what she's done to us. Look at me...look at your situation. She takes and never pays for anything." Cam said the last words almost in a whisper between clenched teeth.

"Let's pray tomorrow morning...that's all I ask. Don't

make any decisions until then?" Annie's sweet voice and question quieted Cam's mood. He took her hand and nodded in agreement.

A long silence fell between the two while Annie navigated the streets to their small apartment. Cam's mood lightened when he saw welcome home signs put up by several church members and as Annie pulled in the parking space beside Cam's full-size truck, he could see a basket left on the steps.

"I love our church, Annie, I want to focus on that. Yes, please come to pray with me tomorrow. I need to get to church soon. Very soon. I really need the atmosphere and the chance to let some things off my chest. I know Who I need." He kissed her hand and smiled playfully at Annie.

Two weeks later to the day Cam left the hospital, Ciara took the same wheelchair ride to her mother's rental car. She was thankful it was an SUV, and she didn't have to sit lower. She slid into the seat and settled her left leg before leaning back and strapping into the seat belt. Her mother's constant attention was wearing her thin and she wished for a moment alone. Her dad stayed at the apartment and would help her into the small space when they arrived.

Ciara rode in silence and was thankful her mom talked to Jan over the Bluetooth and Ciara was mostly left out of the conversation. They talked about her, but her mother and Jan held the full conversation without needing much interjection from Ciara. It was easier to talk to Jan through her mother. It gave a sense that they were keeping up with each other's lives without any real need to nurture a relationship themselves. This helped Ciara tremendously. She felt exhausted with keeping up the small talk and trying to find anything in common with her sister.

As her mother turned onto the small street less than a mile from the storefront and bakery, the anxiety returned. The tightness started in her chest and her heart raced while she fought back vomit rising in her throat. The hospital started her on antidepressants and counseling, but it wasn't giving her the relief she wanted. Ciara's instincts told her to be cooperative and give her parents the illusion she was quickly recovering, otherwise they would stay longer and keep her in the perpetual fishbowl.

Ciara breathed deeply and grabbed a piece of chewing gum out of her purse. She chewed incessantly, and complained about her leg, "I am feeling pain again. I think I may need some more Ibuprofen."

"Sure, honey. As soon as we get to your apartment, I'll fish it out of your overnight bag. I'm so sorry you are hurting...maybe when you aren't in the moving car it will settle down."

"You're probably right, Mom." Ciara attempted to sound breezy, however, she really sounded out of breath. Her heart rate was so fast, she felt like she was running. The cravings for valium and pain killers had subsided and she was thankful the worst withdrawal she experienced was chronic stomach pain. That lasted for the first two weeks in the hospital. They weaned her from all pain medicine, and she spent the last two weeks in the hospital miserable in her mind, but much better in her body.

Ciara did not like the feeling the antidepressants gave her. Her mood was very even all the time, but it wasn't the same as being high. When she was high, she felt more social and ready to take on the world. Since the hospital, she only felt numb. She was always somewhere between relaxed and normal all the time, morning, noon, and night.

As they pulled into the small parking space at her apartment, her stomach flopped at the sight before her. Her dad, Jack Junior, and Bryant were all standing at her front door. Ciara turned quickly to her mother who put the car into park and reached behind to retrieve the hospital bag.

"Why are Junior and Bryant here? I don't want company right now." Ciara felt the panic rise and leaned her head back on the seat.

"Ciara, Junior is your brother and Bryant your good friend. They are both here to help you. You've got to face some of what you've done, honey. They are here to help you make the right decisions." Ciara watched as her mother waved the men over and dutifully swung her leg out of the opened car door. Bryant stood back while Jack Junior offered his hand to his sister and put the crutch firmly under her arm while following her steady one-legged march to the entrance.

Once inside she grimaced at the small space and opted for the accent chair instead of the couch. She needed space and felt trapped by all the people standing in the small room. Bryant grabbed a small kitchen chair and sat in the far corner while Jack Junior sat at the only high barstool by the kitchen island. Her parents sat on the couch opposite Ciara and looked at her closely.

"Mom and I will stay here as long as you need us. You may be facing criminal charges and we know Cameron and his wife have another week to decide how they will testify." Her dad leaned forward and touched her good knee waiting for her to respond.

"I wouldn't blame them if they pressed charges. I feel terrible about what I did. I just want to get life back to normal." Ciara hoped she sounded calmer and more level-headed than she felt.

"Ciara, things can't go back to normal. At the very least the judge will want you to go to rehab. We've got to get things handled before you face criminal charges." Jack Junior turned on the stool and looked down at her. His eyes were expressionless, and she knew he found his chance. She couldn't fight him.

Jack stood and faced Jack Junior. His hand flew forward, and he motioned toward Ciara, "She's your sister, not a client."

Jack Junior shrank back, and Ciara watched as her dad sat back down and her mother patted her leg, "Honey, we are here. You will have to face the consequences and Bryant has agreed to help." Ciara's mother smiled warmly at Bryant, and he smiled to the family.

"I can tie up loose ends here for Caldwell, if that will help her." Bryant looked to Jack Junior and then to Ciara's dad waiting on the men to speak. Ciara had thought for two weeks straight about this moment. She couldn't bring herself to concede everything to Junior. Ciara looked fully at her brother.

"Junior, I want the storefront here in Bayport, my apartment paid for, and my legal bills paid. Other than that, I am ready to sign to be removed from Caldwell Realty." Ciara breathed slowly and was glad to have put into words for the first time in a long while what she desired.

"Ciara, I am glad you are ready to sign, but as your brother, I have to say that starting up your own business here would be fool-hearty in your current condition with your leg and your legal troubles." Junior looked to their father and waited.

"I will stay and help her." Bryant spoke bold and

clear. Ciara's eyes darted to Bryant, and she stared in-credulously. The whole family looked to Bryant.

"Uh, Bryant, Jack Junior is not offering for Ciara to keep the affiliation with the company. You realize that son?" Ciara watched her dad turn fully to Bryant.

"Yes, sir, I realize Ciara will be without the Caldwell name, but we've developed relationships here, we have a client list, and I think I'm ready to start out on my own too. God keeps bringing me to this city, to these people, to Bayport." Bryant relaxed and sat back in the small wooden kitchen chair.

"Bryant, you're crazy. Come back to Orlando with me. You can't make it work here." Ciara watched her broth-er's smug expression and spoke quickly before he talked Bryant out of partnering with her.

"Sixty-Forty, Bryant. We can use both our names." Ciara's eyes brightened as she looked at her dad, "I can keep my name, right, daddy? If we use Bryant's too and change the logo?"

"Fourty-nine-fifty-one and that's my last offer. Cald-well and Ward Realty. I get the fifty-one since I am the only leg work for the next year. No pun intended." Bryant pointed to Ciara's leg in a brace from her ankle to hip.

Ciara sat for a while and looked first to her moth-er and then to her dad. Both looked relieved. Then she looked at Jack Junior who left the conversation and sat engrossed with his phone. His thumb scrolled through texts quickly.

"I accept Bryant's offer. Junior, do we have a deal?" Ciara looked at her brother and leaned forward on her good knee.

"Wh..what..yes...sure. I think you two are nuts, but I think you're doing the right thing by signing." Jack Junior put his phone down and smiled.

"It's decided then, Ciara, you will need to sign soon. I know it is sudden, honey, but your mom and I need you to decide, so we can get the ball rolling with the lawyers and possibly get an extended stay hotel nearby." Ciara's dad paused and took her hand. She didn't want her parents to stay any longer. She mustered her confidence and spoke clearly.

"Daddy, I don't think you and Mom should stay. I am fine. Bryant will be here, so I won't be alone, and Junior is only a few hours away by plane and Jan and I have been talking more." Ciara lied, but she wanted to create the allusion that she was surrounded. The thought of them hovering over her any longer was unbearable. She needed her space. People watching her, made her feel on display and vulnerable.

"Ciara, I'm not leaving you to go to court by yourself. I won't leave you like this. You can't even drive, honey, you need your family close." Ciara saw tears fill her mother's eyes and felt bad about asking them to leave. She loved her parents, but their presence made her feel less capable of handling her life.

"Maybe you should just stay until after court, Carol." Ciara's dad looked at Ciara and winked, "You know I love you, honey, but I do understand your need to get on with your life and have some personal space."

"I'll attend the rehab with Mary Jolly. The last meeting with the lawyer, he all but said he would ask the judge for me to go to drug rehabilitation. You guys met her and that would give you more peace about leaving me here." Ciara relaxed at the thought of getting her personal space again. She had made a good, logical plan that would be hard for her parents to refuse.

"OK, Ciara, if you decide to go to the place Mary Jolly suggested and you keep us in your daily life, I will feel better about leaving you." Ciara's mom relaxed and sat back on the small leather couch.

"Well, family, I have a plane to catch. I am glad to hear that you are getting the help you need. I will have our company lawyer draw up the papers by Monday. Love you guys." Jack Junior rose to his feet and stretched his muscles. After hugging Ciara, his mother, and his dad, he made his way to the small entrance. Bryant followed Jack Junior and gave a quick wave goodbye before closing the small door behind him.

"Your mother is insisting on staying with you on the pull-out couch, so I guess I'm a bachelor tonight at the hotel." He kissed Ciara on the head and embraced Carol before he walked to the door.

"If you two need anything before tomorrow, just give me a call." Jack left, and Ciara's mom locked the handle and deadbolt after him.

"I'm tired, Mom, I think I will go to bed. It's after 8:00 pm and I haven't gotten good sleep in the hospital." Ciara knew her mother wanted to talk more, but she also knew her motherly instincts would kick in and she would let Ciara go and rest.

"Sure, honey, I'll be right in here if you need me. We have a full day planned tomorrow. Goodnight." Carol stifled a yawn and stood to help Ciara navigate the door to the bed.

Ciara melted into the bed and worked for a full thirty minutes to get her leg in a good position. Finally, after using two firm decorative pillows under her knee, she felt relief. Her head hit the pillow and she drifted into deep sleep.

CHAPTER 15

The first week of April came to Bayport in beautiful sunshine and blooming begonias, petunias, and geraniums in hanging baskets lined each street. Cam stood on the corner watching Annie's food truck roll into the parking spaces in front of Glenn's Bakery. It was freshly painted a pale yellow. The new tires with chrome wheels were shiny and gone was the line of sand and grime the former pressure-washing treatment couldn't tackle. The delivery truck lowered the front end and waved goodbye.

He chuckled when he thought about the absence of a name on the food truck. Annie still had not settled on a name. The flanks of the truck were noticeably blank, but it didn't deter her customers before, and he doubted that it would this time when it was up and running again. Annie decided on a grand reopening the last weekend of May.

The repairs were completed a full month earlier than first expected. That gave her three weeks to plan, restock, and to help him. A frown formed as he thought of the storefront beside Glenn's Bakery. The Caldwell Realty sign was gone, and he heard from Hartline that Bryant Ward was now in business there with Ciara.

Annie rounded the corner behind Glenn's Bakery and smiled broadly at Cam, "Why are you frowning? This is beautiful. I hate that you had to suffer with your arm and all...but now it's just beautiful." She ran her hand along the new tire and felt the painted side, "I even have some money to update the kitchen." She winked at Cam.

Cam's mood changed the moment he saw Annie's enthusiasm. "I'm glad I could take one for the team." He raised his arm and pretended to wince in pain.

"Oh, Cam. I was only kidding. Does your arm hurt this morning?" Annie walked to face him and touched his left hand gingerly.

"I'm just joking. My arm is fine, and I get the splint this Friday. That means no cast and I can do more therapy than just squeeze a ball with my hand. I get to move my arm." Cam smiled and reached for Annie.

At that moment Mary rounded the corner and towered behind Annie, "Hey you two lovebirds, when are we eating?" Mary whistled and gave Annie a thumbs up while she walked around the food truck taking in the new paint job and the tires.

"I'm opening in three weeks. I hope you can keep that appetite for a while." Annie followed Mary's perusal.

"Oh, don't worry honey, I'll be your first customer." Mary laughed deeply and moved close to Cam. She grabbed Annie's hand pulling the three together.

Mary looked between Cam and Annie several times before speaking again. Cam knew his friend had information about Ciara. He avoided talking about the decision when it came to prosecution. The police and district attorney were meeting with Ciara's lawyers and anxiously waited for his and Annie's testimony. There weren't any other eyewitnesses.

He stalled for two weeks. Every time he knelt to pray; he would end with an unsettled feeling in the pit of his stomach. His first sermon back had gone as expected. His congregation sat attentively listening to the "leading up to Easter" message. No one noticed he read from his last year's notes.

"I got a call from Ciara's lawyer this morning. She is agreeing to come to Bayport Rehabilitation Clinic," Mary said this quietly and looked at Cam.

"I'm glad she's getting help." Cam's reply was flat, and Annie put her arm around his waist, squeezed and looked fully at Mary.

Annie spoke first and said, "I don't want to press charges against Ciara. I'm ready to give my statement and I'm glad she's getting help." She smiled sweetly.

Mary smiled at Annie and looked at Cam expectantly. The three stood facing one another on the sidewalk while baskets of beautiful flowers swayed in the breeze around them.

Cam looked away from Mary and sighed, "I'm giving my statement at 1:00 today. I'm still praying about what to do...She gets away with everything."

"I understand your sense of justice. That girl has done nothing but cause you trouble." Cam looked back at Mary's eyes and saw the anger and frustration he had been feeling for the last few weeks. He watched her as she frowned deeply.

"I feel a block when it comes to forgiving her. I don't want her to have that kind of power over Annie and me. Annie's free, but I'm still struggling..." Cam couldn't believe how great it felt to finally admit this to Mary.

Annie pulled away and stood in front of Cam, "Sweetie, I ask God to free me almost daily. I have forgiven her, and I realize she will still pay for what she's done in so many ways we can't even imagine. She's pitiful and alone most of the time. We choose to live free. You preach about this forgiveness every week at church. Do you listen to your own sermons? You got to forgive to be forgiven."

Mary clapped her hands together and yelled, "Preach,

Little Annie. If you ever get tired of cooking, just come on down to the clinic and I'll give you a job."

Cam looked at both women carefully. He had so much. He had Annie, his friends, his family, his church. Annie was right. Cam walked to the edge of the bakery window and lowered his head. Annie and Mary did not follow, and he was glad they took his cue. He waited in silence. Finally, he lowered his head and prayed aloud, "Lord, if you will forgive me and let me have communion with You again, I will forgive Ciara." Cam looked up and said a quiet, "Amen."

Mary smiled and slapped Annie on the back, "Well, if we can't eat at the truck, let's get some cake from the bakery. We'll have dessert for breakfast."

Cam breathed deeply and said, "Sounds good to me. I've been eating good with Annie's cooking. I might as well add to it a delicious dessert."

Later that same afternoon, Ciara sat across from the smug Orlando lawyer, Alan Stalling. Jack Junior had retained him for the company and for Ciara. The lawyer was the same person who had her sign away all rights to Caldwell Realty. He spoke in careful concise sentences and rarely changed his expression from a serious, but inquisitive stare. Her mother and father were joining on a conference call. Ciara and her parents anxiously waited for Mr. Stalling to speak.

"Miss Caldwell, we have received all of the testimonies, including the one that was delayed by the injured, Mr. Shivers." He paused studying her face before saying, "It seems the D.A. and the other parties involved won't press criminal charges as long as you agree to attend and complete rehabilitation, restore property, and pay all hospital expenses." Alan Stalling sat back and folded his hands in front waiting.

Ciara's mom spoke over the phone, "Praise the Lord!"

Ciara felt her insides relax and began slow breathing. She could have reached across the table and kissed the older man but thought better of showing that kind of emotion. Instead, she replied, "Mr. Stalling, I am relieved that I won't have to face criminal charges. Now I can get back to my business. Bryant has been alone in our company for far too long. I can't walk well yet, but it's just a matter of time..."

Alan Stalling cleared his throat loudly and said, "Miss Caldwell, you can't be a part of your daily business for at least nine months. The agreement calls for full-time treatment in a facility." He leaned forward and watched her closely.

"What?! Living in a facility? I didn't agree to live on the premises." Ciara stood and reached for her crutch. Her heart pounded in her ears, and she stood balancing on her right leg. She watched as Alan Stalling stood looking down at her. He motioned slowly attempting to get her to sit back down.

As Ciara fell back in the oversized reception chair that had been dragged into a conference room of the office borrowed by her lawyer, she felt hot tears fall down her cheeks. She trembled and listened to both her parents. The voices from her cell phone perched between her and the lawyer did little to calm her. She closed her eyes tightly while attempting to stop the flow of tears.

Finally, Ciara opened her puffy, red eyes and looked fully at Alan Stalling. "Where will I live?"

"Miss Caldwell, that is being arranged by one of the counselors at Bayport Rehabilitation Center...um...I believe it's a Ms. Mary Joll..." Alan Stalling squinted to read the name.

Ciara spoke up, "Mary Jolly...that crazy lady is

deciding my fate for the next nine months. Great...just great."

That night, Cam looked across to Mary who joined Annie and him for a time of prayer at the church. Mary usually prayed alone, but she was offering support. He watched the older woman kneel at the altar while tears flowed down her cheeks. Annie sat cross-legged under the only stage light illuminating her journal. She wrote and prayed.

Cam looked up to the ceiling and focused on the beam rafters. He felt a weight lift as he prayed. He knew God patiently waited for him to respond to the prod to forgive Ciara. It felt good to let it go. The sanctuary was filled with prayer as the three continued to meditate on the Lord.

Cam lifted his head and met Mary's eyes as she now sat across from him, "Mary, how are you so sneaky."

"Boy, I got talents you can't even imagine. Especially in the presence of the Lord. I just get so much from His house." She smiled and raised one of her hands up as high as she could.

"I know you have talents, and the Lord uses you... I'm one of your projects. I remember how you helped me when I first took the church here." Cam motioned around him and pointed to Annie. "And how you helped get us together."

"I feel the nudge to help Ciara too. I prayed tonight. She needs a lot of help." Mary looked full in Cam's eyes.

"She's a shell of a person. I remember seeing glimpses of the real Ciara occasionally. I think that's why I stayed with her so long. Five years and we almost married." Cam shook his head and breathed deeply.

"I've gotten permission from the judge to take her in to live at Bayport Rehabilitation Clinic." Mary pursed her lips and shrugged her shoulders.

"Wait a minute, aren't all the live-in clients, men? How can she stay there for rehab?" Cam raised his brows and shook his head from side-to-side.

"I got permission for her to live with me. She will have to come to the clinic in the day with the other women who are day clients and then back with me at night." Mary shrugged her shoulders and crossed her legs in front.

"Wow, Mary. That's a whole lot of Ciara for you. I will really be praying. I'm not sure which of you I should pray for the most." Cam stifled a chuckle and smiled at Mary.

Annie moved across the sanctuary to sit with him, "What are you smiling so big about?"

"Mary has a new project. Oh, and I think this one is a Mary-sized one. That's for sure." Cam said.

Chapter 16

The next morning, Ciara woke to startling sunlight. The sun shone through the small window illuminating her bedroom and attached bathroom. As she rose and made her way to the bathroom, she heard her phone alerts. She pushed it on and was surprised to see a text from Bryant. She had not seen him since the family meeting and her heart skipped at the chance to catch up on the business. She packed the night before. Her wardrobe now consisted of walking shorts, skirts, or leggings. The beautiful suits and business attire were shoved to the back of her closet and replaced with casual or sportswear.

"I can give you a ride this morning. Don't have clients till 12:00. Need to talk." Bryant's text was just what she needed. She didn't want the rehabilitation van to pick her up and this would be one last chance to get caught up with Bryant. Her cheeks flushed and she ran her hands through the blond strands on her shoulders.

Ciara called the clinic to cancel the van pickup. She then hobbled into her tiny bathroom and started putting on make-up. She gained some weight from the time her mother stayed for a while. Her hair was growing out of the southern puffy hairstyle she adopted for Mayor Nelon. The red in her cheeks gave her a healthy glow and she didn't even need the usual blush routine.

Ciara heard the rap-rap of Bryant's knuckles at her front door. She hobbled to the door forgetting the crutch to make the ten or so steps. Behind Bryant was a cloudless sunny sky. She instantly squinted, "Come in Bryant, I just need to retrieve my bags and stuff." She sounded out of breath and regretted not getting the crutch when she went to the door earlier.

Now she stood precariously close to Bryant and couldn't really move anywhere to let him enter. Bryant extended his arm and moved to stand beside her. She took his tanned arm and let him lead her to the kitchen bar where the crutch sat. Ciara felt the warmth of his arm and was reluctant to let it go.

Bryant reached for the crutch and said, "You should probably keep this close. It would be easy to fall with your unsteady gait." He stared intently at her splinted leg that had been strapped tightly this morning after her quick shower. "How's the leg?"

"It's much better. I'm about to start therapy. I'll be with you in the office before you know it." Ciara smiled sweetly and put the outstretched crutch under her arm.

"Don't rush it, Ciara. You just get better. I mean really better." He looked closely at her. Ciara watched Bryant's eyes fix on hers. He wasn't sure she would recover. He didn't take the bait that she needed to be back to the office sooner than later.

Ciara backed away and went to the bags stacked on her couch. The designer luggage was packed neatly and reminded her of a life she once lived. She longed to rewind and stop her parents from going to Honduras and Jack Junior from having her sign.

"Sorry, I can't carry my luggage," said Ciara. Her shoulders slumped.

"No problem. I think I should be helping you with your luggage. Even if you had two good legs...for goodness sakes...you don't always have to be as strong or stronger than everyone around you," said Bryant.

He moved to the couch and pulled the large oversize suitcase from the couch. He walked to the door while Ciara strapped her overnight bag and purse around her neck and back. They both descended the few steps. She hobbled to the waiting car and placed her bags in the back seat. She went to the door and locked both the door and deadbolt.

As she rode beside Bryant, a familiar itch to go to the office and check with clients came. She waited patiently for Bryant to speak about the company. They were running out of time to be alone in the car. The thirty-minute drive was already ten minutes past, and he was signaling to turn on the road leading to the clinic.

Ciara spoke softly, "How's the business going? Have we had any luck with the Richardson properties?"

Bryant looked over from the road and shifted in his seat. "The Richardson deal is done, and we are looking to make a slight profit this month. It's slow coming, but there was some damage control that had to happen before the client list could remain. We lost the Emersons."

Ciara breathed deeply and let out a long sigh, "I appreciate you doing the damage control. None of the clients know about the rehab. Right?"

"It's a small town, people talk. Do I think people are constantly thinking about and talking about what you did, no, but you need to lay low and get better, It's the only way." Bryant looked at her with his brows creased, and eyes narrowed.

Ciara looked out the window. She steadied her racing heart and breathed deeply. She watched as the scenery turned from bayside to residential to commercial. As Bryant turned into the parking lot to the clinic, Ciara's throat tightened. She fought tears and for the first time since the hospital felt a real craving for valium. She instinctively reached to the bottom of her purse while Bryant looked on. She saw his eyes dart to her hand, and heat rose to her cheeks.

Ciara pulled her hand out. "I just need my gum." She unwrapped the foil around the cinnamon stick and put it in her mouth, chewing quickly.

Bryant shook his head and pointed to the entrance, "Is this where you will be living? Do I take your luggage in there?"

At that moment, Ciara's eyes bugged as Mary made her way to Bryant's sleek sedan. She opened Ciara's door and barked orders for Bryant to put the luggage on the curb. Ciara grabbed her crutch and stood dwarfed by Mary's full frame beside her.

Mary motioned for Bryant and Ciara to stay put and she made her way around the building. Neither spoke as they watched a massive, gold Cadillac maneuver around the building and park beside Ciara's waiting luggage.

"Put the luggage in my trunk and don't scratch the paint." Mary tossed Bryant the keys and looped her arm in Ciara's, "Oh, and leave the keys under the mat."

Ciara watched as Bryant obeyed and followed Mary up the sidewalk and into the clinic doors. Her head pounded, and she spotted a single serve coffee pot in the corner. Ciara welcomed the chance to sit in the over-sized brown leather furniture when Mary barked for her to sit. A young receptionist looked past Mary at Ciara and smiled sweetly, "Can I help you ma'am?" The young lady leaned over the large reception desk.

Mary intercepted the young woman and said, "She's a client and she's with me." The receptionist looked sympathetically at Ciara and moved to sit back down on her stool.

"I would love some coffee about right now. It's my last

vice. It's all I've got. I am allowed to have coffee, right?" Ciara's eyes darted to Mary.

"Yes, girl. You can have coffee." Mary propped the coffee cup under the spout and pushed the button. Ciara watched closely as the dark liquid sputtered into the cup. She focused on the coffee and thought of nothing else. She feared if she took in her surroundings fully, she might have a nervous breakdown. The antidepressants she took as prescribed kept her from the breakdown, but she worried she might be reaching the tipping point. She had mostly lied to the doctors who counseled her about addiction. She used what she called her "Jack Junior" face when dealing with them on the subject.

Her "Jack Junior" face was hard to find here. She assumed Bryant had already gone, or she might have run on crutches back to his car. The feeling of entrapment was beginning to surface, and she focused on the coffee. As Mary extended the cup, Ciara fought the tremble in her fingers and reached for the desired liquid. She smelled deeply first and then sipped the hot liquid letting it soothe her.

Mary sat quietly beside Ciara and took her hand, "Our first group session will be at 9:00. This is a mixed group of men and women. They are at different levels of recovery. I think it will be the best time for you to begin your own recovery."

Ciara looked at Mary and nodded. She focused on calming her senses and finished the cup of coffee quickly and methodically. She stood then and hobbled behind Mary into a room in the center of the building. A skylight was the only light and the sun shone in streams at the center. Chairs were arranged in a circle in the chapel space.

Ciara and Mary were the first to sit. Ciara positioned

her leg in front and thought about the therapy appointments that would begin next week.

"Thank God. I will be able to leave this place to go to
the doctor. I never thought I'd be so glad to go to therapy," Ciara whispered to a young man named, Seth, who
sat to her right.

The young man smiled and nodded. He turned away
from Ciara and shook hands with another guy who entered the room. As young men and women filled the
chairs, Ciara sat quiet and watched on. She watched a
young lady sitting directly opposite her. The thin young
blond was picking at a sore on her arm and rocked slightly back and forth. Her face was drawn, and her clothes
hung on her body. Ciara watched as the young woman's
eyes darted. Something about the woman disturbed her.

Mary began the meeting with prayer and shared a
devotion about Jonah and the great fish. Ciara remembered the story from childhood, how the Jewish proph-
et, Jonah, disobeyed God's directions to go to the city of
Nineveh. Jonah hated the people of Nineveh and didn't
want them to repent to God. He got on a boat that was
going the opposite directions. God sent a storm and Jonah was thrown overboard. He was then swallowed by
a big fish.

Ciara remembered her childhood Bible teacher putting a little figure of a dark-headed, bearded man inside a
cardboard whale. Her little child's mind wondered what
Jonah did in the belly of a whale for three days. She always loved the ending when the teacher would pull a little string and Jonah would fly out of the whale's mouth
and of course he then went and obeyed God.

Ciara thought carefully about Jonah while the other
people talked about their week and half of them even
admitted to using drugs again. Ciara looked down and

whispered under her breath, "You idiots, why would you tell everyone here that you used again?"

Ciara's daydream about Jonah was broken by Mary, who introduced her. She was relieved Mary didn't give her last name. She didn't want these people to know she was a Caldwell. Her plan was to endure this and never let anyone know a Caldwell was here.

"Hi, I'm Ciara. I had an accident and now I'm here." She twisted her hair and bit her bottom lip.

"I know what you mean, I had an accident too. Addiction happens to a lot of unsuspecting people. They start with a little fun with friends and then..." The hollow rocking woman, someone called Kate, spoke quickly and bared her arms. Tracks of needle marks and bruising traced down them both. Ciara's eyes bugged and she shook her head, no. She went to stand but was stilled by Mary's hand.

"Our time is up and it's time for chapel. Let's all pray and I'll see you back on Friday." Mary bowed her head and began praying for each person by name. When she got to Kate's name, Ciara closed her eyes tight and spoke to God for the first time in a long while, "Help that poor girl."

Ciara was unimpressed with chapel; the music was subpar, and the message was predictable. She sat dutifully and plastered her face with a cordial expression. Several times she took careful mental notes of how the more advanced students reacted to each part of the day.

Ciara didn't see Mary until the afternoon. She made it through lunch which consisted of lettuce, tomato, a carton of milk, and the bottom of a wheat bun. A questionable breaded chicken patty and chips were offered too, but Ciara couldn't bring herself to eat them. She took one, of course, but cut it into small pieces and pushed it around her plate to make the others think she was eating. She opted for a third cup of coffee and felt a little jittery from all the caffeine, but at least she had some energy.

Ciara watched as each of the women, including Kate, walked out the tinted glass doors. She looked around the classroom space she entered at 1:00 and noticed only men sitting in the desk chairs. The room looked like a high school classroom. Jeremy Clay in a nice, polo shirt and pressed, dress slacks stood at a white board. She had seen him in the bakery and the night Bryant brought her to the clinic to get sober.

"I'm Jeremy Clay, I'm the director here and I'll be training you in this class. I am also a counselor. We will support you as needed." He smiled and extended his hand.

"My wife is Caroline Clay. I believe you met her?" questioned Jeremy.

Ciara nodded and smiled, "I did."

Ciara took his hand dutifully and sat in a desk on the front row. That had always worked for her in high school. Stay close to the teacher and ignore the nonsense behind. As Jeremy began explaining the physical and psychological effects of drugs, Ciara began another daydream. This time she was back in college and starting valium. What Jeremy was saying made perfect sense. The valium was the problem. She shouldn't have used it. There was probably something else she could take instead. Jeremy began classifying drugs and listed them on both boards.

"Well, there goes that. I can't take anything. God help me. What about my anxiety? What about this feeling that is smothering me?" Ciara questioned softly.

She felt eyes watching her from behind and saw

Jeremy looking with raised eyebrows. She felt her face flush red and her eyes widen.

She dropped her head quickly and rested her eyes on the lukewarm cup of coffee in her hand. She took a big swig of it and instinctively took out a piece of gum. The combination of cinnamon and bitter coffee was acrid, but she didn't care. It kept her from reacting and that's what she needed to do right now. Staying low profile was her new motto. Jeremy continued the class, and the attention moved away from Ciara.

Ciara smiled as Jeremy approached her after the class, "Where are all the other women? Where is my room?" She said the last part in a whisper not wanting everyone in the class to know she was staying on site.

Jeremy smiled at Ciara, "Mary Jolly didn't tell you? You won't be staying here. This facility only houses men. Hence all the women are already gone. They are staying with local church people. You are staying with Mary."

Ciara reeled on her one foot and leaned heavily on the crutch. Her knuckles turned white as she gasped and swallowed her gum. It stayed at the top of her throat threatening to make her vomit, "I had no...no...idea that was where I'd be."

Jeremy patted her white knuckles and said, "Miss Caldwell, Mary's your only hope. No one else would volunteer to let you stay with them. The truth is much of the town is either mad at you or scared of you. Take my advice and be really good to Mary."

Ciara nodded to Jeremy and quickly made her way to the front reception area. Tears threatened again. It wasn't just that she didn't like Mary Jolly, who was good friends with her ex-fiancé, but it was also that she was afraid of her. Mary watched her close and examined her every move. She made Ciara nervous with her scrutiny.

"God, why? You know I need my space. I need to be able to be alone and relax and do my thing. I'll die if I have to keep on the public face," Ciara prayed quietly and turned at the sound of footsteps behind her. She swiped the tear from her left cheek and caught her breath.

Her shoulders relaxed at the sight of Hartline standing beside her, "Oh thank God, someone I know. I'm surprised you would visit me in a place like this. You don't belong here." She punched him on the shoulder and smiled.

"Ciara, I do belong here. This is where I got sober and got the help I needed. Have you not heard anything about my story? I haven't always been an upstanding churchgoer. God changed my life forever." Hartline teared up and wiped at his cheek while Ciara looked on speechless.

"Wow, you came here too. Isn't the food just awful." She lowered her voice and mouthed, "Smuggle me some smoothies and that amazing cake of yours." Ciara looked around to see if anyone was watching.

"I'll bring you some cake and a smoothie, but it'll have to be on Saturday, when you can have visitors and food brought in from outside," Hartline said this loud and craned to see down the clinic hallway.

On cue, Mary stepped out of Jeremy's office and walked toward Hartline, "What are you two conspiring?"

Ciara huffed and fixed her stoic expression to greet Mary, "When do I go with you to your home?"

"Oh, so Mr. Clay's given you the delightful news. We will leave in about fifteen minutes. Your luggage is still in my car, so I guess all that's left for you to do is fill out your journal." Mary pointed to the student workbook.

"So that's why all those people were taking notes.

Great, now I have homework. I should have looked in this thing and filled it out earlier," said Ciara.

Hartline said his goodbyes and exited through the front doors. Ciara watched the door for a while before collapsing into an oversized chair. She began imagining Heartline dropping her off at her office. She could sleep in the reception area until Bryant got there, and he could take her to her apartment after work. She could meet with the lawyer and never come back to the clinic.

As her pulse raced at all the possibilities outside of the clinic she reached for her handbag and shoved her hand to the bottom. Her fingers scratched the bottom cloth lining and moved methodically around. Finding nothing, Ciara pulled the bag to her chest and breathed out.

"There are no more pills, and I'm stuck," she whispered to herself.

It was impossible. She was court-ordered to the clinic and Mary's house, and no judge in this town would change the requirements. She looked at the journal and saw week one sprawled across the first page. She would do what she must to get out of the clinic. Whatever it took.

As night approached and Ciara rode in the massive car beside Mary, Cam and Annie furiously worked in the food truck. The electrician was done hooking the truck back into the box and all that was left to do was get the new appliances installed. The oven and crock pot were heavily damaged in the impact when the swinging serving window struck Cam's arm and swung into the truck cracking and breaking glass.

Cam hummed a worship song while Annie shined the surface of her new counter, "Do you think we should talk to Bryant next door? I think it might be neighborly for us to make amends. God's been talking to me more about forgiveness."

Cam stopped humming and smiled. "I think you're right. He didn't have anything to do with Ciara's foolishness. We should probably at least clear the air."

The two left the truck and emerged onto the sidewalk. The streetlights and pretty string lights in the trees were illuminating the shop windows on the street. Cam held Annie's hand and adjusted his sling before pushing into the glass door to C&W realty. The new sign was vinyl and covered the large engraved wooden one from before. The clinging bell brought Bryant out of his office, and he walked toward them. Bryant's eyes widened and his brows raised.

"Hi, Bryant, Cam and I thought it would be neighborly to come by and greet you. We understand you are still working out of this building and were hoping all hard feelings could be behind us." Annie smiled sweetly and extended her hand to Bryant. Cam stood beside her with his right arm draped on her shoulder.

"Oh, Thank you Jesus. I thought maybe you guys decided to sue this business instead." Bryant smiled broadly and took Annie's hand and then Cam's.

Cam winked and said, "You mean we could still do that?"

Bryant's shoulders slumped as he stepped back looking at their faces. Cam saw the fear in Bryant's eyes and quickly shook his head, no.

"I'm just kidding, man. We aren't going to sue. We've prayed a lot and hope that Ciara is getting the help she needs."

Bryant sighed and nodded in agreement, "The main reason I am still here is because I feel responsible. I can't get it out of my mind that I contributed to her downfall."

Cam studied the other man's face for a moment before speaking, "Bryant, I don't think it's healthy for you to operate your life feeling responsible for things you can't control."

"I know, I've been reading my Bible a lot and praying, but I can't shake the feeling. I think it will take some time. If I could just see her get better, I'd feel better too." Bryant ran his hand through his hair and sighed.

"Annie and I will pray too. I know Hartline is praying and Mary Jolly is counseling her. She's in the best place possible to get help. Trust God and don't feel responsible. Whatever you did to contribute, in the end she made her own choices." Cam put his right hand on Bryant's shoulder.

Bryant nodded in agreement for the second time and said, "Does this mean that I can get food from the truck now? I've been smelling that food for over a year now and never been able to taste a morsel."

Annie smiled and said, "First meal is on the house and when we need to buy some overpriced, beachfront property you can help us, right?"

Bryant chuckled and raised his right hand, "I'll make sure it's not overpriced. That's my job."

"Deal." Cam and Annie waved goodbye and walked out the doors.

At that moment, Mary and Ciara wheeled Ciara's large suitcases from the car into the large garage. Ciara took in her surroundings and realized she was in a very impressive house. It was old, historic, and in mint condition. "Wow, I could sell this for a pretty penny."

"It's not for sale, honey. This is my family inheritance." Mary dragged the huge piece of luggage up a flight of stairs.

"Everyone has a price...that's all I'm saying." Ciara

counted windows when she entered the great room. The furniture alone was worth a fortune. She looked at the pictures on the walls. One familiar face of a very handsome young African American man hung prominently on the wall. He was holding a young lady's hand. Her ebony skin was flawless, and she had a toddler with pigtails sitting in her lap.

"What's his name? I know him. He's from Atlanta, right? He helped with the prospect on the Westin house...he's Bernard Jackson." Ciara looked at Mary inquisitively.

"Bernard Jackson is my son, and he now runs the company my family started. His dad left us years ago and it has been just the two of us until he met sweet Tia." Mary smiled sweetly at the picture.

"No way, that's just too coincidental...does everyone know everyone around here." Ciara huffed and swiveled on her crutch.

"Ciara, I think you need to eat and rest. I've called for Chinese takeout, and I've had your room prepared. I like my privacy, and no one's lived here with me for quite a while. So, in other words, I'd like to keep my space." The doorbell rang, and Mary smiled and moved to the door to retrieve the food.

After eating her lion's share of Kung Pao chicken and rice, Ciara rubbed her tummy and asked where to take her luggage. She realized she may have to navigate a huge staircase. She couldn't imagine a room being on the main level for her.

"Follow me." Mary directed Ciara to the master suite on the main level. A huge walk-in closet and bathroom was attached to a beautiful bedroom. Ciara's eyes filled with tears, and she brushed at her cheek before Mary could see.

"Isn't this your room? I can navigate the stairs. You don't have to give up your space for me." Ciara's voice was hoarse and trembled slightly. The drama and weight of the day was starting to weigh her down. She could not get her emotions in check and without the pills, she couldn't find any synthetic way to cope.

"Girl, I can't have you falling. Those stairs are hard for a two-legged person. Besides, I don't want to lug that massive bag you brought up there. I have eight bedrooms to choose from, as well as the beautiful skylight and telescope my father had installed. I'll get more praying done up there." Mary pulled the large piece of luggage past the rug and dropped the handle.

"Thank you," said Ciara.

Mary left the room while Ciara rummaged through her suitcase and found pajamas. She stood in the warm shower until her good leg fell asleep from the extra weight. When she fell in the large bed, it took less than five minutes to get comfortable and fall asleep.

Ciara dreamed about the young woman, Kate. She woke at 2:15 am with sweat dripping down her back and her pillow twisted around her injured leg. She worked to untangle it and kept trying to get the image of the woman out of her mind. As she drifted back to sleep, she dreamed she saw Kate again. Kate was sitting across from Ciara at the clinic, but this time she was wearing Ciara's cream suit. It was buttoned to the top and the young woman's stringy blond hair was twisted in a bun.

She wore Ciara's expensive high-heeled shoes, and she held a designer purse to her chest. She fumbled with the purse latch and thrust her needle-pricked arm into the oversized bag and pulled out a prescription bottle. Ciara jumped at the sight and yelled, "Give me my stuff! That's mine. You can't have my stuff! You can't have my pills!"

She woke again with her heart racing and her mind whirling. The panic attack was lasting longer than usual and there was no escape. She couldn't go to the medicine cabinet and get what she needed. She couldn't try to convince her mother for cold medicine or Benadryl.

Ciara felt her chest tighten and she rose from the large bed. She reached for the crutch at her bedside and walked out of the room into the great room. Maybe there's something in Mary's house. She was an older woman. She's probably needed medicine. Ciara slowly made her way in the dark on her good leg and was careful not to make too much sound with the crutch on the beautiful cherry wood floor.

She looked in the kitchen cabinets and found only Tylenol and ibuprofen. There wasn't even wine in the fridge or cabinets. She gave up her search and walked slowly back to the great room and to Mary's desk. She riffled through the desk drawer and pushed her hand far back into the small top drawer. She pulled out paper. She quietly pulled the chain on the desk lamp and read. It was the deed for the Bayport Rehabilitation Clinic.

"Mary, why would you have the deed to the clinic?" Ciara whispered.

Ciara opened a manilla folder under the paper and read the agreement between Jolly Realty and Bayport Rehabilitation Clinic, "Mary gave the building to the clinic. What?"

At that moment Ciara heard footsteps above her head. She sat motionless as a door creaked and a toilet flushed. She turned out the small light and made her way back to bed. She lay very still with the crutch beside her in bed. Ciara didn't remember falling asleep, but the next time she woke, Mary stood over her shaking her shoulders.

"It's time to get up. Wow, girl do you sleep with your crutch too. You really do have a lot of insecurities." Mary rushed out the door leaving Ciara in a groggy state. She rose slowly and massaged her temples while dangling her good leg over the side of the overstuffed mattress. The king-sized poster bed dwarfed her small frame and she had to scoot forward a foot to find the floor beneath.

After a quick shower and pulling on a sundress she met Mary in the kitchen. The two ate toast and eggs and Ciara drank deeply from her black coffee. Mary read from a devotional book and Ciara reached for her phone to check real estate listings from her text messages.

"I hope Bryant is paying attention to this beachfront. It would be a shame to miss this deal," Ciara said.

Mary's eyes peered over the rim of her red reading glasses as she lowered her book. "You got a long day at the clinic, let Bryant handle that," Mary said while standing and collecting her car keys.

"I know, Mary. I just like to stay in touch with the business," Ciara said.

Mary nodded for the door while Ciara rose and retrieved her crutch and handbag. She followed Mary to the garage and sank into the passenger seat. The drive took thirty minutes and neither woman spoke. Gospel music played, and Ciara fought the urge to check the listings again.

As they entered the clinic, Ciara felt more comfortable with the schedule. She was relieved the group wouldn't meet again until Friday. No more baring our souls and maybe no more interaction with Kate. Mary even agreed to let Bryant bring paperwork for Ciara to sign even though it wasn't time for her to have visitors.

Ciara watched the clock and was relieved when it was

time for lunch. Bryant entered the small room where she sat alone at the small table. He sat across from her and looked conspicuously out of place in his suit pants and neatly pressed golf shirt. She was delighted to see the new emblem on his shirt. C&W Realty.

She smiled at him and reached for the pen he held out in front of her. He brought her a smoothie and got special permission to give it to her. Mary smelled it and motioned him to the dining hall. "I'm glad to see you, Bryant, and I like the shirt," Ciara said while signing beside all the flagged places.

"Ciara, you look great. I'm glad to see you eating too." He pointed at her plate where she had a hamburger patty cut into pieces and a piece of lettuce, tomatoes, a carton of milk, and a bottom wheat bun.

"I'm not eating this," she whispered behind her hand, "I just eat the veggies and bread and milk. Thanks for the smoothie." Ciara took a giant sip of the acai concoction and pointed to her temples. "Ouch, I got a brain freeze."

Bryant pointed to her leg, "When do you start therapy? How's it feeling?"

"It's fine, and I start therapy next week. I'm ready to get started," she said quietly.

Mary entered the dining area and nodded to Bryant, "Mr. Ward, your time's up. Saturday is visitation and Sunday is church. Ciara's visitations will begin as soon as she's been here for four weeks."

Ciara's eyes darted to Bryant, and she fought the urge to reach for him. His face was expressionless, and his strong hands were still. She never noticed Bryant's hands before now. Her eyes dropped to her own small hands. They trembled slightly while she fought to still them in her lap.

Bryant rose to his feet and smiled at Mary, "Yes

ma'am, I don't want to get Ciara in trouble." He winked at Ciara and her stomach flopped. His usually gelled hair was falling forward on his forehead, and she resisted the urge to push it back.

"Maybe I could go to church with Bryant on Sundays. Since the chapel is mostly men on Sunday and I must go somewhere with a family. It's the only church I know around here." She looked imploringly at Mary.

Mary shrugged, "I don't see why not. I'll take you to Bryant's church on Sunday morning in four weeks after you're settled in here and you can come to my church on Sunday night." She winked at them both and grabbed Bryant's arm leading him out of the kitchen. She called back at Ciara, "It'll be fun for the three of us."

Ciara sat stewing at the thought of Mary sitting with her at church. The woman would probably sit between her and Bryant. Mary would love the choir and the message while Ciara would steal glances at Bryant. She smiled when she thought of him. She thought about Bryant through afternoon chapel, prayer time, and during her counseling session with Jeremy and Mary.

Mary and Ciara sat in Director Jeremy Clay's office. Jeremy spoke first and broke Ciara from her daydream. Her gaze was fixed on the small window above his head. She was imagining Bryant swooping in and carrying her out the double glass doors of the clinic to his waiting Mercedes. "Ciara, you are doing very well in your journal, and very well in each phase for this week. You always speak appropriately. We've even had other clients think you were staff. It's hard for them to believe you have any addiction issues."

Ciara brightened at his assessment of her progress so far. She mentally calculated she currently had an "A" at rehab. That was to be expected. She never got a lower grade in anything else.

Jeremy shifted in his seat and looked to Mary, "But we have concerns...Mary and I worry you are doing too well. Your reactions are controlled and very measured."

Ciara frowned and recalculated. "I guess I'm making my first "B" ever, huh?" She looked at Mary and waited for her to speak.

Mary took her hand and said, "What Jeremy is saying is that you seem fake. Not real. And we worry you are progressing on the surface, but there's something brewing deeper in you that isn't being dealt with. You really shouldn't be grading yourself right now."

Ciara's eyes darted from Jeremy's face to Mary's. This was not Jack Junior's negotiating table and neither of the counselors had manipulation in their expressions. "What does fake mean? I mean I know I sometimes don't share my feelings, but it makes me more anxious and more upset. I've learned to handle that stuff myself."

Jeremy leaned forward and questioned, "How do you handle it yourself?"

Ciara racked her brain for the answer, "I guess I think about it and talk myself out of being upset...and I try to relax...and I get alone so I can be myself." She didn't mention what came to her mind next. She would find valium or pain pills or vodka.

Mary patted Ciara on the back, "Well, now we want to help you with more strategies than what you just mentioned. Ciara, we are here for you. Your first new strategy is going to be telling director Jeremy or me one truthful feeling, idea, or embarrassment every day."

Ciara winced, "Is this going to be confidential? I got the Caldwell name to keep out of the mud."

Jeremy and Mary looked to one another and then at Ciara. Jeremy spoke first, "Of course, it's confidential.

We are both trained counselors and would never betray your confidence."

Mary then added, "Do you think you could start today?"

Ciara huffed and said, "Of course, I don't want to stay fake." Her sarcastic tone was ignored by Mary and Jeremy.

Mary looked at Ciara and raised her eyebrows, "Answer this then: Why did you go through my desk drawer last night?"

Ciara's eyes bugged for a split second before she regained her blank expression, "I was looking for something."

Mary prodded, "Can you tell us what you were looking for?"

Ciara turned the questioning to Mary and asked, "Why on God's green earth would you give this million-dollar property to the rehab? My God, you could have done so much more with that money."

Mary dropped her head and looked back up, "Ciara, that is my private information. Please keep that information to yourself. Now, what were you looking for?" Jeremy patted Mary's hand and squeezed her shoulder.

Ciara sighed and waited before saying, "Ok, I know this will set me back in treatment and it may make you two to think bad of me, I am no thief, and I wasn't looking for valuables...I was looking for pills or wine. I felt the tightness in my chest again and wanted some relief to sleep." Ciara breathed out slowly and slumped back letting her head rest on the back of her chair. Telling the truth to these two felt good. It had been a long while since she was honest with anyone.

Mary spoke quietly, "That's what I thought. I heard you in the kitchen first and realized you were snooping in the cabinets."

Ciara looked to both and said, "Am I in trouble, are you going to tell the judge?"

Jeremy spoke up, "No, Ciara, we aren't going to tell anyone. You confessed and now you are on the road to recovery." He bowed his head and began to pray. Ciara watched the top of Jeremy's head wide-eyed.

Later that evening Ciara pulled her leg into the car and sank into the oversized seat. Mary didn't speak and flipped on gospel music. A beautiful African American female voice bellowed out. A few words about God and forgiveness caught Ciara's attention. She didn't know the words, but she felt the song deep. Her shoulders relaxed, and her hands rested in her lap.

As they entered the garage bay, Ciara smiled broadly. Her current mood did not make sense to her. She would have to sit at the table and eat with Mary and then she would have to fill out her journal, and then she would have to stand in the shower until her foot felt numb, but the routine gave her some pleasure. Somehow.

"What is happening to me? I'm wanting to spend time with a crazy lady and eat lots of fattening foods," Ciara whispered to herself as she hobbled up the stairs anxious to hear the doorbell. There would be some great food and her stomach rumbled at the thought of more Chinese or maybe some takeout Italian with garlic bread.

CHAPTER 17

Three weeks later, Cam woke at 2 am dripping sweat. The Bayport mild spring was quickly giving way to the intense summer heat. The air conditioner would soon run at night. He was alone in bed and Annie was not beside him. He looked at the bathroom door and didn't see any light or hear any sounds. As he walked into their small living area, he found Annie lying on the couch with her laptop perched beside her on the small coffee table.

Cam bent over Annie and gently shook her shoulders. She slowly opened her eyes and squinted. He loved the way her nose scrunched up when she was trying to figure things out, "Hey sweetie, did you forget where our bed is?"

"Ummm...Cam? No...no...I was just looking for new recipes and I must have dozed off here." She slowly rose and reached for her laptop and clicked it on. Cam noticed the fine cuisine website.

"You are expanding the menu honey?"

"I don't know why. I keep feeling like I need more recipes. It's been an obsession with me since the accident. The truck oven and prep space barely allow what I already cook." She pressed her thumbs into her temples.

"Annie, if it helps you to plan and keep your mind busy, I don't see any harm in your obsession. Maybe God's trying to tell you something about your future." Cam pulled her to her feet and kissed her tenderly. She wrapped her arms tightly around his waist and rested her forehead on his chest.

Cam sighed lightly and said, "You ready for bed now? You got a big day tomorrow at the truck. It won't be long till you're cooking all the time and I'll have to stand in line to get any attention." He winked and led her out of the living room.

He stopped before he crossed the threshold of the bedroom. He watched as Annie snuggled under the sheet and her tall slender form settled on the queen-sized bed. Her steady breathing and still form let him know she was slipping back to sleep. He followed her to the bed but did not lay down. Instead, Cam knelt and started a quiet prayer.

"Heavenly Father, Annie is unsettled and I'm afraid she's lost her peace. I pray You help her. But if You are talking to her about more recipes and bigger dreams give us the open door," Cam's whispered words caused Annie to stir. Her lips turned into a smile, and she giggled.

"A storefront named Westin House. I like it." She began slow breathing again and turned facing Cam. She was talking in her sleep. He felt his heart skip a beat at the thought of what she said. Her dream was still there, and God was orchestrating something big for the two of them. Cam got into bed and held Annie in his arms. As he drifted to sleep an excitement settled on him. It was only a matter of time, and they would embark on a new journey.

The next morning, the beautiful summer sun shone brightly on the streets. Ciara moved methodically behind Mary and spoke little as they entered the rehabilitation building. Her full leg brace was now replaced with a walking boot that extended to her knee. She studied the outside architecture of the building while Mary ascended the stairs. Ciara hadn't really thought much about the building before today. The more she looked and counted windows, the more she became curious, "Mary, what was this building before?"

"Can't you figure it out. You know real estate. What was its former purpose?" Mary raised her eyebrows to Ciara in a challenge.

Ciara scrunched up her nose and followed Mary into the reception area. The front foyer was pretty and had an antique light fixture dangling in front of a tall window above the entrance. The current chapel was directly in front.

"Was this a church? No, wrong location in the city for that," said Ciara before Mary could comment. She raised her hand to her chin.

Mary, eyebrows raised, stood beside her. Ciara craned her neck to look down the small hallway.

"It was a wedding chapel?" questioned Ciara.

"Good going, girl, you might just make a real estate agent yet. You got an eye for property." Mary smiled wide and motioned for her to follow. Ciara meandered behind Mary down the hall past Director Jeremy Clay's office. Her boot scratched the tiled floor as she followed. Her mind whirled with images of the former use and traffic in this very location. Both women turned and stopped in front of a double door.

Mary turned and looked at Ciara, "What is this room?"

Ciara was beginning to enjoy herself. She passed the coffee pot and didn't reach for her cinnamon gum as she usually did. Normally she would have a cup in her hand and have already put at least one stick of gum in her mouth. It felt good to skip the routine and not go directly into the group meeting or a classroom. Lately, she had also been working as a tutor for struggling readers. It gave her something to do and helped pass the time. One of her paces for recovery was to work.

Ciara looked full at the double doors and noticed the beauty of the solid wood, painted white, and the twin, gold doorknobs.

"It's the bridal room."

Mary shook her head, yes, and said, "You're right, but there's more to it than you think."

"If it's a part of this place then it has to have a practical purpose now." Ciara sniffed and shook her head up and down. "Yeah, it's definitely used for something."

Mary smiled again. "Step into my office."

Mary opened the double doors revealing a beautifully furnished room complete with an en suite powder room. A massive ornate mirror stood in the corner and Ciara's sandaled foot sunk into the plush shag rug.

"Wow, this is where you disappear every day? I thought you might be walking around the city praying for everyone and finding vagrants to bring back to the clinic. I didn't realize you were luxuriating in the back." Ciara smiled and giggled at the thought of Mary hanging around in here and then entering the institutional side barking orders at all of them.

Mary frowned. "Girl, you better not give my secret away. I can't be having my private life interrupted all times of the day. I got to have a place to pray and take care of things."

Ciara smiled. "I won't say anything. It just goes to show, you can't judge a book by its cover. Maybe you shouldn't be so hard on me about my shallow expensive pursuits, that's all I'm saying."

Mary huffed and motioned to Ciara, "Let's get to group. I think your favorite vagrant Kate might be coming today. Her parents are dropping her off again for the day program. I told them she needed more intervention, but she keeps convincing them to let her stay with them. Without a court order, she just won't get the help she needs."

Ciara frowned and trembled slightly at the mention of Kate. She had not encountered her since the first week at the clinic. The dream she had the first night came flooding back. She swooned and fought to balance between her boot and sandal while following Mary through the halls toward the chapel. Her heart raced, and she reached for her gum.

"I'm getting my coffee Mary. I'll join you in a minute." Ciara looked down and tried to sound nonchalant, even though she felt light-headed.

"You drink way too much coffee. That's got to be cup number three since you woke up this morning. I need to start charging you personally for all you drink." Mary didn't turn to look at Ciara. Instead, she entered the chapel. Ciara thought about following Mary without going to the front or the dining hall to get more coffee, but she would get her coffee, and chew her gum, and think about valium in this group session too.

As Ciara joined the group, she balanced her cup on the chair beside while digging through her small over the shoulder wallet purse. She opted for breath mints instead of gum. Her jaws were aching from all the chewing.

Kate sat opposite Ciara again. She wore the same clothes and had the same hollow look in her eyes. This time, however, she showed no interest in Ciara. Instead, she rocked and stared at a new young woman who sat wide-eyed. Ciara had never seen the woman before. She figured the woman couldn't have been much older than eighteen or nineteen.

Mary opened in prayer while Ciara watched Kate. Kate stared and picked at a sore on her hand. Her eyes rested on the new woman's pretty, ebony skin. It was flawless, and her hands were adorned with several expensive rings. Her manicured nails were neat and trim, and she clutched a designer bag. As Mary finished praying, a worship song played loud and clear. Kate continued to rock back and forth and stare.

"She's jealous of the new girl. She sees her beauty and wealth and it reminds her of her poor pitiful state," Ciara whispered to Mary.

She didn't know how she was able to size up the situation so well and waited on Mary to comment. Mary waited for everyone to finish their journals and prepare to share with the group. Ciara shook her head and sighed loudly.

"Am I becoming you, Mary. Oh God, I'm becoming just like you? I'm getting wise and I have a little pooch in my stomach. It's over, I'll never get my girlish figure back," Ciara whispered while looked at her middle section.

"Ciara why don't you stop brooding or freaking out or whatever you're panicking about right now and tell everyone about your recent victories...or setbacks." Mary leaned in toward Ciara and locked eyes.

Ciara looked closely at Mary. She breathed out slowly.

"You should call on someone else," Ciara muttered.

At that moment Kate began to convulse wildly. She shook and fell to the floor. Before Ciara had time to react, Mary was kneeling over Kate and barking out orders for the group to get help. Jeremy entered the room and dialed 911 while Mary checked Kate's pulse and breathing. The ghostly frame settled into a limp position while everyone in the circle stood over.

Mary held Kate's wrist feeling for her pulse. She looked up to the group and said one word, "Pray."

At that same moment across town, Cam and Hartline paced the sanctuary of Bayport Community Church. They prayed in their usual places. Both men were praying for addiction recovery. They had no way of knowing what Ciara was witnessing at the rehabilitation clinic, but their prayers were joining hers. All three were asking God to help and all three were asking for lives to be spared and lives to be changed.

Ciara squeezed her eyes shut and mouthed her prayer, "Oh God, save her life. Oh God, help Kate. Oh God, don't let her die."

At that moment, paramedics entered and knelt beside Kate. Ciara was reluctant to move from the motionless body. She felt the need to stay close and continue to pray. She knew the paramedics were performing life-saving maneuvers, but she also felt she needed to keep praying.

"Kate needs You, Lord," Ciara said. Tears formed in her lids, and she blinked several times.

Kate was given a shot of Narcan, and she roused slightly. The paramedics wheeled her out of the chapel and through the double front doors. The paramedic truck lights shone through the doors and into the chapel. Ciara stood until the taillights faded. Her hands were tight by her side. Mary took her hand and led her to sit down. Most of the group scattered and Jeremy talked to the new woman who Ciara heard him call, Shara.

Ciara swallowed the last of her mint and looked down at the lukewarm coffee. She swirled the liquid and shook slightly. Mary sat quietly beside her and waved to Jeremy. He nodded and continued to talk to Shara.

Ciara wanted to move; she wanted to stand. She wanted to do something, but couldn't seem to find the strength, especially on her booted left foot. She studied the boot and placed her elbows on her knees. She looked at Mary and shook her head up and down for a full ten seconds before saying, "I need God, too. I need to be able to get a prayer through to Him and know it."

Mary smiled and grabbed for her hand, "Dear Lord, Ciara wants to talk to You. Please help her to keep talking to You and let her know You're hearing her. Thank You Father."

Ciara smiled and said, "Amen."

"Girl, it's time you get to church. This Sunday. I'm taking you." Mary tapped Ciara on the back and left the chapel. Ciara heard her footsteps down the hall and figured she was going to her special office. As she listened further, she decided to make her way to the dining hall. Ciara knew by now getting in the line early meant no one else touched her tomato and lettuce and sometimes she would get the thicker cheese slices to go with her patty of some sort.

She wouldn't eat the patty, of course, and now she didn't even cut it into small pieces. She just sat at her table and grabbed for her journal. "I have so much to write about now," she whispered to herself. She thought of seeing Bryant and her stomach flopped. "Oh Lord, help me to keep a steady mind and my sanity around him. Thank you," she prayed.

CHAPTER 18

Sunday morning in Bayport called for air-conditioning and caused churchgoers to forgo any extra layer of clothing. Pastors opted for golf shirts and light trousers instead of button-down shirts and slacks. Ciara nervously sat next to Mary and second-guessed the plain sundress she chose earlier that morning. It made sense to blend in at church, but she didn't like her limited options since she hadn't shopped since last season.

"What if everyone's wearing long dresses this summer instead of knee-length," she said to Mary on the ride.

"Ciara, you try way to hard," Mary said.

Mary led Ciara through the regal church building. They stopped at an usher and Ciara tried to hide her booted foot behind her and balance on her right foot. The long conversation Mary was having with the older man was wearing on Ciara.

"Hey, Mary. I know exactly where to sit. Can we go now?" questioned Ciara.

Mary looked at her and nodded for her to show the way. Ciara hobbled to Mayor Nelon's seat and motioned to the seat behind. Bryant would probably still sit in this section. Church people were creatures of habit. Nine times out of ten they always sat in the same place.

Mary sat first and Ciara followed behind. She wanted desperately to leave room for Bryant but thought better of making it obvious to Mary she was saving him a seat. Soft music played from a recording and the choir entered quietly. Ciara was anxious to see Bryant and was disappointed when she still didn't see him at five minutes before the service was to begin.

Ciara stood obediently beside Mary when the choir director asked everyone to rise to their feet. At that moment she noticed a hand waving. To her left and in the third center row, Bryant sat flanked by Mrs. Nelon on one side and a beautiful tall redhead on the other. She waved back and frowned slightly. She swallowed her gum and choked while Mary noticed Bryant and waved her jeweled hand.

The pastor asked for everyone to bow their heads in prayer. "Is he sitting with Annie Shivers?" Ciara whispered to Mary.

Mary nodded, no, and lowered her head in prayer.

Ciara looked past the bowing heads long enough to realize the young woman was not Annie Shivers.

"My mind is playing tricks on me," Ciara whispered under her breath. She noticed the beautiful auburn-haired woman holding Bryant's hand during prayer. Ciara's face flushed and she breathed deeply for a full three breaths before mouthing, "Amen."

She stood through worship until her right foot cramped. She then sat deflated into the seat and waited for the sermon. The eloquent southern voice of the pastor kept Ciara's attention, however when he finished her mind raced again with the thought of the woman next to Bryant.

"Who is she? He hasn't spoken to me about her," Ciara said.

Mary's eyes locked with Ciara's. "That's not why we are here. You need to get your mind on something besides Bryant Ward and his new girlfriend." Mary was right. She shouldn't meddle in Bryant's personal life. Ciara had no contact with him since his last visit a month ago.

Mary took sermon notes and didn't miss one word just as Ciara expected. She watched as the older woman raised her jeweled hand in praise during the last song and prayer. Mary looked at Ciara as the congregation were told to stand. Ciara caught her eyes before the prayer.

At the closing prayer, Ciara looked to the rafters and said her own quietly, "I know Mary is watching me. Watching how I react in every situation. Oh Lord, I'm tired of being watched. Please give me some space. Amen."

The service ended early, and Ciara dutifully followed Mary. The two of them walked to Bryant. As they approached he turned and greeted Mary first. Ciara stood quietly. Her heart pounded in her ears, and she couldn't find the words to say to Bryant. Her cheeks were hot, and she fiddled with a long blond tendril while Mary and Bryant talked about the sermon. The red-headed woman stood close behind Bryant and talked to Mayor Nelon.

"Hi Ciara, you look great. How's it going?" Bryant stepped past Mary to stand in front of Ciara. He looked impeccable with his gelled hair and pressed golf shirt. His recently tanned arms made Ciara think about ocean front properties. She imagined him standing in front of a posh, little beach house painted in a tasteful cream-tangerine. She imagined an ocean breeze blowing through his hair and the sun warming his arms while he rattled off the amenities provided by the newly built beachfronts.

Ciara smiled at Bryant and spoke softly, "It's good. I've been busy with..." She wasn't going to say she had been busy getting clean from her pill addiction. Awkward silence fell between the two and the auburn-haired woman turned to stand beside Bryant. She stared while waiting for Ciara to speak.

Bryant looked between the two women and smiled. "Ciara, this is Taylor Emerson. She's making an offer on a newbuild on Bay Breeze Drive." That meant they didn't lose all the Emerson group. Somehow, they kept this one. Ciara's eyes narrowed slightly and followed the young woman's perfectly manicured hand as it lightly brushed Bryant's forearm. Ciara had a suspicion of how they held this client.

Mary moved beside Ciara and offered her arm to help steady her. Ciara had been standing on one foot and balancing with her toes on the other. She was relieved to shift slightly and use Mary to take some of the pressure off.

Bryant's eyes filled with concern, and he reached for Ciara's small pale arm, "Is your leg doing better?" His movement forward left Taylor standing precariously behind. His gaze locked on Ciara's booted leg. Ciara felt exposed and regretted the knee-length sundress from last year's wardrobe. Taylor's manicured feet were tanned and the long silk dress she wore shimmered at her ankles. Ciara felt deflated and frumpy standing close to Taylor. It didn't help Taylor was taller than Ciara causing her to have to look up to talk to her. Bryant and Taylor looked like the perfect pair ripped out of the latest fashion magazine.

Mary spoke next, rescuing Ciara from Bryant's interrogation and Taylor's intimidating presence, "I think it's time for us to go. I've made reservations at Sunset Pointe for lunch today and I don't want us to miss it." She shook Bryant's and Taylor's hands and turned Ciara toward the back, double doors leading to the foyer. Ciara quietly said her goodbyes and followed Mary. Her gait was slow, and the booted foot and crutch grabbed the attention of the deacons flanking the swinging wood doors. The two older men looked at Ciara and in a grand gesture opened both doors letting her pass.

Ciara shrank behind Mary and was exhausted when they both emerged from the decorative, brick front. She moved as quickly as possible down the handicap walk. Ciara dropped into Mary's Cadillac and tilted her head back sighing deeply.

Neither of them spoke as Mary drove to the restaurant. Ciara played with her food while Mary checked her text messages from Jeremy. He had news about the hospitalized Kate. Apparently, she was fighting kidney failure.

"Oh Lord. Help that poor girl," Ciara prayed.

Ciara daydreamed about selling the new build houses on Bay Breeze Drive. She imagined herself in her cream suit. Her skin tanned slightly and her feet in wedge leather sandals. She tapped her unpainted nails on the counter beside Mary while pushing her salad around with the small fork. Mary's phone rang and Ciara caught bits and pieces from the conversation. Jeremy was on the other line and Ciara guessed the two of them discussed what to do with Kate and how to handle her parents. Ciara was beginning to understand the rehab lingo and knew what Mary meant when she mentioned "enabling behavior."

The conversation made her uncomfortable and she forced her mind to continue her daydream. She did not want to consider her own parents in the equation of enabling behavior. Ciara was learning that addicts find people to help or enable them to continue risky behavior when they are no longer able to sustain the addiction themselves. Ciara frowned when Bryant came to her mind.

"Bryant was more an enabler than my parents," she mumbled to herself. She thought of Bryant driving her around all the time and covering appointments for her when she was too inebriated.

Mary dropped her phone in her bag and looked at Ciara, "Did you say something?"

Ciara looked up and put her fork down. "No, I was just talking to myself." Mary smiled and winked at Ciara. "That's fine, just don't start answering yourself."

Ciara shifted in her chair and drank deeply of the spiced tea in front of her. Mary introduced her to the honey-sweetened liquid and Ciara ordered it every chance she got. Mary waved for the server and paid for the two of them. Ciara's current financial situation was quite troubling. The next two paces in her recovery process included financial responsibility and something called "restitution." After defining the word from her journal, she learned that sometimes addicts needed to pay others back for the losses they caused, hence, restoring things to the people in their lives.

She was glad the apartment and hospital bills were all paid by her inheritance and insurance. She had a place to live and a storefront for the realty business. A small stipend from her cut of the profits was coming in from C & W Realty. She currently had three bills to pay. A fee to Bayport Rehabilitation Center, her cell phone, and a payment to keep utilities on at her apartment. All three were automatically paid from her account. The rest was left in the account, and she hadn't looked at the balance. She usually lived with accountants and Jack Junior keeping watch on her spending and saving. Now she was on her own.

She had a real lack of experience with living on a budget. Her insurance company paid for the liability damages to the food truck and injury to Cam, however, they would not pay for her wrecked car. She really regretted drinking the vodka and taking the pills when she thought about losing her beautiful car.

Ciara's car was junked for parts, and she barely found enough money to pay off the dealership. Now, she had no car and only a small amount of money to buy another. The amount in her account would be small and insignificant compared to her previous lifestyle before her parents left for Honduras. She didn't want to face the issue, so she avoided it. The thought of spending weeks on the subject was very unappealing to her.

Ciara's troubling thoughts about money and restitution rumbled through her mind and she felt depressed. She felt her energy slipping as she thought about recompensing people in her life. Who had she wronged? Who did she still owe? Ciara figured she wouldn't make an "A" on this pace. She couldn't find anyone left to pay back.

She paid a lot to everyone in her life. Jack Junior got what he wanted and had full control of the family company. Jan and her parents were still living their lives exactly as they wanted. Bryant had a business and new beautiful heiress girlfriend, and Mary mentioned Annie Shivers got her food truck upgraded. Ciara felt miserable. She was doing nothing but paying for her sins and there was no end in sight.

Her melancholy was interrupted by the vibrating tone of her cell phone. Mary was turning into the double driveway of her beautifully bricked home as Ciara reached into her designer, oversized shoulder bag.

"Hello, this is Ciara Caldwell." She couldn't resist using her business tone developed over the past two years at Caldwell Realty.

Jan's steady feminine voice sounded on the other end of the call. "Hi sis." Little voices shrilled in the background. Ciara could hear giggles and what sounded like small footsteps running around a tiled floor. She could imagine Jan standing at the cluttered kitchen island while three small children raced around her small figure. Baby Grace was probably sitting on Jan's hip or in the baby swing close by. Ciara had only visited twice, but both times she experienced the same managed chaos of her older sister's home.

"Hi, Jan." Ciara flipped down the visor and smoothed her eyebrows while reaching for her lipstick. She mindlessly found the tube and applied two coats while she listened to her sister's monologue about their parents and the daily life in Honduras.

Ciara felt eyes watching her and asked Jan to hold for a moment. She placed the phone on mute and looked at Mary, "Why are you staring at me?"

Mary didn't move and sat facing Ciara for a moment before speaking, "Maybe you should tell Jan about your recovery process. Or maybe, tell her about your recent crush on Bryant?"

Ciara felt heat rise to her cheeks and her eyebrows shot up. She pursed her lips and they slipped under the double coat of gloss. She sighed and scrunched her nose up at Mary, "How do you do that? How do you know everything I'm thinking and feeling? It's just weird and intrusive. May I have a moment with my sister?"

Mary shrugged, "Suit yourself you little fake. I'm trying to get you some real people in your life. The kind who love you no matter what, but you got your own way I guess."

Ciara huffed and looked down on Mary while exiting the car. "By the way I don't have a crush on Bryant. He's my business partner...that's all."

Ciara carefully navigated the few stairs from the garage while clicking her phone off mute. She continued her small talk with Jan. She had to keep in contact with her sister so her parents wouldn't feel the need to hurry to her side. It was Ciara's compromise. She turned at the last step and saw Mary still in the driver's seat. The older woman smiled at Ciara and motioned for her to enter the house. Ciara turned and ambled to her room.

"Sis, I think I need to lie down for a while. Apparently, I am going back to church tonight with Mary. I think I may need my strength." Ciara sat on her king-sized bed. It swallowed her small frame. She removed the sandal from her right foot and unstrapped the boot from her left. Arranging a throw pillow, she propped her leg and sat back on the overstuffed upholstered backboard.

Jan spoke slowly and quietly, "Ciara, I think you should give this church a chance. You may like the more relaxed atmosphere of the little church that Mary attends. I looked them up online after our last conversation. You may need this tight knit community church. They will love on you."

Ciara laughed at the thought of a group like Mary surrounding her. They would size her up in a quick second and then start deciding on the best course of action to fatten her up. Then they would all work on getting her to let her hair down while worshipping in wild abandon. "Sis, I don't think I need any more loving on me...Mary's enough. She feeds me every chance she can, and she snoops in all my business. I don't need more people; I just need less Mary."

Jan prayed for Ciara and said a quick goodbye while Ciara dropped her phone beside her. She fumbled with the embroidery on the overstuffed bedspread and listened as Mary entered the great room. The footsteps on the grand staircase and above her head led Ciara to believe Mary was done with the conversation. Relieved, Ciara closed her eyes.

That same afternoon down by the bay, Annie and Cam stood outside the food truck and welcomed the shade cast by the Bradford Pear trees lining the sidewalk. Annie tilted her head to the left and sized up the blank flank of the food truck. Its newly painted surface glowed in the setting sunlight. "I just can't decide on a name...I'm sorry Cam. I know you want me to, but nothing seems right." Annie squinted and put her hands up in a rectangle. She looked through her hands and shook her head left to right.

Cam laughed and said, "I don't think you have to name it. I just thought you might want to try again now that it's more presentable."

Annie smiled back and said, "Do you have a name?"

Cam's eyes darted up and he thought for a few seconds before recalling Annie's recent words. She had been talking in her sleep and probably wouldn't remember what she said. "What about Westin House?"

Annie looked puzzled and sighed, "That doesn't sound like a food truck name."

"Do you like it? Would it sound good for a restaurant?" Cam wanted to get the idea out in the open. He also wanted Annie to feel comfortable continuing her dream.

"I do like it for a restaurant. It has a good ring to it and for some reason, it sounds familiar." Annie looked directly at Cam. Her red tendrils had escaped the bun at the top of her head and the wind blew on the back of her neck.

"You came up with it." Cam winked playfully at his

wife. His tanned face and arms glowed in the setting sun. He caught a glimpse of himself and Annie in the bakery window reflection. They were a perfect couple, and he was proud of his marriage. They had waited and found each other at a pivotal time in both of their lives.

"How did I come up with it? It is my family name, but I've never thought about using it for a restaurant... at least I don't think I have. Have I?" Annie looked puzzled at Cam.

"You said it in your sleep. You were talking in your sleep and told me." Cam grabbed her hand and pulled her to him.

As he embraced Annie, he caught sight of Hartline in the bakery window. It seemed several congregation members needed to stop by their businesses on this beautiful, sun-filled, Sunday afternoon. Hartline waved back and pointed to his watch. Cam looked at his own and panicked.

"Annie, it's almost time for Bible study. We better lock up and hurry or we'll be late." Cam moved toward the truck and entered quickly. Annie followed close behind. The two of them locked up in record time and sprinted toward his truck. Cam looked over at Annie while he drove the few miles to the church. She looked presentable for Bible study despite the smell of cooked onions that permeated both of their shirts. He stifled a laugh at the thought of standing before the adult class while the smell of Annie's smoked sausage sauce filled the room. He could just imagine a couple of the guys with stomach's growling looking at their watches.

North of the bay, Ciara woke to the sound of Mary humming and clanging pots and pans in the kitchen. Ciara had never seen Mary cook and was curious to see what she was doing. She quickly covered the path between the master bedroom to the full-size kitchen with the decorative, large island equipped with a farm sink and plenty of counter space. Ciara stopped at the edge and caught a glimpse of Mary kneeling at a lower cabinet and rummaging through plastic bowls and dishes with lids.

"Are you cooking for us tonight?" Ciara startled Mary who looked back and motioned for Ciara to come beside her.

"Girl, no. I don't cook, but I do need to bring something for after service social. Now I just can't find my cake platter."

"So, you're baking? Ciara looked inquisitive and began organizing the various plastic containers according to size. They were scattered throughout the floor and on the counter above.

"I don't bake either. Hartline made me a strawberry cake, but I can't show up with the Glenn's Bakery box. That would just be tacky." Mary bugged her eyes at Ciara and put her hand up motioning for her to help her stand.

Ciara laughed, "I totally understand." She then spoke softly, "Fake."

"You just mind your business. No one thinks I made the cake. They all know better." Mary huffed and grabbed for her stool to look above her double refrigerator. She celebrated when her fingertips struck the cake platter and handed it down to Ciara.

"Ciara, we got to hurry. No one cares if we're late, but if we wait much longer we'll miss all the music. I need that praise break in my life to keep me uplifted and cheerful." Mary pulled the Glenn's Bakery cake from the box and put it on the platter. The lid was equipped to cover and lock keeping the contents fresh and unharmed.

Ciara brushed through her hair, brushed her teeth, and decided to put the sundress back on. Mary never gave her any indication about what to wear and the last thing Ciara saw Mary wearing was her rhinestone accented blue jean dress. So, she figured the sundress would be fine. The one thing Ciara hated more than anything else was to stick out and feel uncomfortable around a lot of people she didn't know.

In the garage, Mary stood by Ciara while she arranged her booted foot into the car. She then handed her the cake, "Keep it steady, please."

Ciara rode beside Mary holding the cake dutifully. She glanced out the window and listened to Mary's gospel music. Her right foot tapped to the tune, and she felt like humming to one of the hymns she remembered as a child. Her eyes widened as they turned into a little town about twenty minutes from Mary's house. The town was old, and few storefronts had operational businesses. There was a laundromat, a used furniture store, and a corner pharmacy. Most of the storefronts were boarded up or in bad repair.

Mary turned the car and parked in front of an old theatre. Light glowed from the glass doors and the sign was bright. Ciara strained to read what was on the movie marquis but couldn't see from the front parking angle. "Are we going to the movies? Church movies? Do those exist?"

Mary shook her head, no, and motioned for Ciara to hand over the cake. Ciara stepped out of the car and retrieved her crutch and small designer handbag. She was getting around better without the crutch but was afraid to leave it behind in case she had to stand for a long period of time. If she wasn't careful, she would be in the boot for a longer time. Her leg was healing, but a small fracture in her ankle remained.

Ciara followed behind Mary and noticed first the loud gospel music muffled only by two swinging doors. They stood on a red carpet with yellow movie reels imprinted. Ciara's arms goose pimpled at the sound of the strong gospel voices singing in unison. She could make out strong sopranos and altos.

The two of them moved past several faces, but no one turned or seemed to notice. Mary led Ciara to the front row of theatre seats and stood beside her while she settled her crutch and handbag. Ciara looked around the room and saw everyone on their feet, hands raised, and voices lifted. She stood beside Mary and settled her booted foot on the carpeted floor.

A full choir sang for the next thirty minutes while everyone in the theatre sang along. Ciara didn't know the words to most of the songs but caught on to the choruses quickly. Especially the ones with scripture reference. No one looked around at anyone else and Mary had been in the same "praise" posture the entire time. Ciara began to relax and sat to give her foot a rest. Being the spectator to this worship time gave her a few minutes to unwind. It was weird how the atmosphere full of people could give her a moment alone, but strangely that's exactly how she felt.

A tear ran down Ciara's left cheek and she consciously moved to wipe it away. She looked left and then right. No one was looking or noticed she was crying. The room was full of worshippers all talking to God.

She heard people in call and response saying, "Amen," and "God is good." For the first time in her life, she thought about the house of God as a place for Him not for people. It made no sense how this place which many would call an "undesirable" and "unsightly" place for God's presence, would be the place she realized the gathering of the church was for God.

Ciara shook her head and focused her thoughts on the elderly preacher who stood at a podium while a young woman took a mic and stood beside him. The choir stood, the people stood, and Ciara stood again. Despite her foot and the awkward stance, she stood. There was a moment while standing that Ciara felt she was standing before God Himself. Her eyes darted to the tiled ceiling and to the stage and back to Mary. Everyone waited. A few people continued to mouth praises and one gentleman called out, "Praise God," which resulted in a cacophony of responses, "Amen."

The young woman around fifteen with beautiful braids around her forehead and a stunning white dress began to sing out strong. The lyrics were displayed above her head on a projector screen and Ciara looked up above the woman to read each word. The sound of her powerful female alto voice resounded in Ciara's chest. The tears began flowing freely now. She felt a strong hand push some tissues into her hand and she didn't look over but took them. She wiped her face and attempted to stop the tears.

The song ended and the pastor introduced himself as Pastor Carter. The congregation sat and Ciara reluctantly joined them. She didn't want the moment of worship to end. She felt peace and freedom for the first time in a while.

She listened as the pastor spoke loudly and quickly about Jesus' teachings in Matthew. Ciara remembered from her childhood the teachings were called the Beatitudes. She listened as his sing-song voice with an occasional shout read out each of the "blessed are." Ciara's mind caught on the first Beatitude, God blesses the poor and realizes their need for Him for the kingdom of Heaven is theirs. She read and reread this in her Bible. In her notes at the bottom, she found where blessed was translated "happy." It didn't make sense.

Pastor Carter ended his sermon and a keyboard player played behind him. The congregation was quiet, and Ciara bowed her head and closed her eyes while the pastor prayed. He offered for those who needed to pray to come forward to the front aisle and pray together with him and his prayer team. Ciara watched as Mary moved forward with several others and stood facing everyone. People began to stand in front of the prayer team, and they prayed together. Ciara felt a strong desire to move forward. She couldn't understand where all these feelings were coming from. It was not like her to get emotional at church.

Before she talked herself out of moving from her seat, she went and stood in front of Mary. She stretched out her hands and Mary took them. The two stood quiet while Ciara bowed and quietly called out to God, "Oh God. I want You and I want Your presence in my life."

She looked up and was surprised to see tears flowing down Mary's face.

"Ciara, you took the right step tonight. Pursue Him and don't look back. Now you have returned to God. Now you have Him to help guide you. Reading your Bible and prayer will see you through." Mary pointed her right hand to the ceiling and held Ciara's hand with her left. Ciara felt a lightness on her shoulders and chest. The tears came, but now they felt happy for some reason. She had heard countless others describe the feeling and now she understood.

Ciara smiled at Mary and whispered, "I need to call my sister. I got to tell her what happened to me."

Mary nodded back in agreement and Ciara made her way through others at the front aisle and retrieved her handbag and crutch. She walked out the double swinging doors and left the building. She stood on the sidewalk in front of Mary's car and dialed Jan's number. She couldn't stand still and paced on the crutch while holding the cell phone with her shoulder.

Ciara reached Jan's voicemail but waited patiently to leave her long message, "Hi Jan, I went to Mary's church, and I talked to God, and I feel so different, and I just wanted to say that happy are the poor who realize their need for God, for theirs is the kingdom of Heaven. Goodbye...love you guys. Oh, and please tell Mom and Dad."

Ciara wasn't satisfied. She thought about calling her parents, but with the time difference it wouldn't be wise. She thought about calling Jack Junior but decided against that, since he wasn't the type to celebrate religious experiences. Then she thought of Bryant.

"Oh, Bryant would love it. He would understand," she said while dialing his number.

Her pulse raced when his strong voice answered, "Hi Ciara, is everything alright?"

She felt a little childish and wished he hadn't assumed she always called with bad news, but she shook the thought and began to recite the same speech she left on Jan's voicemail, "I just thought you'd like to know and would understand. Bryant, it's amazing to be in God's presence. To know He's listening."

Bryant's voice spoke out strong, "I have been praying for you to meet with God. This is so wonderful. Now my business partner and good friend is a believer. You don't know how much I've wanted this for you, Ciara."

Ciara's eyes teared up again, "Thank you so much for the prayers and thank you for not giving up on me." She smiled through the tears and hoped she didn't sound too emotional. This was all new to her and the huskiness in her voice from crying was enough indication of her emotional state. She didn't want to start sobbing while Bryant was on the phone.

Ciara sniffed and said, "Bryant, I'm still working through paces at recovery. I know I have a lot to learn and things I got to face, but now I feel a new energy to do it. It's nice to have you and crazy Mary. I appreciate it. It won't be long until I'm back to help in the office, but the next six months, I will only be able to come on weekends to help."

"Take it easy and don't come back too soon. I don't want the pressure to set you back." He sounded like a father and his tone bothered Ciara. She didn't want him to think of her as a child. Her heart skipped a beat, and she forced her mind back to business talk.

"I will take it easy. Don't worry I've got the hounds of Heaven in Mary to keep me straight." Ciara chuckled and began to laugh.

Bryant laughed too. "You know it has taken me three months just to get her to trust me. Even now I feel her gaze on me and I shudder."

"Awe, she's not that bad. I think she's mostly bark and not bite, but then again I don't want to cross her." Ciara said a quick goodbye to Bryant when she saw Mary exiting the theatre building. She was humming and made the ten steps in four strides to stand in front of Ciara.

"You ready to go home?" Mary smiled and opened the passenger door for Ciara.

"I thought we had to stay after service for the social thing." Ciara looked at Mary puzzled.

"No ma'am, I don't eat potluck." Mary made her way to the driver's seat and cranked the car while Ciara settled in the seat beside her.

"Ms. Mary Jolly, you never cease to surprise me." Ciara giggled and rolled down her large passenger window letting the cool night air lift her long blond tendrils. The stars were in full view and left Ciara looking heavenward. They passed all the rundown storefronts like before, but Ciara barely noticed. She took in the beauty of the night and hummed along with Mary's gospel station.

CHAPTER 19

June and July came and went with the fervor of tourist season and record high temperatures rolled into one. Annie and Cam spent all their time and resources keeping the food truck stocked and purchased a new top air conditioner to keep up with the ovens and weather. Cam had weekly therapy visits for his arm and was now in a splint and could help Annie more. The church was doing well and had record attendance for Easter.

Both Cam and Annie were excited with the growing church crowd and celebrated with a weekend getaway to their former honeymoon spot. The rest and relaxation was short-lived when the 4th of July crowd stood before the food truck. They hired Tony Glenn to run the counter since he was out for the summer, and both were not excited to hear school would start back mid-August this year and they would lose Tony during lunch hours and football practice.

Cam frowned as he sliced asparagus. Annie had shown him multiple times, but he didn't seem to catch on to her technique. His thoughts went to the storefront with the C & W Realty sign out front. He knew Ciara was spending Saturdays there and some Sunday afternoons too. The proximity of her to the food truck caused him to pray more. He would frequently touch the sides of the truck or close his eyes tightly and ask the Lord to watch over them.

This Saturday morning however, Cam didn't feel

the need to pray for safety. Instead, he felt to pray for a restaurant. Ciara and Bryant's storefront would be perfect, but he chided himself on coveting his neighbor's property. He searched for another location but soon realized he couldn't afford them. Commercial properties in their town were few and far between.

Mary had kept him and Annie abreast of Ciara's progress and both were glad to hear she was doing well in the program. Cam caught a glimpse of Ciara a couple of weeks ago and couldn't help but notice her calm demeanor. Ciara didn't know Cam could see her through the small truck window, and it was rare for Ciara to come out of the front entrance of her business. But that Saturday she stood for a moment facing her storefront. She sized up the window, looked over to the food truck and then reentered her front door.

Cam thanked God for allowing Annie's business to flourish and prayed for her to get the help she needed to keep up the pace. He hated to admit it to himself, but he prayed for summer to end soon and for the fall slow down to come. He was afraid, though, that the word about Annie's amazing meat pies was out and even with the absence of the tourist there would be a steady stream of customers. Tony Glenn promised the fall, football crowd would come here. He assumed Annie would change business hours in the fall and they would be spending Friday nights at the truck.

At C&W Realty, Ciara hung up her office phone and was relieved to have made the return calls in record time today. She and Bryant agreed she would do the office work on the weekends, and he would be free to show properties all day Saturday and occasionally after church on Sundays. Ciara had been delighted at the thought of being alone for five straight hours on

Saturdays, however, after her first month, she found herself hoping Bryant would join her before her time was up.

She did not ask him to pick her up or drop her off. It felt too forward and made her feel vulnerable. Sometimes Mary would drive her and sometimes the rehabilitation center van would drop her off in the rear of the storefront. Getting her license back and buying a small economy car were in the works and Jeremy was helping her contact the judge. It wouldn't be long until she would be driving again. Her left foot was in a small walking boot and the crutch was no longer necessary. Ciara celebrated these steps.

She had given up the thought of resuming the life she led before, and surprised herself, when in counseling she admitted, "I wouldn't trade my peace for a thousand BMWs."

Ciara's thoughts wandered to the food truck outside of Glenn's Bakery. Why didn't Annie Shivers give the truck a name? It was so odd. With the insurance payment she could have afforded lettering. Her thoughts continued with the truck. She noticed the crowds outside the window when she had gone to the reception area to check appointments from the front desk computer. She and Bryant had not made enough to hire a receptionist, but they were getting close.

Bryant was working hard and had closed some very lucrative deals, but Ciara liked to think the recent upswing in profits was due in part to her assistance on the weekends. She thought of Annie and Cam in the food truck and chuckled when she thought of Cam as a sous chef. She didn't recall him ever cooking anything. Then she thought of how hard they must be working. An image of Annie and Cam cooking, cleaning, and serving burst into her mind's eye.

"Lord, they need help," she said.

Ciara didn't know where the prayer to help the Shivers came from. She looked heavenward and said, "I don't think they'd welcome my help, though, Lord."

She shook her long, blond hair and pushed it over her shoulders. She heard Bryant enter the back door and give a clear, "Hello." Ciara's heart skipped and she moistened her lips. She resisted the urge to put on more lip gloss. Mary mentioned one day that it looked very vain to apply make up all the time. Ciara had taken the critique to heart and didn't reach for her make up bag.

Bryant stopped at his office and didn't come to Ciara's. She was disappointed but refrained from going to him. She felt like a silly schoolgirl when she was around him now and tried not to spend too much time in his presence. It was difficult to fight the urge, but she was getting much better at impulse control. She limited her coffee intake and was weaning off the gum and mints.

Ciara reached for her sticky note with the Bible verse-Let patience have her perfect work. It was good to remind herself of scripture. She was now experiencing more than just peace from her Bible study and prayer life. Now she was experiencing joy. The last time she spoke with her mother and father, all three laughed for most of the call.

When she did interact with Bryant each Saturday or Sunday afternoon before she left, she would replay the moment until she had the conversations memorized. Ciara fought the urge to pray for Bryant's affection. Instead, she prayed she would not succumb to her feelings and ruin her relationship with Bryant or with God. On the days Mary picked her up from C&W Realty, Ciara would look out the window when Mary asked about

Bryant. Mary would usually smile a big, toothy smile and wink or say something like, "Your business partner sure is a cutie."

Ciara was glad to be done with the finance pace and sobered at the thought of how much money she went through because of the accident. She now kept her own budget and carefully balanced her account each week. It was her least favorite thing of the week, so she made sure to reward her hard work with a piece of Glenn's Bakery cake.

Now she was working through the restitution pace. It was hard for her to find a way to pay anyone back since her insurance and inheritance had restored property and health to each person she harmed. Her prayer time on this pace was filled with a lot of questions to God. She knelt in her office and prayed silently, "Father God, I don't know how to do this restitution thing. Help me. Amen."

Ciara rose to her feet and walked to the glass doors out front. She looked out and stared at the blank side of the food truck.

"Cam and Annie need help. They need inexpensive workers. I can't cook and they wouldn't want my help," she said while frowning at the thought.

Just then a thought occurred to her. One of the women in group on Friday, was praying for a job. That's it. She needed to call Mary and get her on the job of connecting the Shivers to the clinic. They needed workers and the clinic needed a place to train their graduates to go out in the real world.

Ciara was congratulating herself for thinking of others and helping her neighbors when Bryant walked up behind her and placed his strong tanned hand on her shoulder. Her skin heated at his touch, and she turned around to face him. They stood looking at each other and Ciara giggled slightly, "Bryant, you startled me."

Bryant stepped back a step and grinned, "I didn't mean to scare you. I just wanted to check to see if you needed a ride and maybe could get some dinner. I'm starved and I'm tired of eating alone or with clients." He brushed through his gelled hair with his hands causing it to fall on his forehead. Ciara resisted the urge to brush it back.

"Sure, I can call the clinic and tell them I don't need the van today." Her voice was quiet and breathy. Ciara attempted to square her shoulders and look past Bryant to her office door.

Bryant stepped aside and she walked past him brushing his arm. Her own arm goose pimpled and she reached out for it as she dialed the clinic office number. Ciara attempted her best professional voice as she spoke with one of the interns who drove the van. "I will be back in time to leave with Mary. Thanks."

Ciara grabbed her handbag and switched off the office lights. She didn't even take care to organize the top of her desk. Her personal finance statement was still on top and color-coding pens were strewn about. She smiled and closed her door. It would just have to wait until tomorrow afternoon.

Bryant led Ciara to his waiting Mercedes. It sat under the streetlamp in the back parking area. She glanced over and waved at Hartline who was throwing boxes into the dumpster. Bryant waved too and smiled big as they exited the parking area. The street was beautiful on this late summer night and Bryant opened his panoramic sunroof. The top of Ciara's hair blew slightly with the breeze, but she didn't mind. Even the smell of the smoked sausage and onions from the food truck didn't bother her. In fact, she was embarrassed when her stomach growled.

Bryant looked over and said, "I guess I'm not the only hungry one?"

Ciara smiled and grabbed her small stomach. "I haven't been with Mary at all today, so I kind of forgot to eat. She keeps me on track with meals. Otherwise, I might not ever eat."

Bryant laughed and pointed to his smoothie cup in the holder between them. Ciara nodded back in agreement. "It seems we have something in common," she said.

Ciara sat quietly while Bryant switched the radio stations. He landed on the local Christian station. Ciara hadn't listened to contemporary Christian music in a long time. Mary always listened to the gospel station and the van's stereo was broken. The clinic played a CD from time to time, but it wasn't from the latest playlist.

She liked the new sound and swayed when a worship song came on. The lyrics were clear, and she felt her heart fill with the words about Jesus. Bryant knew the words and sang along with the song. He drove with one arm while the other rested on the armrest between them. He looked at Ciara at each stoplight. She caught his gaze and tried small talk but gave up when he smiled and turned the radio up louder.

He studied her face at the stoplight in front of the country club. He frowned and pointed to the sign, Bayport Country Club. She looked from the front window and smiled at the neat rows of palm trees lining the entrance. They swayed from the bay breeze.

"Is this Ok? I don't want to bring up any bad memories or anything," said Bryant.

"Bryant, this is fine. By the way I don't remember

anything about this place except for being here with Mayor Nelon." Ciara's eyebrows rose and she stared back at Bryant.

"You don't remember meeting clients here and drinking?" Bryant questioned in a half whisper. Was he regretting coming to the country club?

"I do remember some of it, but I'm ready to face some things and I'd like to make better memories here." Ciara felt a confidence come to her and pointed to the entrance.

"That's great Ciara, I'd like to take you here for the right reasons. They have some of the best crab cakes and the chef is from Orlando. I sold him the last beachfront from the new build." Bryant parked the car and ran quickly to Ciara's side. Her face flushed red when he opened her door and extended his hand to her. She accepted it and rose from the leather seat.

As the two entered and stepped to the reception desk, Ciara looked to the large bar. There were several men sitting on barstools, and she could smell the alcohol from where she was standing. The smell made her stomach turn.

"Well Lord, I guess You have taken the desire from me," she whispered.

Ciara followed the host to the table donned with a pressed white tablecloth and small light in the center. The table was situated over the bay waters and the moonlight reflected beautifully from the black water. Her eyes quickly adjusted to the dim light, and she looked at the menu. As the server approached, Bryant gently took her menu and smiled, "Let me."

Ciara resisted grabbing the menu back and ordering for herself. She softened when she saw his big grin and listened as he ordered for them both. Evidently, he knew the cuisine well because he didn't even look at his menu. He was taking charge and she wasn't used to giving up control.

Ciara smiled at Bryant when an appetizer arrived with a heaping amount of fresh shrimp and a delectable soup bowl filled with creamy grits. "Yum." Ciara ate her grits and a shrimp while she watched Bryant do the same. His dark hair was combed back, and she was hoping it would fall back on his forehead again. It made him look less austere and more approachable.

Bryant's eyes sparkled when Ciara cut into her freshly prepared salmon and took a bite. Her stomach was full, but the tasty salmon was hard to resist. She ate as much as she could and sat back holding her stomach. "I'm done. I can't eat anymore."

Bryant smiled and said, "It's good isn't it. I think we would drink a lot less smoothies if we had food like this around all the time."

"I'd gain fifty pounds! No thank you." She smiled and grabbed his right hand. Ciara quickly moved her hand back and started to speak. She was flirting with Bryant, and she couldn't resist him.

Bryant moved forward and took Ciara's hand. He looked closely at her and studied her face. She watched on silently as he held her hand and sighed loudly. He was getting the courage to tell her something very important. A panic rose from her stomach to her chest. What if he was going to tell her that he was dating Taylor Emerson, or leaving the company, or leaving Bayport? She was not in the state of mind to handle any true confession from Bryant. Something told her he was going to say something that would change their relationship.

Bryant was intoxicating to her. He made her feel out of control and vulnerable. She was not ready for anything heavy, Her worst fear was he would leave her. When had she gotten so attached? Was she in love with Bryant?

Ciara rose to her feet knocking her plate into another platter. Bryant's eyes widened and he moved to stand too. Ciara motioned for him to sit down. "I need to go to the restroom. I'm not used to eating this much..."

"Sure, are you alright? You look white as a sheet. Do you need me to walk you there?"

"No! I mean, no. I will be back shortly." Ciara made record time with her booted foot. She found the foyer bathroom and quickly entered a stall. She lowered the lid and sat for a moment before her heart stopped racing. She pulled out her phone and called Mary. She was relieved when the older woman's voice boomed out, "Ciara Caldwell, where are you?"

"Oh Mary, I'm at the country club with Bryant and I ate a lot of food and I'm in love with Bryant. I just figured it out. He's like a drink to me. Or he's like a pill to me... am I making sense. Oh, I just need Jesus to help me." Ciara heard the toilet flush beside her, but she didn't care. She needed Mary's advice and strong support.

Mary sighed deeply and said, "I thought this would eventually happen. Ciara, it's not wrong to be in love with Bryant. I just don't know if you are quite ready to deal with the complications and drama of love. Not deep love where you have other relationships and connections with him. Do you want me to come and pick you up?"

Ciara thought for a moment. It would be easier to ride back with Mary, but she would have to face Bryant again. He would eventually tell her his heart and she feared she would not be a part of his big reveal. "No, I will get him to take me to the clinic, if you will wait for me there."

"Sure, honey. I'm here. You're really growing up and taking responsibility. Don't panic. Pray." Mary hung up leaving Ciara to her own thoughts. Ciara began to pray silently that God would help her. When her breathing calmed, she checked her makeup in the bathroom mirror, and exited the restroom.

Bryant stood in the foyer with a questioning expression. He moved toward Ciara and took her arm. Taking some of the pressure from her fractured ankle. Ciara held his arm and walked beside him. They drove in silence to the clinic. The swoosh of the open sunroof was the only sound. Ciara prayed until Bryant turned onto the clinic road. When he entered the parking lot, she turned and faced him.

Bryant shut off the engine and looked at Ciara. "I apologize, Ciara. I feel like I pushed you tonight. I have been wanting to talk to you for some time, but I realize you are not ready. When you are, will you tell me?"

"You are one of the best friends I have. Of course, I'll tell you. I hope I didn't ruin your evening and meal." Ciara looked down at her hands and sighed.

Bryant moved past the console and grabbed Ciara's left arm. He then lightly kissed her left cheek. When he moved back, she could still feel where his lips touched her cheek. Her pulse raced and she looked over at him. Her eyes widened, and she moistened her lips.

"You didn't ruin anything. I am praying for you and believe you are becoming a great woman of God." Ciara smiled and moved to open the car door. She stood outside the passenger door and grabbed her handbag. When she looked up he winked, and her stomach flopped.

"Goodnight."

"Goodnight."

Fall in Bayport brought some relief from traffic and the heat. A recent cold front left everyone feeling refreshed. Ciara spent every other Saturday at the office for the months of September and October. She didn't tell anyone she was avoiding Bryant, and Bryant didn't attempt to interact with her except for business and the occasional small talk. Ciara would feel his gaze and smile at him, but other than that she steered clear of him.

Ciara was graduating from the rehabilitation program in December and her parents and Jan were coming into town for the occasion. Jan and Ciara were going to stay in the apartment and her parents were staying at a bed and breakfast nearby. No Thanksgiving plans were being made, and Ciara was relieved when Mary suggested the two of them host the rehabilitation clients at Mary's house. Mary was driving to Atlanta for Christmas and decided against a family Thanksgiving too.

The streets of Bayport were pretty in the summer, but the Christmas decorations meticulously put up in early November were even prettier. They were breathtaking. Ciara loved to see the lights come on at sunset. The town was quiet and beautiful and helped her set a new precedent of peace for November. The last two Novembers were filled with regret and started her on a path of self-destruction.

Ciara drove her new little, economy sedan through the streets and in front of the storefronts. Her mood was light, as she listened to the local Christian station. She was learning all the songs, but still flipped it over to the gospel station for part of the time. She had to get her praise on like Mary said, "To keep her cheerful."

Ciara passed the food truck and parked in front of C&W Realty. She sat in her car for a short while and looked at the storefronts. She looked over at the large print on Glenn's Bakery and read aloud, "Best Bakery in the South." She nodded her head in agreement. She then looked at the food truck. Annie was still inside with Shara, one of the women from the clinic. She was probably giving her lessons and Ciara imagined the beautiful Shara, with her perfectly manicured nails, scooping out onions to sauté. Ciara laughed at the thought.

Ciara looked at the side of the truck. The pale-yellow flank still shined, even in the dim lighting of the storefront Christmas lights. Bryant added a tasteful Christmas wreath on the C&W door. It was given to him by a client, and it provided the only decoration the respectable business donned. It suited Ciara fine although she was starting to respond more favorably to the little town's love of all things holiday. The little, lighted reindeer for this season were set to come on right after Thanksgiving. They were there waiting in the moonlight.

The side of the food truck was still blank. No name lettered the side. Ciara frowned and thought for a while longer before exiting her car. A cool breeze made her arms goose pimple, and she pulled her little jacket close to her abdomen. She unlocked the storefront door and clicked on a lamp at the reception desk. She passed the coffee pot and congratulated herself for her one a day mantra. She now had one stout cup of coffee each morning and no more.

Ciara sat in the sitting area and began to pray. For

some reason, she wanted to pray at the office. Everything in her life was working out, but the business with Bryant was unresolved. How would she work beside him at their current stand still? She was afraid he would leave or marry Taylor or decide to stay in the partnership as is forever. She would die inside if she stayed right here with him, and nothing changed.

"God, I don't want my current relationship to end with Bryant, but I don't want it to stay the same either. I'm just too scared to know what he really wants to do after I graduate. Please help me keep my peace and my joy," Ciara prayed.

Her eyes snapped open when she heard voices on the sidewalk. She closed the blinds to the reception window and peered out through a slit. She saw Annie standing with Shara as the clinic van pulled up. She smiled at the sight and congratulated herself on her part in helping. "Restitution," she spoke quietly.

She felt the word permeate her body as she continued to look at Annie. "Restitution. Yes, I've finished that pace," Ciara said.

"Restitution," she said it again and tears filled her eyes. "I hear you, Lord. I'm just not that good of a person. I'm still learning how to give," Ciara said to the tiled ceiling.

Give big. Ciara felt the words and looked at the truck again.

"What if I give the storefront to Annie?" Ciara questioned.

She rose to her feet and looked around frantically to see if anyone else was in the office. There were no natural sounds, but she heard her own heartbeat in her ears loud and clear. Then she felt the peace and joy wrap like a blanket.

"I can do this," she said to the empty office.

The idea was exciting and freeing to Ciara. She quickly rose to her feet and paced the tiled floor. The details flooded her mind. She thought of how to draw up the paperwork and she thought of how to get Annie to agree to sign. She looked at the walls the contractors had constructed and realized they could be easily removed. Bryant insisted on keeping the industrial kitchen intact, although they replaced cheap office appliances for the industrial ones. She made her way to the kitchen and looked with her amateur eyes at the plugs and switches on the walls. She assumed they were not changed out by the contractors.

She quickly exited the glass doors and raced to Annie who stood with the van taillights illuminating her face. The two women's eyes locked as Ciara smiled broadly. She calmed her breathing and asked Annie to join her inside. Annie's eyes widened and she walked reluctantly behind Ciara. As the two entered C&W Realty, both women moved to the sitting area. Ciara sat and waited for Annie to sit down. She motioned for her to take the couch. Annie slowly sat on the couch but leaned forward as if she might run out of the door any minute.

"Annie, I know this is strange, but I really need to talk to you." Ciara tried to quell her excitement. She sat back and sighed deeply, happy to be starting the conversation.

"Yes, Ciara I am a little scared of you right now." Annie's eyes narrowed and then widened as she watched Ciara.

"I was praying, and I realized there is one thing left for me to do for my recovery." She waited for a few seconds.

"That's awesome Ciara, but what do I have to do with

that?" Annie clasped her hands in front and shifted forward on the office couch.

"I want to give this storefront to you." Ciara smiled from ear to ear and waited anxiously for Annie's reply.

Annie's eyes widened again, and she let out a small giggle. "You can't be serious. This is your business, Your livelihood. Are you taking something, Ciara?"

"No, Annie, I've been sober for months now. I am sure this is what I want to do. The storefront belongs to you. God will provide for me. I've been given a lot of things in my life. You were supposed to be given this by your mother as an inheritance. Mary told me the whole story. I couldn't possibly in good conscience keep you from your inheritance." Ciara congratulated herself on her monologue and sat back ready for Annie's agreement.

Annie paused mid-sentence and began to cry. She looked down and then around the room. Ciara could imagine her mind counting the windows and checking out the floors and ceilings.

"We should pay you something for it. My mom still has about half of the money. She's had to live on some and she gave me some for the truck, but we could pay you something." Annie sniffed and gave a half smile.

"I don't want you to pay anything. It is yours. I will call the lawyer now. I can't pay for all the legal fees, but I can give this to you free and clear. It's totally mine." Ciara's eyes filled with tears, and she giggled. "I have never felt so good in my life...well since visiting Mary's church six months ago."

"Ok, I'll accept it. My mom will pay for the legal costs of getting it in my name. Oh, my goodness, Ciara. Are you sure?" Annie trembled and she stood hugging herself.

"I've never been surer." Now let's call Mary and get

the ball rolling. She'll be the one to help us right now. The two women waited on the edge of their seats while Mary let out a loud, "What!" She then began to ask Ciara if she was sure and after being convinced Ciara was in her right mind and really wanted to give Annie the storefront, she gave them the number to a local lawyer.

After they made an appointment for the next morning, Ciara said her goodbyes to Mary and Annie. She watched after the other woman until seeing taillights leave the backlot. Her heart raced. Who should she call now since Mary knew? Her mind went to her parents and Jan and then she thought of Bryant.

"Oh no, Bryant and I don't have a business office or storefront any longer. How will he feel about this? This may be the one thing that drives him away from me forever," she said through clenched teeth. Fear began to replace her former peace. She should have talked to Bryant first. He deserved to know first. She picked up her phone and looked at the display.

"I should call Bryant," she said flatly. Her thumb hovered over his name in her contacts. She breathed deeply before lowering her thumb on his number. The phone rang straight to voicemail. She quickly pressed the end call button and slumped into the oversized chair in the reception area. Ciara squeezed her eyes shut and looked up to the tiled ceiling. She couldn't tell him in a message. It had to be in person.

"Oh, Lord. I will be obedient, and I will trust You even in this," prayed Ciara.

Later that same week, Cam woke to the sound of Annie praying. He heard a sing-song prayer rising from their bedroom beside a little window. Annie was sitting cross-legged at the foot of the window as small rays of sun fell on her head and the floor in front of her. Cam blinked twice and could almost see an angel standing behind his wife. Her head was lowered, and she rocked forward and back. He stretched and followed to sit next to her. His back was against the wall and his head touched the wooden windowsill.

Annie looked over to Cam and smiled, "Your crazy ex-fiancé is giving us our storefront."

Cam smiled back and made a grand gesture heavenward, "Annie, I think God is giving us our storefront. He's just using Ciara to do it." He kissed the top of her head and lifted his arm around her shoulders. He noticed how strong she felt despite her thin frame.

"Annie, you have worked hard your whole life and now you're about to work even harder," said Cam.

Annie smiled sheepishly and said, "You're right. God is blessing us. I listen to your sermons and Bible study. It's just when it involves me that I have a hard time believing. I resented everyone and everybody for so long, it's hard to stop even when a gift like this is coming my way. I think the fact it is coming from Ciara Caldwell is the miracle I needed." Annie grinned widely, "I've prayed more for that girl than anyone else. Now look what God is doing."

"You've been praying for Ciara?" Cam looked squarely at Annie and studied her face.

"I have a whole journal of prayers right here." Annie lifted the journal filled with her small, neat handwriting. The cover was bent, and a few pages were dog-eared.

"All this time I've seen you writing in that I thought you were praying for a restaurant. I was praying for her too. Not because I still have feelings for her." Cam paused and tensed. He relaxed when Annie nodded in agreement, "I was praying because I thought I was still responsible for her."

"Cam, I was praying for her because I was her at one time." Annie flipped to a journal page.

"You were a spoiled rotten brat who went through sports cars like you change shirts?" Cam chuckled at the thought of Annie at the spa barking out orders for a perfect manicure.

"No, silly, listen." Annie pointed to a page and began reading, "Dear Lord, I realize I am constantly hiding, hiding behind my circumstances, hiding behind Mom and our house, hiding behind Mary and her boldness, hiding behind Cam and his devotion to You, and hiding behind Ciara Caldwell and her storefront. Please help me come out of hiding."

"Ciara was hiding too. She was hiding behind her money," said Annie.

Cam nodded in agreement as he thought further.

"She was also hiding behind her pills. That's when I started praying. I didn't realize how much she was really hiding, and I certainly didn't realize how painful it would be for her to come out of hiding, but now..." Annie sighed loudly and wiped at her cheek as a tear ran down.

"Now, she's free, really free." Cam hugged Annie tightly and pulled her to her feet, "We better get ready, so we won't miss our appointment." Annie looked at her watch and pushed past Cam.

"You're right, I will make sure to put on a little extra make-up this morning and wear something beside a chef's jacket. I will be sitting across the table this morning from the lovely Ciara Caldwell."

Cam laughed at the statement and bowed before Annie, "Correction, Ciara has to sit across from the beautiful and talented Mrs. Annie Westin Shivers."

At Mary's house that morning, Ciara sat at the kitchen table and ate toast while Mary waited for the coffee pot to finish dispensing the strong, black liquid. Ciara spent most of the night on the phone with her parents and Jan. Most of the Caldwell family members agreed and were excited with Ciara's decision. Even Uncle Jim texted Ciara and gave his blessing after mentioning how great the publicity would be for the Caldwell name.

The only Caldwell Ciara hadn't heard from was Jack Junior. However, it wasn't her family she was most concerned with telling. She asked everyone to keep it quiet until she talked to Bryant. Her heart skipped a beat when she looked closely at her text messages. She scrolled to Bryant's last text. It was a simple, "Goodnight." She was more in love with him now than ever. The thought of losing him caused her to put her phone face down and drink a large gulp of her coffee Mary had placed in front of her. The liquid burned her tongue and caused her to cringe and open her mouth wide.

"Slow down, Ciara. You want to have all those taste-buds intact when we go to the country club later today." Mary exited the kitchen leaving Ciara staring at her toast.

Ciara picked up her phone and looked at Bryant's number for a full five seconds. She mustered the strength to press the button. A text alerted her, and she stopped. She had avoided Bryant for two weeks. She attended Mary's church and went into the office when she knew he was meeting with clients. The secret wouldn't keep much longer. Cam and Annie would want to get started and telling Bryant couldn't wait.

As Ciara lifted her phone, she read Jack Junior's text. "What the heck are you doing? That's all you got little sis. Think twice before you give your greatest asset away. Bryant is your partner and he's upset. How could you do that to him after he left to help you. Don't be mad when he comes back to Caldwell." Jack Junior's text rolled in Ciara's mind and tears filled her eyes.

Ciara dropped her head to the table as Mary reentered the kitchen. She came and sat beside her and put one of her strong hands on her shoulder. Ciara began to cry more and felt a little exposed to be sitting at Mary's kitchen table sobbing. She straightened her back and looked at Mary.

Mary smiled and spoke, "Ciara, you don't have to go through with this. It's Ok. No one would blame you if you decided not to proceed." She handed Ciara a napkin and watched as Ciara blotted at her eyes. The tears continued, but Ciara sighed deeply and calmed her breathing.

"Mary, I do want to proceed, more than anything. Now Bryant knows and I'm losing him. Junior wasn't supposed to tell him. I was." Ciara began to sob again as she handed her phone to Mary. She tried to breath slowly and moved to the water tap and ran some water into a juice glass while Mary read the text from Jack Junior.

"Bryant is a good man. How do you know he's against the idea? Have you talked to him?" Mary spoke quietly. She sat still on the other side of the large mahogany kitchen table and held her mug in both hands. Ciara watched her raise the glass and take a sip.

"You read the text from Junior." Ciara closed her eyes and began taking slow deep breaths, "Mary, I'm in love with Bryant. It's more than the partnership I'm losing. I'm losing the man I love too."

"I thought as much. Give him time. This could just be a big shock. He loves the Lord, and I've seen him show his dedication to you in amazing ways. You do what you know is right. If it's right to give the property to Annie, then do it. If not, don't. I know this for certain, you'll never go wrong by doing the right thing." Mary pursed her lips and began to pray.

Ciara began to pray too. She felt the heaviness leave as she listened to Mary's prayer.

"I trust You, God, and I will do the right thing no matter what it costs me. Please give me strength," Ciara prayed.

Mary drove Ciara twenty minutes to the lawyer's office with Gospel music blasting over the stereo. It was Mary's favorite CD and Ciara suspected she pulled it out for her. The songs were strong and powerful and helped Ciara focus on the task at hand. She felt courage fill her heart and she pushed the Bryant issue deep down while studying the buildings as they passed.

"Mary, I think I will continue with my business. I realize I don't have an office, or partner, or money, but I know a lot and I have you." She smiled and settled into the large, leather seat.

"I have no doubt you will. I agree." Mary smiled showing all her sparkling white teeth, "With me and Jesus, you can do anything you put your mind to."

Ciara laughed deep and sat quiet for the remainder of the ride. The two of them pulled into a newly built cluster of bricked businesses. According to Mary, they were recently finished, and many Bayport businesses were relocating to be closer to the interstate traffic. The proximity to the Interstate with large billboards facing traffic, was a big draw.

As Mary and Ciara entered through double glass doors, a receptionist led them to a young lawyer's small office. Ciara looked around the room and saw a large conference table in the corner. The young lawyer, named Jeffrey Lott, motioned for her to have a seat while lifting a large manilla folder. He joined them at the head of the table. The seat across from Ciara was empty causing her heart to skip a beat when she thought of Cam and Annie. Having to make small talk made her very nervous.

"What am I going to say? Sorry I rammed your food truck and broke your arm Cam, but here's my business," she whispered to Mary. Mary cut her eyes to Ciara and shook her head, no.

Ciara shook her head at the statement and was relieved when Annie Shivers entered the room alone. Mary rose to her feet and stood a little awkward looking between Annie and Ciara. Ciara smiled at Mary and motioned for her to sit at the other end of the table between the two of them. Mary raised her eyebrows and followed Ciara's directions.

Annie spoke first, "I drove myself. I felt like I should do this alone. Cam's at the church and my mom put some money in my account. I don't know why, but I just wanted it to be me for a change..." Her voice trailed off and she caught a glimpse of Ciara.

"I know what you mean, Annie. I felt the same way, but I did bring both of us our guardian angel, Mary. If that's Ok with you." Ciara winked Mary's direction and watched as Annie smiled and stifled a giggle.

Mary shifted in her seat and mumbled, "Guardian angel, Lord, these two are making fun of me. They know I'm not anything of the sort."

The lawyer began opening the folder and explained the steps for transferring ownership. The title search and insurance were discussed. Annie looked on wide-eyed. Ciara passed over her recently recovered license and signed at all the places indicated by the lawyer. Before she knew it the lawyer had closed the manilla folder and handed a copy to her and Annie.

Ciara rose to her feet and watched Annie as she wiped a tear from her cheek. At that moment, she saw

what Cam must have fallen for. Annie was not just pretty; she was also very tender and kind. She was exactly
what Cameron, the pastor, needed in his life. Ciara shud-
dered at the thought of her cold, aloof, former self standing with Pastor Cameron Shivers as his wife.

Annie walked around the conference table and
hugged her. She felt the strong thin arms and at first resisted hugging her back. Then, her eyes filled with tears,
and she embraced the other young woman. "Thank you
for forgiving me even when I didn't ask for it."

Annie smiled and took Ciara's hand. "You are forgiv-
en, and I believe you are also free."

Ciara smiled big and pointed to Mary. "Want to go eat
at the country club to celebrate?"

Annie smiled back and said, "No, thank you. I've got
a lot of work ahead of me and besides that I'm allergic to
seafood. All that place knows how to make is crab cakes
and shrimp."

Ciara's eyebrows rose in a question, and she began to
ask, "How can a chef be allergic..."

Mary moved between the two ladies, "Let's get going
before we lose our reservation. There are plenty of chefs
allergic to seafood. Don't let that keep you from trying
some of Annie's meat pies."

"Oh, I won't. I can try all that food I've been smelling
for the last year." Ciara smiled at Annie.

"Come by anytime. It'll be on the house," said Annie
with a grin.

Annie, Ciara, and Mary exited the small office.
Blinding sunlight made each of them raise their hands
for shade. Annie walked to her small car and waved as
she drove away. Mary led Ciara to her car parked at the
edge of the businesses well away from any other cars.

Ciara followed and felt her stomach growl at the

thought of the crab cakes she had enjoyed with Bryant a few months back.

"That's what I will order. In honor of Bryant and what can never be," Ciara whispered. She sighed deeply and resisted the urge to check her text messages. She left her phone on silent and pushed it deep inside her over-sized handbag.

As Ciara navigated rows of cars parked in front of a storefront gym, she looked down at her watch at the same moment Mary stopped walking. Ciara walked into the back of Mary and dropped her handbag. Mary winced as Ciara stepped on her toes peeking out of her open-toed sandals.

Ciara looked up and gasped as she looked past Mary's car to a shiny Mercedes parked neatly beside. Bryant sat on the hood of his car and his legs were crossed in front. His arms were crossed in front of his chest. His face was without expression, and his eyes were hidden behind sunglasses. Ciara put her hand to her chest and nervously stood at the edge of Mary's trunk facing Bryant.

Mary recovered from rubbing her toes and looked full at Bryant, "Would you like to talk to Ciara alone?"

Ciara snapped out of her former stare and looked at Mary, "No Mary, I think you should stay close."

Bryant spoke steady and strong, "Yes, Mary. I'd like to talk to my partner alone. Thank you."

Ciara watched Mary move to the driver's side of her car and start the engine. She almost ran to the passenger side. Ciara moved from Mary's car and stood in front of Bryant.

"Bryant, I need to talk to you..." Ciara couldn't believe how weak her own voice sounded. She mentally scolded herself on her cowardice.

"You think?" Bryant moved from the hood of his car and closer to Ciara. She could see his freshly shaven face and noticed his tight jaw. She wanted to reach out to him and apologize for destroying their business together, but she couldn't find the words.

Bryant reached for Ciara's small hand and said, "Follow me." Ciara looked up and had to shade her eyes again. The sun was high above her head and the light and heat was beginning to be unbearable in the parking area. She followed him hand-in-hand to the shade of the storefronts. He walked past the lawyer's office and the gym. They both ascended a small, outside staircase and stopped in front of a second-floor storefront window. There was no sign out front and Bryant stopped and faced her.

"You're scaring me, Bryant. I thought we were going to talk." Ciara's regular voice returned, and she squared her shoulders back. She resisted putting on her Jack Junior face. She had conquered that tendency recently and didn't want it to resurface now even though this was the perfect moment for it.

"I'm not mad at you, Ciara. I'm hurt." Bryant sat on a window ledge at the vacant storefront. He breathed out loudly and lowered his head. He looked up again and removed his sunglasses. His eyes searched her face. "Why didn't you tell me you were giving the office away?"

Ciara moved in front of him and lowered her eyes from his questioning gaze. This was her moment to be honest and vulnerable. She knew she needed to tell the truth. No one was there to soften the blow or to save her from Bryant's utter rejection of her.

"Why are you hurt? You're not mad, you're hurt?" Ciara questioned. Her mind began to connect the dots. He's hurt because he has feelings for her too. This realization helped bolster her courage and she breathed deeply. He shuffled his feet and crossed his arms. His shirt sleeves were rolled up and she could see the tension in his tanned arms.

"Bryant, I was afraid to tell you. I was afraid to lose you." She waited and searched his face. She wanted to reach for him. Her hands shot forward, but she quickly moved them back to her side. She watched his body language. He continued to cross his arms and would hardly face her. "And I wasn't just afraid to lose my business partner, I was afraid to lose you."

Ciara watched as Bryant's posture relaxed a bit and a small sigh escaped his lips. A slight smile came to Bryant's face. He turned and faced her. She saw his brown eyes bright and bold. They were locked in her gaze, and she felt breathless.

"Ciara, I have something to show you." He pushed lightly past her and moved to the glass doors covered on the inside with brown butcher paper. He pulled out a key and opened the door. Ciara followed him into a construction zone. Saws sat on tables and wooden walls stood erected in small office spaces. Her gaze went to sheet rock standing against a far wall.

"Are you selling this? I didn't think we were selling anything like this. Just the beach property?" Ciara turned away and began counting office spaces. At her best count she came up with three offices and a reception area.

"This is mine. I live in the back and work on this on the weekends. I sold my condo and put a down payment on this when we got our commission checks." Bryant smiled with pride and pointed to a door leading to the back.

Ciara's mind whirled at the thought. This whole time

Bryant was finding a way out of their partnership. Her heart sank and she turned away from him. A small tear escaped and rolled on her cheek. She moved to the window at the reception area.

"I did do the right thing, didn't I, God? Now Bryant is free to have his own business too," Ciara whispered to herself as she walked to the far wall. Ciara closed her eyes tight and turned back to Bryant.

"I'm very glad you did this, Bryant. You deserve the best and I am so glad you still have your business." Ciara smiled slightly and nodded her head up and down. "Yes, you deserve something out of all this mess I created."

Bryant walked to Ciara and took both of her hands. He pulled her to him and embraced her small frame, "Silly Ciara, I don't want to have my business. I want to have our business." He kissed the top of her head and pulled her away to look carefully in her eyes. Ciara looked on and began to relax. "Our business?"

She saw a big grin cross his face and felt her heart leap at the sight.

"You really mean it. You really want to stay business partners and friends?" Ciara questioned.

He smiled and nodded. She wanted to embrace him again, but was still reeling from the last encounter. It would all be back to normal. Her smile faded. Back to normal. That wouldn't work for her. Not with the feelings that she now had for him.

"I can't do it. I can't sit across from you while you date Taylor Emerson or some other socialite..." Ciara's words trailed off as she stepped back two full steps. The distance didn't seem to help calm the beating in her chest.

"Bryant, I appreciate you thinking of me, and I do want to keep the business. It's just that..." Ciara wished at that moment she had insisted on Mary staying close.

It was so hard to keep her courage standing here in Bryant's storefront, with Bryant offering her to stay partners.

Bryant's brows furrowed and he frowned slightly, "What else do you want Ciara? Is this not enough?"

"Yes, Bryant. This is perfect and I want to do it so bad. I just..." Ciara closed her eyes tightly and prayed.

"God help me say the right thing," she whispered.

"It's too soon after your recovery. I understand. I keep pushing you and wanting you to do more than you should. It's just I care a lot about you." Bryant looked away from Ciara and moved to the door. His right hand was on the long bar handle as he looked back.

She needed to tell the truth. She needed to go to Bryant and tell him the truth. Ciara moved toward Bryant and lowered her eyes. She fought to find the courage to tell him she was in love with him and couldn't just be his business partner. She stopped right in front of him. The sun shone through the tinted door behind Bryant. She focused on him and cleared her throat.

"I need to be honest, Bryant. It scares me to death. It's something I've not been good at for a long time, but I really should..." said Ciara.

Ciara looked down and whispered, "I'm in love with you, Bryant. It wouldn't be fair to you and Taylor Emerson or whoever else you date for me to pretend to just be your business partner when I really want more." Ciara's face flushed red, and she shuffled her feet.

Ciara felt Bryant's hands on her arms, and he spoke strong and clear. "Ciara, look at me."

Ciara looked up at Bryant's smiling face.

"Well, say something." She frowned slightly.

"I don't love Taylor Emerson and I don't want to date anyone...except for you. I've been in love with you, crazy

Ciara, for a long time now. Whatever made you think I didn't want us?" Bryant winked and hugged her close. Her face rested on his chest, and she could hear his heart beating wildly. He pulled away and smiled.

"You've been in love with me too. How did I not know this?" Ciara backed away and walked in circles blowing sawdust from various wooden ledges. She smiled from ear to ear and began giggling. "I think we should tell Mary. She's probably worried to death about me." Ciara looked at Bryant again and watched as he motioned for her to join him at the door.

She followed him to the door, and he paused before opening it, "One more thing before we find Mary." Bryant lowered his head and met Ciara's lips with a gentle kiss. Her shoulders relaxed as Bryant pulled her close. His chin rested on the top of her head.

"Taylor Emerson, huh, I thought that made you jealous," said Bryant.

Ciara frowned and hit at Bryant's arm. "That's not funny. I was going through a lot right then." She smiled and winked at Bryant. "I was green with jealously. I wanted to push her down and walk on her with my hard, booted foot."

Bryant laughed as he took her hand, leading her downstairs. They passed the office where Ciara had just signed over ownership of her property. She pulled on Bryant's hand. He stopped and turned toward her. Her hands fell to her side, and she motioned him under an awning above the law office.

"I'm sorry I didn't tell you about giving the storefront to Annie. It may take a while for me to trust. It's new for me." She smiled and took his hand again.

"It's new for me, too. I wanted to be mad at you, but I'm not. I don't know if I could have sacrificed like you did." He smiled, revealing the dimple he had on his right cheek. Ciara reached to his face and stood on tiptoes to reach his lips. She kissed him sweetly and then rested her forehead in his chest.

They embraced until they heard a tap on the window beside them. Jeffrey Lott stood at the window with his fingers pulling down the metal blinds. He frowned and shook his head, no. He shooed them away with his other hand. Bryant smiled broadly and gave a thumbs up to Jeffrey. They obeyed and moved from the awning and back into the direct sun.

"I guess we are being good neighbors again," Ciara said as she stifled a giggle.

Bryant led Ciara through the parking lot and back to his Mercedes. As expected, Mary sat in her car beside Bryant's watching the two emerge from the building. Bryant held Ciara's hand tightly and opened the passenger door to Mary's car.

Mary smiled broadly and then scrunched up her face. "What are you two grinning so big about? Who swallowed the canary?"

Ciara turned to Mary and said, "I'll explain it all on the way to the country club. Let's go eat."

"Is Mr. Ward joining us at the club?" Mary asked as she left the parking lot. She kept one eye on Ciara and the other on the road. Ciara continued to grin and hum a sweet tune.

"He is." Ciara said quietly and looked at the small flowers on her sundress. She sighed big and looked over at Mary, who looked a little out of character with the questioning gaze she continued to fix on Ciara.

"Well, Ok. I'll give the country club a heads up that we'll have a guest joining us." Mary reached for her phone while Ciara continued with her silly grin.

"Bryant's going to be joining me a lot in the future." With that statement Ciara turned up Mary's Gospel CD and rolled her window down. Tears ran down her cheeks and she smiled up through squinted eyes. She was happy to see the sun go behind a small cloud. She looked at the electric blue sky and shouted.

"Blessed and happy are the poor in spirit for theirs is the kingdom of God."